"You're so different, Joy. Different from any girl I've been with."

She lifted her chin. "Is that good or bad?"

"Good." He kissed her. "Really good."

He kicked off his boots and pulled his shirt over his head. Her gaze landed on his chest. He was all muscle. So unlike her own curvaceous body.

In any other circumstance she would have probably run away, her insecurities taking over as she looked at a man so hard, lean, and powerful. But she was too turned on; her body needed him, and as he pulled off his jeans and boxers, she could see he needed her, too.

His hands on her thighs were rough as he lifted her and pushed her against the wall. She couldn't help but notice that he picked her up with no visible effort. . . .

He carried her to the top floor, walking straight to his bedroom and resting her on the bed.

Then he kissed her and smiled down at her. "I want you to stay here tonight."

Praise for Lilli Feisty and Bound to Please

"Terrific . . . Fans of realistic erotica will enjoy *Bound to Please*."
—HarrietKlausner.wwwi.com

"Sexy . . . Don't let this one pass you by!"
—*TheRomanceReadersConnection.com*

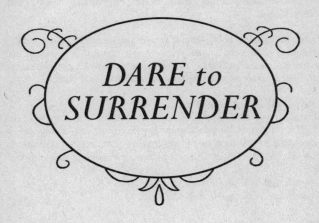

DARE to SURRENDER

LILLI FEISTY

FOREVER

NEW YORK   BOSTON

Copyright © 2010 by Lilli Feisty
All rights reserved. Except as permitted under the U.S. Copyright Act of 1976, no part of this publication may be reproduced, distributed, or transmitted in any form or by any means, or stored in a database or retrieval system, without the prior written permission of the publisher.

Cover design by Claire Brown
Book design by Giorgetta Bell McRee

Forever
Hachette Book Group
237 Park Avenue
New York, NY 10017
Visit our website at www.HachetteBookGroup.com.

Forever is an imprint of Grand Central Publishing. The Forever name and logo is a trademark of Hachette Book Group, Inc.

Printed in the United States of America

First Printing: February 2010

10 9 8 7 6 5 4 3 2 1

For Jay.

Acknowledgments

I would like to thank my wonderful editors, Amy Pierpont and Alex Logan. Also, my agent, Roberta Brown, deserves a big hug. My Smutketeers, my family, and all of my friends—thank you for helping me write during a very difficult year. And Dana, thank you for always picking up the phone.

DARE to
SURRENDER

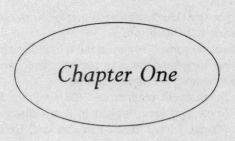

Chapter One

Half of being successful was luck, right? So, as she entered the elegant surroundings of the museum fundraiser, Joy Montgomery prayed she was about to get lucky.

Scanning the crowded, oversized room, she searched for a blond man with green eyes to die for and a long, lean body she would never forget.

There, in the corner! Her gaze landed on him and her breath caught. He was more gorgeous than she remembered. He held himself away from the crowd, which seemed to fade away when he caught her eye for just a second before a group of guests blocked her view.

A petite brunette came toward her. "Joy! I'm so glad you made it!" she said, and gave Joy a hug.

"Wow." Joy looked around the third floor of the San Francisco Art Museum, the atrium of which had been reborn into a reception hall for the year's biggest fundraiser. The walls were adorned with the museum's best pieces from their collection, and the high ceiling opened to the night sky. The large space echoed with conversation, making it difficult to hear.

"So, I see he came." Joy eyed the tall, lanky photographer, trying to ignore the way her heartbeat seemed to speed up whenever she looked at him.

Ruby Scott, event planner and the neighbor Joy had come to know and love, looked in Ash's direction and frowned. "Yeah, I have to say I'm shocked. He quit his photography, despite the fact that this museum wanted to do a show for him." She shrugged her petite shoulders. "He just seems lost somehow." She brought her attention back to Joy. "And it's such a shame he's not taking photographs now. He was really on the brink of something amazing."

Joy blinked. "Pardon me? What do you mean he's not taking pictures anymore? I don't understand."

"Who really knows? Artists can be so unpredictable."

Shit shit shit! Joy had banked on Ash's being here, and he was. But if he wasn't taking photographs anymore, how was she supposed to lure him to the gallery she worked for? Her boss had told her to find an up-and-coming artist, someone edgy. There was nothing edgier than Ash Hunter's sexy photographs.

"If he's not taking photographs, what's he doing?"

"Not teaching anymore, I know that. He used to be in the Navy. I'm wondering if he's considering returning to security."

"He doesn't look like security." Joy took in his faded jeans, T-shirt, leather jacket, and black boots. His dirty blond hair was too long, and he looked like he hadn't shaved in a day or two. He looked like . . . an artist.

Ruby shook her head in his direction. "I know. But I

think it's in his blood. He's not happy unless he's on the go, and he's been in town ever since . . ."

Joy turned back to Ruby. "Since what?"

Smiling, Ruby shook her head. "Never mind. Anyway, apparently he was quite the hero in his day. Not that he'd ever admit it."

Ash could stop speeding trains and scale tall buildings—it still wouldn't help Joy keep her job.

Conveniently, a waiter happened to be passing by with a tray of champagne glasses. Joy plucked off two flutes and downed one, then looked up to find Ruby staring at her, her face tilted, her blue eyes questioning.

"Everything okay, honey?" Ruby asked.

"No," Joy said, waving her now-empty flute in Ash's direction. "My boss wants him—his art, I mean—as an exclusive for the Cartwright Gallery. If I don't come back with some sort of agreement, I'll probably be fired."

"They can't fire you for that!" Ruby said. Though her slight frame appeared relaxed, Joy saw that the woman's gaze never rested anywhere for long. She was constantly taking in the environment, watching for any possible detail that might be less than perfect.

But everything was flawless. From the display of a light show on the far wall to the smoked salmon canapés being passed by a waitstaff that seemed to be made up of supermodels, every last detail had been immaculately attended to.

Ruby Scott was the epitome of detail-oriented. Joy Montgomery was, in a word, not.

"Listen, sweetie. I have to get to work, but we'll talk about this later—I promise we'll think of something! Right now, don't worry about it. Just enjoy yourself."

Ruby took Joy's empty glass and flitted off to consult with the caterer.

Joy watched her go, her slim body fitted into an impeccably tailored dress. She wondered how one became detail-oriented, a perfectionist. Joy was a lot of things, but none of those traits were on the list. She could have finished off another degree with the cumulative time she'd spent looking for her keys, she never remembered any of her three brothers' birthdays, and she was always late to work.

And she never seemed to be able to put together an outfit with the flair that some women, like Ruby, naturally seemed to possess.

Like tonight. The flowery dress had seemed an appropriate choice when Joy had pulled it out of her closet earlier that evening, but now, in a sea of black fashion, she shifted awkwardly on her flats, feeling very out of place in the bright fabric. Also, unlike most of the other women at the event holding tiny clutches, Joy had her ever-present oversized bag slung over her shoulder. But she had a panic attack if she went anywhere without it. The bad thing was, she tended to collect random miscellanea along the way. Every few weeks, she dumped the contents of the bag onto her bed and was always surprised at how much crap she'd managed to shove in there.

Sighing, she turned her gaze to the paintings on the wall. The gala was a reception for a big museum fundraiser, but no one except Joy seemed to be appreciating the wonderful collection displayed around them. Like that piece on the far wall. Her gaze fell on a vivid abstract and she found herself moving forward, drawn to it. The dazzling colors calmed her; the flowing composition soothed her. Stopping a few feet from the piece, she uncurled hands she hadn't even realized had been clenched and stared.

"You like this?"

Joy snapped herself into the present. She'd been so lost in the art that the room had faded, and she hadn't noticed Ash approaching. Now he stood next to her, but he wasn't looking at the painting. He was looking at her, his eyes intense, unblinking, and the most beautiful shade of green she'd ever seen—tinted emerald as if laid directly from an artist's palette—

Shit. Every time she started describing a man in art terms, she knew she was in trouble. What had she said about Cartwright? Oh, that the shadows of the sharp features of his face were like a study in chiaroscuro.

Big mistake.

She pulled her bag tighter and nodded. "Yes. It's, um, very moving." *Really intelligent, Miss Art History Major.* And it was then that she remembered Ash was an artist himself and was probably thinking she was incredibly dull.

Then she remembered the type of artist he was. She pictured one of the bondage photographs she'd seen at Ruby's place, and a tiny erotic awareness tingled over her. Because Ash Hunter didn't do landscapes or still lifes or abstract art. Ash Hunter tied women up in ropes and photographed them.

Ash Hunter was considered to be a master of bondage. A tall, sexy, kinky man who actually made erotic art artistic.

At least, he used to be that man. Now it seemed he was just tall and sexy, and she had no idea about the kinky.

She experienced an urge to find out.

"Joy, right?" he said, and she discovered his voice was still scratchy and deep, just as she'd remembered from the one time she'd met him outside her building. She'd been late for work and had burst outside, slamming the door right into Ash's shoulder.

"Yes, that's right; I'm Joy. Montgomery." She brushed a stray lock of hair behind her ear. "And you're Ash. Ash Hunter. Oh! How's your shoulder?" Her face heated as she remembered their last meeting.

Ash frowned slightly. "Yeah, it took awhile, but I recovered from the incident. Had to have minor surgery, but it's all good now. Just a few twinges every now and then." He rubbed his right shoulder as if massaging a sore muscle.

She jerked back. "What? Oh my God! I'm so sorry; you should have told me! My insurance could have covered it. Though I don't have any insurance, well, just a basic plan that probably wouldn't have helped. Either way, I am *so* sorry."

But he was smiling now, the little lines near his eyes crinkling, and she had the unfounded thought that they didn't crinkle often.

"Joy. I'm messing with you."

Relief flooded her and she bit back a smile. "You asshole."

He quirked a brow.

Crap. First she couldn't shut up, and now she'd just called him a bad name.

"I'm sorry; I didn't mean that," she said. "About you being an asshole."

"Yes, you did." But his green eyes were softer than before. Like the artist had added a touch of yellow . . .

She tossed the thought aside. "Fine, but you have to admit it wasn't nice of you to keep me going like that."

"You're right. It was very, very wrong."

"Now you're just humoring me," she said.

"Maybe."

Silence stretched between them, until she finally had to say something before she exploded. "Actually, I wanted to talk to you about something. Professionally. Do you have a minute?"

He looked at her a second too long and then nodded. "Yeah. But it's so loud in here I can barely think. Come with me."

Leaving no room for argument, he turned and walked to a metal door. Punching a code into a box, he turned the handle and opened the door, pausing to hold it with one of his long, lean arms so she could head through first. As she passed him, she barely brushed his shoulder and the heat from his body jolted through her like electricity.

Great. She was hot for the bondage-artist-turned-security-specialist whom she was supposed to be wooing to the Cartwright Gallery so she could keep her job.

Crap. That was abso-fucking-lutely the last thing she needed.

As she passed beneath him, Ash caught a whiff of vanilla and his balls tightened. And as he watched the redhead take a few steps in front of him, her flowery dress swirling around her knees, he nearly went hard. Joy Montgomery. She wasn't his type, and yet something about her made his blood run hot. It had that day he'd met her in front of Ruby's building, and it still did.

Stopping, she turned and looked at him, not noticing the lock of wild red hair that fell out of the bun she had piled high on her head. He decided not to tell her; for some reason he found her dishevelment endearing, which confused him. Everything in its place, that was his credo. And everything about Joy seemed slightly out of place.

He shouldn't like that, especially not now.

"Why do you have the security code?" she asked.

"Because I have some art here, and I'm too paranoid to let anyone touch it except me." He moved past her and led the way down the hall to the last door on the right. Then he pushed inside and flipped on the light.

Clearing his throat, he crossed his arms across his chest. "So, Joy. What did you want to talk to me about?"

But she didn't seem to hear him. Silently, she stared at a marble sculpture as if it were Jesus.

She took a step closer to the three-foot piece. "My God," she whispered, releasing her huge gray bag and letting it fall to the floor with a thud. "This is . . . beautiful."

He got compliments on his art all the time, so why did his face heat from her words? "You think so?"

"I think it's amazing." She moved her hand as if to touch it but floated her palm a few inches from the piece. "It's so . . ."

"Indecent?" He laughed wryly.

"Sensual."

"I guess that's one way of putting it." It was a sculpture of a man and a woman, their elongated limbs entwined, wrapped around each other. Rope bound them, wrapping and dipping between the forms, appearing and disappearing in the crevices of the sculpted marble.

"So you're going to show these here?"

He kicked the tip of his boot against the desk. "Um, no."

Her eyes widened. "What? Why?"

Why did she seem so concerned? He shrugged. "Because I'm taking a break from all this. Besides, they're not very good. I'm just an amateur."

"No. These are modern and yet . . . there's something classic about them. The woman is bound, yet still iconic somehow. Power, beauty. Reminds me of ancient Roman work." She bit her lip as she grinned, impish. "They were naughty, too."

He just shook his head. She had no idea what she was talking about.

"I know what I'm talking about. Stanford art school and all that." She began digging through her giant purse and finally pulled out a card. Handing it to him, she said, "I work for the Cartwright Gallery. I would love to show these."

"So that's what this is about? You're trying to get me to show at your gallery?"

"Yes. We'd be delighted to represent you. Both your photography and your sculpture."

He stepped back. "No way. I'm done." He had way too much going on, too many people depending on him to waste time taking pictures and tinkering with marble.

"I'm having a really hard time believing that." She turned her head slowly, releasing his gaze at the last minute, to stare at the marble piece again. "I can't tell if they're making love, or bound against their will . . . or both." Her voice was soft and pensive, as if she was thinking aloud and had forgotten he was even there. She walked around the sculpture, her eyes taking in the naked forms, and he saw her breathing go a bit shallow, saw her eyes darken. She bit her fingernail, and he saw her hand was trembling slightly.

"Oh, Lord," he said, walking to her, and she inhaled

sharply when he closed in. He could smell her arousal. "You're getting turned on by a sculpture."

"I am?"

"Are you?"

"Maybe," she said softly, her gaze darting over his face. "I like art."

Just like that, a vision hit him, of Joy, bound. Restrained. *His.* Desire flooded him and he could not resist drawing closer, felt his body tighten with awakening. "Tell me what else you like." It seemed insane to be talking to her this way, but he couldn't stop, and he took one of her wrists in his hand and encircled her. Despite her full breasts and hips, she had a small frame, and he took a moment to feel the elegant bones beneath her soft skin. "You have such delicate hands, Joy."

She scoffed and shifted uncomfortably. "That's ridiculous!"

"Do you like to be tied up?"

"That's a preposterous question!"

"Do you?"

She inhaled, looked to the side, and he thought she might not answer. But then she turned back, lifted her chin, and met his gaze. "I . . . I don't know. I've never done it."

He tightened his grasp around her wrist and was satisfied when she gasped; it was a gasp of pleasure. "Never tried it?"

"No."

Her wrist in his hand, he backed up, backed her against the desk. "That's a shame."

"I'll be sure to rectify the situation as soon as I meet another man who's into bondage."

Her words sent an unfamiliar twinge through his gut; he wasn't used to feeling jealous. He never cared enough to be jealous. But the thought of another man binding her made something inside him constrict. Better to put that thought right out of Joy's head.

Releasing her wrist, he lowered his mouth and placed a soft kiss at the base of her neck. "No other man, Joy. Me. Let me." Lust thundered through him, and he knew he wouldn't take no for an answer.

"This is crazy. . . ."

"I know."

"I want your art," she said, but her eyes were dark with desire for more than just his art.

Stubborn little thing. He kissed her on the other side of her neck, and she braced herself on the desk, dropped her head back to allow him better access.

"Meet me tomorrow night, Joy. Come to my place and we'll talk."

And I'll tie you.

"No," she whispered.

He froze. "Is there someone else?"

He hadn't survived being a SEAL with shoddy observation skills, and he picked up on the way the muscles in her neck tensed at his question. But she hadn't answered yes, so he let it go. For some reason, the thought of her having some other guy sniffing around only made him more aggressive. Possessive.

He slid his hand into the curve of her waist, felt her warmth through the loose fabric of her dress. Her body felt tight when he'd expected soft. With his fingers, he grazed the dip of her waist, palmed her rib cage and gently cupped her breast. A visible shudder ripped through her, and when he lightly touched her nipple through the fabric of her dress and bra, she moaned.

"Tomorrow night?" he asked again, this time against her lips.

"I see so much of you in that piece."

She was gazing over his shoulder, presumably at the art. "It's sensual and restrained, demanding yet flowing. It's sex and yet more than just erotic." She looked at him. "It's obviously your work."

He just stared at her.

"Why are you stopping this? Creating art?"

He pushed away. "It wasn't meant to be a career. I needed a break, a distraction."

"From what?"

"Listen, I really don't want to talk about that right now." He scribbled his address on a piece of paper. "I'll see you tomorrow night."

"Is this your only sculpture?"

She must have seen his gaze dart to the wall cabinet, because she jumped up and yanked the doors open; damn, she was more observant than he'd given her credit for. Inside were a few dozen pieces, ranging from six inches to a foot high. Her gasp was audible. "Oh, holy fuck!"

"You have a mouth on you, don't you, sweetheart?"

She glanced over her shoulder. "Sorry. It's just that these are amazing. You have to show them!" Straightening, she turned to face him. "Seriously. Let me—I mean the gallery—represent your sculpture."

"No."

Just then his cell vibrated, and he saw a text from Ruby telling him to get his ass out there to meet one of the owners of the museum. Somehow she'd pried out a promise from him to schmooze with the bigwigs tonight. "Damn. I gotta go. Just turn off the lights and shut the door behind you."

Lifting her chin, she stared at him. "I'm not done with you."

He met her stare. "I'm not done with you, either. See you tomorrow night. Eight o'clock—my place." Giving her no time to protest, he walked out the door and let it shut behind him with a firm click.

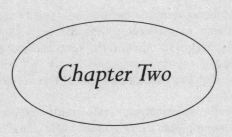

Chapter Two

Joy stared at the closed door. Excitement buzzed through her, and she wasn't exactly sure why. Well, Ash's hands on her body, the way he kissed her—melted her—was an obvious reason. But her gaze drifted to the erotic sculpture, and she felt it in her gut, in her heart and between her legs. She'd always been responsive to art, but this was ridiculous. This was a physical reaction; just looking at it made her damp, made her nipples tingle.

And yet there was nothing vulgar about the piece. As she ran her fingertips over the cold marble curve of the female's breast, she was touched by the beauty of it and how it made her want to be that woman. Powerful submission. She'd never felt the desire to be bound, but that was all changing as she touched the smooth marble rope sculpted by Ash's hands.

It was a crime to keep these pieces hidden. She moved to the cabinet where more than a dozen smaller, varied versions of the larger sculpture rested. Glancing over her shoulder to make sure the door was firmly shut, she gently lifted one of Ash's sculptures and held it in her hands. So beautiful, so smooth; it made her pulse race. Glancing at the dingy metal cabinet and back to the art in her hands, her heart sank at the idea of returning it to such a dull home.

When she was nineteen, she'd lived in Paris, as an art history student. During a private tour of the Louvre, she'd discovered the museum had hundreds of works in storage and had nearly cried when she'd found out the majority of the massive collection would never be seen by most people. She felt a similar reaction now, and before she even knew what she was doing, she pulled a wool scarf out of her bag, wrapped the piece of marble in the thick, soft knit, and placed the whole thing in her purse. Then, with a deep breath, she did as Ash had asked: She turned off the lights, shut the door behind her, and left.

Clutching her oversized purse to her chest, Joy paused just a few feet from the museum exit. Her belly was a blender of anxiety as she looked through the glass doors. Was she really going to do this?

Deep breath. Push through.

Damp San Francisco fog hit her bare arms as she ran down the stairs, and she fully expected alarms to go off, or Ash to chase her down, yelling, "Stop! Thief!"

But none of those things happened. As she hurried up the street, her heart began to slow down and her hands went from full-out shaking to minor trembling. By the time she hit Market Street, she could breathe normally again.

Almost.

What had she done?

Oh, just stolen a piece of art from a museum.

She'd stolen. A piece of art. From a museum! Museums were sacred, a sanctuary in a world that seemed to value art less and less every day.

Pardon me, why am I in this handbasket, and where are we going?

Hell. She was going to hell. Or jail. Probably both.

And if Ash noticed the piece was missing, he'd be the one to send her to either of those places. If he found out what she'd done, how could she ever explain herself?

It's for his own good.

Don't be ridiculous. This is for you, Joy.

Shaking the voices out of her head, she briskly continued her pace up Market Street. She could have taken a cab, but she needed to burn off some of the excess energy coursing through her blood. Because she'd committed a crime.

A felony, in fact.

What the hell had she been thinking?

That those pieces were too beautiful to be kept in an old metal cabinet. That maybe if she showed her boss one piece by Ash Hunter, he wouldn't fire her. And if she couldn't come to an agreement with Ash, she would, of course, return it. But hopefully everything would go according to plan, and meanwhile she could keep her job and convince Ash to let her curate a show for him and no one would be the wiser.

You're not thinking, Joy. You never think.

Her grandmother's words slammed into her head; how often had she heard them? *Impulsive, irresponsible, hasty.* She'd been hearing it her whole life, and now, striding through San Francisco with a piece of stolen art in her handbag, Joy thought maybe her grandmother was right.

But it was too late now. She couldn't just go up to Ash and say, "Oopsie! Look what happened to fall into my purse!" So she kept walking.

The neighborhood became more dodgy as she headed west, but Joy barely noticed the panhandlers and wackos as she whipped around a corner and headed up the hill. A man asked her if she wanted to buy some "good shit," but she politely said no and went on her way. She had found that most "bad" parts of cities could be successfully navigated if she walked fast and looked like she knew where she was going. San Francisco, Paris, Rome, Munich— they all had their bad sides, and Joy had been mugged only once. And that had been in Barcelona; it was a very unpredictable city.

Now she hugged her purse close to her side. If anyone tried to steal from her, she would have to use her rusty self-defense moves. No way was she letting this artistic treasure out of her hands.

On the way, she paused briefly to admire a spray-painted mural. The graffiti was beautiful, and she recognized the artist. Well, she recognized his work, even if the artist himself was a total mystery. His murals just appeared, as if overnight, and they were special. She recognized the pure, raw talent of the artist, and not for the first time she wished she knew who had created it. She dug a business card and the tape she carried for just this purpose out of her purse and stuck the card to the wall. She had no idea if the artist was getting her cards; he certainly had never called her. But she couldn't help but hope he would, someday.

Catching some movement out of the corner of her eye, she quickly turned and continued on to her destination. Minutes later she was in the lobby of a huge, old apartment complex and running up three flights of stairs. As usual, an array of appetizing scents accosted her as she made her way upstairs. Her mouth began to water, and as she got closer to Erica's door, Joy's stomach was downright grumbling at the spicy scent of curry coming from apartment 305.

Erica was Joy's oldest and best friend. At thirty-two, Erica had recently ditched her ten-year stint as a waitress to attend culinary school. Like many of the students, she lived in this building, which was just across the street from the San Francisco Culinary College. Because it housed mainly culinary academy students, the decrepit building was always permeated with an array of delicious scents, and, in the heart of a semester when everyone was practicing for midterms, the smells escaping through apartment doors were downright mouthwatering.

Tonight was no different. Joy rapped on the door, and seconds later Erica was there, smiling and pulling her inside. "You made it!"

Joy hung her coat on a rack. "Of course. And I'm starving!" Apparently thievery could make a girl hungry, but she kept that little discovery to herself. "Something smells delish."

Erica pulled a white kitchen towel from the pocket of a floral apron. Underneath she wore a sleeveless blue sundress that was probably vintage from the fifties. The old-school dress contrasted nicely with her thin arms, which showcased her colorful tattoos.

"Come into the kitchen." Erica wore her pinkish hair in

a high ponytail, and she brushed a strand behind her ear. Her alternative look didn't negate the fact that Joy's best friend was gorgeous—tattoos, pink hair, pierced nose, and all.

The apartment was small but cozy. An old, worn table and the mismatched chairs surrounding it took up most of the space. The kitchen was tiny but perfectly organized, with pots hanging from a rack over the stove and spices lined up and clearly labeled on a wall rack. Erica's place was the exact opposite of Joy's in terms of organization.

Joy took a seat on a well-worn upholstered dining chair, placing her bag gently beside her.

"Taste." Erica placed a spoon before Joy, and she took a bite of green curry.

Joy's eyes drifted shut as a wave of curry-induced ecstasy washed over her. "Oh my *God*. You've added a bit more lemongrass this time, haven't you?"

Straightening, Erica looked pleased. "Damn, woman. You're good."

"Learned from the best."

She thought she saw the faintest blush tinge Erica's cheeks, but that seemed highly unlikely; she'd never seen her friend blush in all the time she'd known her. Of course, she'd never seen Erica take a chance such as dropping her reliable job as a waitress to join the competitive, male-dominated chef world, either. But Joy never thought she'd commit an art felony. After tonight, she was beginning to think anything was possible.

"So! Tell me about the gala. Did you get the exclusive you were looking for? Did you get Ash Hunter?"

Joy shifted in her seat, the thought of Ash—of his hands on her skin—causing her body to heat. "Not exactly."

Erica glanced over her shoulder. "What do you mean, not exactly?"

Arranging the silverware on the table, Joy avoided Erica's knowing eyes. The woman knew her all too well. "We still have some details to work out."

"But you think he's willing to work with you?"

Me, Joy. Let me. His words flooded her head, and she felt the back of her neck heat.

Repressing a shiver, she nodded. "I think so. We're going to, er, talk more tomorrow night."

Erica opened a bottle of chardonnay, poured two glasses, and set one before Joy. "You like this guy."

Joy shook her head. "Not like that. I don't think." She couldn't think. "I don't know." Her wrist still tingled where he'd held her.

Delicate hands. She laughed and shook her head. "It doesn't matter. I need him—his art, I mean—or I'm going to get fired."

Erica placed two huge bowls of curry on the table. "I seriously doubt that, Joy. I mean, not after what went down between you and Cartwright."

Joy heard the bitter edge to her friend's words but ignored it. Sometimes Erica could be a tad overprotective. What had happened between her and William Cartwright, the man from England who owned all the galleries world-wide, was that she'd had a weeklong affair with him, had fancied herself in love, and then he'd gone back to London without so much as a thank-you or good-bye, unless one counted the dismissive e-mail he'd sent when he returned to London.

Joy didn't.

"Have you even heard from him lately?" Erica spooned

a heaping bite of curry into her mouth and chewed with vigor.

"Just work-related stuff," Joy muttered, not wanting to admit some of those "work-related" e-mails had definitely been flirtatious. Like when he ended one with a *P.S. What are you wearing?*

She'd ignored it.

"So if your boss here wants to fire you, just go over his head."

"No way. I'm not using sex as a means of keeping my job." Joy took a bite of curry, closing her eyes and savoring the salty-sweet flavor.

"You like it?"

Joy opened her eyes to find Erica watching her expectantly. "I love it. Thanks for this; I needed it." Glancing at her bag, she took another few gulps of wine and ignored the flutter of nerves when she remembered the stolen item inside her purse.

"Everything okay?" Erica asked, refilling Joy's glass.

"Yes." Again she brought her wine to her lips and took a deep swallow. "Definitely. Everything is going to be just fine."

An hour later, Erica put a slightly tipsy Joy into a cab and sent her home. She waited until the taxi's lights had faded before she turned and went back inside her building. Just like every time she said good-bye to Joy, she wondered when the woman was going to see how beautiful she was, how good she was. In fact, she was so pure of heart she made an easy target for assholes like the owner of the gallery she worked for, that loser Cartwright, to prey upon.

Fingering the amethyst pendant hanging on a silver chain around her neck, she bounded up the stairs back to her apartment. Joy didn't think Erica knew how much he'd hurt her, but she did know. When Joy hurt, Erica practically felt it herself.

When they'd met, Erica had been waitressing at a hip restaurant popular with Stanford students. Serving a bunch of preppies wasn't exactly Erica's dream job, but she made three times the tips that she would have in any other area.

Thanks to a ludicrous zoning regulation, she'd been forced to go to school with the upper class her entire life and, as a result, had always been the outcast. The poor kid. The girl in the hand-me-downs.

Despite Joy's privileged upbringing, she was somewhat of an outcast herself, and she came into the restaurant often to study. Always alone, Joy would pore over her huge art history books as she ate crème brûlée and drank coffee.

One night some frat boys were giving Erica a hard time, trying to get her to leave work and go back to their place. When one went so far as to put his hand on her arm, Joy had jumped up and thrown hot coffee in his face. Erica could tell Joy had been surprised by her impulsive action, but ever since that moment, they'd been the best of friends.

In her apartment, Erica cleaned up the dishes and sprayed down the kitchen. Then everything was clean, and there was nothing left to do. Tapping her foot, she looked around her empty apartment. Something on the floor caught her eye, and she bent to pick the item up. A ponytail holder. Joy was constantly losing the things. Smiling, Erica went to the dresser, lifted the lid off a box, and dropped the piece of elastic inside, where it joined about twenty of its friends. Yeah, Joy was a bit of a mess sometimes, but she was an intelligent, lovable, beautiful mess. And if one more guy hurt her, he'd have Erica to answer to.

The sculpture was even more beautiful than she remembered.

When Joy arrived home, she placed it on her dresser and tried not to stare at it. She needed a distraction, and she had just the thing. After she changed into leggings and a half shirt, she pulled out a DVD and slid it into the player. She'd started belly dancing about four years ago, and it was her secret passion, one only she knew about. Far too insecure to ever dance in public, she performed her hobby only at home, in her bedroom. It always distracted her from her worries, and the exotic music seemed to sink into her bones, inspiring her to move. But now, as she danced to her most recent belly-dance DVD, for some reason she couldn't totally distract herself from the sculpture on her dresser. It was like the figures were watching her. Her first audience. Was that why she danced extra hard? She worked up quite a sweat as she moved her hips, undulated her abdomen, and snaked her arms. And after, as she changed into an old T-shirt, washed her face, and brushed her teeth, she couldn't stop her gaze from drifting back to the sculpture's sensual form.

It was turning her on.

And every time she looked at it, she saw Ash's intense green eyes, saw his lips tilt up in that cocky smile, felt his warm hands on her body. Remembered what his lips felt like kissing her, breathing against her skin.

As she climbed into bed, her nipples hardened, recalling the way his thumb had lightly grazed her sensitive flesh. His hands were . . . magic hands.

Magic hands?

She pulled up the covers to her chin. He had her thinking like a ninny, thinking with her body and not her brain. She was too smart for this, too smart to fall for a charmer like him.

Like Cartwright.

Do not go there.

But her gaze drifted back to the sculpture, and she felt her body's own arousal. The miniature image of a female form, sitting cross-legged, her arms bound behind her body with rope. It looked so real, the way the woman's head was tossed back slightly, as if in ecstasy.

Much like Joy had probably looked earlier that night, when Ash had stepped between her legs and kissed her throat.

The thought sent a throbbing to her sex, made her open her thighs just a bit, but it only made her feel empty, made her crave something, even if she wasn't sure what it was. Powerful submission. Every time she looked at that sculpture, that's what she thought of, and she realized she was curious to know what it was like. And she was positive she knew a man who could show her exactly that. Hell, for some reason, he even seemed to want to, which was strange. She wasn't exactly a model, and she'd seen his work, knew what he was used to, and it wasn't Joy. She was the opposite of tall and thin, and the thought of him seeing her less-than-perfect naked body sent a jolt of fear shooting through her.

But she couldn't help but wonder. *If* she agreed to let

Ash tie her, what would he do? Would he tie her hands behind her back, like the sculpture? Just thinking about it made her wet, and she slid her hand under the covers to lift the hem of her T-shirt, to reach underneath and pinch her nipple.

Would he do that? Would he pinch her, taste her, bite her?

Would she let him?

She imagined she was helpless. She imagined it was his hands roaming across her skin, reaching between her legs and sliding under her panties. She spread her legs and imagined it was his mouth biting on her nipple until it stung and she gasped, until she moaned aloud. She could almost feel what it would be like to be powerless as he spread her labia open with his hands and stroked her, using his long, beautiful hands to finger her clit, used those fingers to fuck her, harder and deeper, until she was screaming for release, and all the while tied, vulnerable to his touch. . . .

She arched against her hand, rubbed harder, used her own wetness to slide her palm around her pussy, to work herself. She wanted Ash to fuck her. She wanted to feel his long, hard body against hers, touching her, using her.

The thought was shocking, wrong, even. What modern woman wanted to be used by a man? But as her arousal built, as her own moans of pleasure filled the room, her mind wouldn't release the idea, and as she pulled her clit tight between her fingers and pulled, she imagined it was Ash's teeth sucking her flesh.

She tried his name out loud, softly at first. "Ash," she whispered into the stillness. A shock of pleasure bolted through her, so then she whimpered, said it louder. "Ash."

Losing it completely, tossing her head as she pinched and pulled and tugged, crying out, "Ash, yes, Ash!" She came against her hand, her nipple squeezed tight between her other fingers, her body shuddering beneath the covers as she cried out. And even as she climaxed, she was thinking she *wanted* Ash to do to her anything he wanted.

Anything at all.

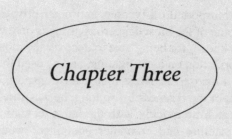

Chapter Three

So, are you in?"

Ash looked across the diner table to where his old military buddy, Juan Romero, sat across from him. He hadn't seen the special-ops soldier since Ash had left five years ago, but the five-foot-eight wall of muscle looked even more solid than he remembered. Judging from the huge pile of pancakes the guy had just consumed, Ash concluded he was spending a lot of time at the gym burning calories since he'd been discharged.

Ash preferred cheeseburgers for breakfast and shoved the last bite into his mouth. "You only need me to monitor? No fieldwork?"

"We need a contact here, someone who speaks the language and can get the local data on road conditions. You still have your contacts overseas?"

Ash nodded, adrenaline already sparking in his blood. No amount of security clearances would get him the first-hand information he'd need to keep the ground crew safe as they transported oil tycoons and other private parties across some of the most dangerous grounds on the planet. Ash was known for being able to uncover the most up-to-date information on local fighting, and he used that information to devise the safest routes for transport. Despite being out of the business for so long, he was sure he'd be able to catch up quickly with the latest technology, and today's satellite and computer equipment would only allow him to be more accurate than ever.

Romero drained the rest of his coffee. "So. I've already got a signed contract for a year of private security duty in Iraq. I've handpicked my team. You remember John, Andy, and Christof, right?"

"Definitely." They were all ex–special-ops guys, all the best at what they did, and Ash had executed many missions with them, including that last ill-fated operation.

"I just need a computer guy here at home to manage everything and make sure our gadgets work."

Ash leaned back, staring at his ex-teammate across the red Formica table. The diner was themed with 1950s decor, complete with an old jukebox and a black-and-white-tiled floor. With his military haircut and crisp shirt, Romero looked like he would have fit right in had this actually been the fifties.

Unlike Ash. He was anal about most things in life except his appearance. He hated worrying about his hair, and he often forgot to shave. It was incongruous to the rest of his personality, but there it was.

He'd hated that part of the military, having someone else tell you to cut your hair and what to wear, exactly what time to go to sleep and get up. But Romero was offering private work, so he wouldn't have to worry about any of that.

Ash said, "I gotta tell you, Romero, your timing couldn't be better. Turns out, I'm between projects at the moment, and I've been looking for something."

Romero chuckled. "Ain't we all?"

"Are we?" He'd predicted he'd grow out of this feeling when he hit thirty, but, at thirty-five, Ash was more restless than ever.

"And you wouldn't have to leave the area. I know that's important to you because of your mom and sister. How are they doing, anyway?"

"You know. Fine. The usual." He ignored the look of sympathy that flashed through Romero's eyes. "Count me in," he said, purposely changing the subject.

"Great. I expect to have things going in the next week. Are you sure you're up for this?"

Ash nodded. "Definitely."

Romero brought his coffee cup to his lips and swallowed. "So, Hunter, what have you been doing with yourself these past few years, anyway? I know you were in private security after you left, but when did you quit?"

"About a year ago. The company I was working for got bought out, and I was outsourced." He shrugged. "I had stock, though, so I didn't have to worry about money."

Romero whistled appreciatively. "Nice. And since then you've become a man of leisure?"

Ash hesitated, for some reason uncomfortable sharing his erotically artistic endeavors with his special-ops teammate. "Yeah. I guess you could say that." Romero's words stung. Ash already felt guilty for taking time off, for taking photographs when he should have been working.

Yeah, he had money in the bank, but he had a family to worry about, a mother and a sister who needed him. He was all they had—he'd never forget that.

"It was hard to find men who weren't attached. You know, to a wife and kids." Juan grinned. "Somehow I knew you'd still be a bachelor, though."

Ash fidgeted with his fork, laughing wryly. "I guess I just haven't found the right girl." But an image of Joy flashed through his head, with her bright red hair and sparkling hazel eyes. Her skin had felt so good beneath his hands; he could get used to that feeling.

"It's for the best," Romero said. "Guys like us aren't made to settle down. We get antsy, you know what I'm saying?"

Ash did, all too well.

Romero grinned. "Well, I need you here for now, so don't get too antsy on me yet."

"I won't, Juan. I'm signed on now, and you know I'll have your back."

Romero reached across the small table and gave Ash a soft punch to the arm. "You always did, Hunter. You always did."

The next day, Saturday, Joy came up with a million reasons she should cancel going to Ash's that night. As she sat at her desk in the gallery, she kept peeking at the number one reason, which was hidden in her file drawer, the tiny sculpture she'd stolen from Ash Hunter.

It was as sensual as ever, and her little self-love the night before hadn't dampened her reaction to the piece one bit. Even now, looking at it made her tingle everywhere. And knowing Ash had crafted something that caused such a reaction in her made her excited and scared to see him again.

Excited because she wanted those hands on her body.

Scared because she'd stolen from a guy whose life seemed to revolve around defense and security.

"Well, well, look who's on time for once."

Joy looked up to see her boss, the portly Mr. Panos, waddling over to her desk. Straightening, Joy met his dark, accusatory stare. "Good morning, Mr. Panos. How are you today?"

"I'll be better if you tell me you got that exclusive I've been asking for."

She shut the drawer. "I'm working on it. I have a meeting with a promising artist tonight."

"Good. In this economy we need a big name right now, and something edgy. I'm depending on you, Joy. Your fancy art history degree may look pretty on the wall, but if you can't sell art, you need to start thinking about teaching or something. You know what they say, those who can't *do* teach. And those who can't teach, teach art history!"

Joy bit her tongue to keep herself from retorting. Instead she watched Panos waddle away, his backside ticktocking from side to side like a huge pendulum. She picked up her pencil and released her anger through some free-flow cussing: *Fuckwad dicknose bucket-of-lard asshole...*

There. She drew little hearts and flowers around the words, and when she felt calm again, she took a deep breath, tore up the paper, and threw the tattered pieces into the garbage.

Their receptionist, Andrew Xiao, pushed through the

front door and placed a paper cup on her desk. "Nonfat latte."

"Thanks. I need this. I just got reamed by Panos. Again."

With his Mohawk, black mod boots, and wool sweater, Andrew looked like he'd just stepped out of an Urban Outfitters catalog. Sipping his coffee, he rested one skinny, jean-clad hip against Joy's desk and rolled big brown eyes. "Panos is such a moron," he said in a low voice, and still the words echoed in the empty space.

Looking around the gallery, she sighed. It was dead. "We had one couple come in earlier, but when they didn't find any impressionist landscapes, they left in a hurry."

Coffee cup in hand, Joy started pacing the concrete floor. "The problem is location. We need to be down on the East Side where all the other modern galleries and shops are, not on Union Square where the art scene died five years ago."

"No shit. Fortunately this place seems to be more of a hobby for the owner than anything else. I doubt he'll shut us down."

Joy paused in front of an enormous abstract. The artist was slowly moving her work to the east galleries but was letting Joy keep a couple of pieces, mainly because Joy had begged her to. "We're losing our artists."

"Have you thought of applying anywhere else?" Andrew asked gently.

"The thought of starting at yet another gallery . . ." It seemed every time she changed jobs, it was just proof that her art history degree had been as useless as her family had told her it would be. There was always museum work, but she loved finding new artists, exposing the public to new and exciting cultural finds, seeing their looks of delight after Joy hung a piece on their walls. She shook her head. "I just can't do it, not yet."

She looked around the space, at the same art that had been hanging on the walls for months. The place was starting to look stale, even to her. "We just need something amazing to set us apart, to make people want to come here."

Andrew looked skeptical. "Any ideas?"

Her gaze went to her desk, and she pictured the stolen artifact inside. She gave Andrew a tiny smile. "You know what they say, right?"

"Every rose has a thorn?"

"Besides that," she said, rolling her eyes. "They say sex sells." And all Joy needed was the sex to sell. And she knew just where to find some.

Joy clenched her shaking hand into a tight fist and rapped three times on Ash's door.

She hoped she looked okay. What did one wear to a professional-possibly-could-end-up-in-bondage date?

She'd changed about ten times before settling on a plain brown knit dress. She'd worn her hair down and attempted to tame it with smoothing gel, and she'd even put on some green eye shadow in the hopes of giving her boring hazel eyes some life.

On her feet were her usual flats. It was either this or tennis shoes. Unlike most girls, Joy didn't have a shoe fetish, and her closet displayed this by its dismal selection. Every time Joy entered a shoe store, she tended to get overwhelmed by the choices and always left empty-handed.

Now she wished she had worn some sexier shoes. Heart thumping, she waited for him to answer the door.

What if he knew about the sculpture? What if he was angry?

What if he tried to kiss her again?

What if he wanted to tie her up? The idea had been at the back of her mind ever since last night, and she knew that she could be persuaded.

Easily persuaded.

No, no, no. You stole from him; you can't have sex with him!

The door opened, and he was there, grinning at her, those little lines around his eyes crinkling again. He wore jeans, a T-shirt, and boots. For one second, she forgot why she'd been scared to come here.

"Joy. Come on in."

"Thanks." She dipped her head and crossed inside, taking a moment to feel the warmth of his body as she passed. Why did she always seem to heat up whenever she was anywhere near his vicinity?

Stepping inside, she took in the spacious flat. The style reminded her of her oldest brother's modernist decor. The old building space had obviously been remodeled, and the style was eclectic mid-century, most of it open space. Huge windows took up an entire length of the far wall, and Joy gasped aloud when her gaze landed on the beautiful view of the San Francisco skyline.

The kitchen was to the right, with modern concrete countertops and stainless-steel appliances. It seemed to shine, as if it was rarely used. In fact, the entire place was spotless and orderly, from the carefully arranged bookshelves that spanned the wall next to the glass dining table to the uncluttered desk under a spiral staircase; Ash Hunter was obviously a neat freak.

Strange. You wouldn't guess from his appearance.

Pulling her bag off her shoulder, she went to the low, brown sofa, above which hung a huge black-and-white photograph of a naked woman, bound in rope from ankle to shoulder, suspended, hanging horizontally in midair. Mesmerized, Joy dropped her purse onto the couch and then shrugged off her coat and dumped it onto the cushions, all the while staring at the photograph. She couldn't see the woman's face, which was hidden by her long dark hair that hung nearly to the floor, but she could see the curve of her breasts, her nipples, and her ass. Joy's pulse ratcheted up another notch. What was it about Ash's art that made her so aroused?

"You like that?" He picked up her purse and coat and hung them on a coatrack.

She nodded. "Very much. It's a shame you don't want to take photographs anymore. I can't believe you're just giving up." *And maybe I can persuade you to change your mind.*

"Yeah." But she heard something in his tone of voice, as if he was unsure, and the way he was staring at her made her think she'd give up her collection of silk scarves to know what he was thinking at that moment.

"Is your studio here?" she asked.

He jerked his head to the left, and she followed his gesture to a large alcove. His photography studio, obviously. There was an old-fashioned camera on a tripod and several umbrella lights scattered around the floor. Joy took a step toward the staging area, where a large piece of black fabric hung opposite the camera. Then she turned and gasped.

Right. The rope bondage—that was what was making

her heart race, what was perpetuating that erotic nuance that was hanging heavy in the air. And it wasn't like she could ignore it; the rope was directly in her vision now, multicolored nylon looped around pegs, dotting the entire opposite wall, forming colorful circles from floor to ceiling.

She found herself moving toward the wall, much as she'd done with the painting last night in the museum. She reached out and stroked a length of red cord, the material soft yet sturdy-feeling beneath her fingertips.

It reminded her of his sculptures, and her body responded; between her legs a small pulse began to beat as she thought of the photograph, of the sculptures in the museum, the one in her desk. Of Ash and his hands, what they were capable of, both artistically and physically.

She felt him behind her, felt his fingers as they moved her hair off her neck, and then his lips softly brushed the top of her spine. Her eyes fluttered shut as the heat from his mouth seemed to spread all over her skin.

"I can't keep my hands off you," he whispered, nipping at her earlobe.

Her knees weak, she turned to face him and met his gaze. *I don't want you to.* She shook the thought out of her head. It was wrong, so very wrong to want him so badly. She had to resist. She had to remember what was at stake. Her job, her honor, and she was way too attached to her home to trade it in for a jail cell.

But he was making it so very hard to focus on anything but him, touching her, looking at her with those deep green eyes. Cupping her cheeks in his palms, he brought his face toward hers, and then he was kissing her, his mouth slanting over hers as he slid his tongue inside her mouth. She kissed him back, thinking for a second that she'd never had a kiss quite like this, like she was losing herself completely as everything around her faded. Like she was losing herself.

She pulled back. "Does every girl you meet end up tied up on the first date?"

"Pretty much."

"I'm not every girl."

"I see that." He looked her over in a quick, hot glance. "I like that."

"I want to talk about the gallery, about your art."

He backed her against the wall, and she felt a length of rope pressing against her upper back. A shudder ripped through her, landing right in her sex.

"Are you sure?" He pressed his mouth to hers, nipped at her bottom lip.

"Yes . . ." And then she pushed her tongue into his mouth.

But soon he took over the kiss, and when he pulled back, her body felt slack.

"You know you want to be tied, sweetheart. Admit it."

"Yes, but—"

"That's all I needed to hear."

He kissed her as he pressed his hard form against her body. His hands, more roughly now, roamed over the fabric of her knit dress. Her waist, her hips, her arms; he seemed to be touching her ubiquitously.

"Let go, Joy. Don't think."

"Was I thinking?"

"Trust me."

"God . . ."

He continued to kiss her; she continued to melt. She

felt him take her hands and press her wrists together to bring her arms above her head. He was stretching her, and she arched against him, wanting to feel him against her breasts. Wanting to feel him everywhere.

How could she want this? It was too much, too fast.

"Tell me what you want, Joy."

And yet there was no hesitation in her answer. "Whatever you want, Ash. I want you to do whatever you want. To me."

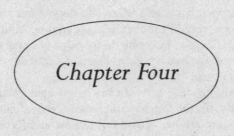

Chapter Four

She saw the corded muscles of his arms loosen, the only sign that he'd been anxious she might say no.

It took only a couple of minutes, and just the process of him binding her, the feeling of the corded material wrapping around her skin, made her pussy go wet, made her entire body hum with lust. When she felt him tie her off, she tested the rope, and while it wasn't uncomfortable, it was secure. Her wrists were bound, like she was his prisoner.

"You all right?"

"Yes." She was more than all right. The act of submission made her pussy ache in a way she'd never experienced and, surprisingly, calmed her.

Smiling, he pulled her arms tight above her, his body stretched against hers, something she was quite sure he did on purpose. Against her hips, she felt his erection through his jeans and her dress; goose bumps erupted over her arms.

He stepped back, and when she tugged her arms, she realized she couldn't move; he'd secured her to the wall.

"Ash?" She was hovering on the edge of being anxious and thrilled, the two emotions mingling until she couldn't tell them apart.

He took her face between his palms again and kissed her, gently, for the longest time, until she was calm, until the ropes around her wrists felt almost comforting, like they were part of her. Submitting to him, she stopped fighting, and then he got on his knees before her, moving slowly to kiss her body as he made his way down. When he nuzzled his face against her hip, kissed her hip bone through the fabric of her dress, she lost it, lost all control.

"Ash . . . I need you." Between her legs there was a want; she was pounding with need—for him. She'd never felt a need like this. Ever. The bonds heightened every sensation coursing through her, and she welcomed, claimed, each one.

He lifted the hem of her dress until it was pushed up around her waist. For a second, she thought she must be out of her head, because normally she felt very self-conscious when she was exposed. And she'd never been so vulnerable with someone she barely knew.

But now, that sense of anonymity seemed to entice her, and she stretched her body, arched, let his hands move under her dress to feel her skin. She saw desire in his eyes, and it made her feel sexy, feminine. Maybe it was the ropes, being bound and helpless, giving herself to him; she felt a bit as if she were floating. She felt her own smile on her face as she waited for him, watching Ash's gaze, which was now focused on her panties, her swollen clit.

He glanced up. "Do you like being tied, Joy?"

She nodded.

"Tell me you like it." He placed a soft, warm kiss in that spot he'd been staring at, his breath muffled through the lace of her panties.

"I like it, Ash. I like being tied by you."

"I don't know what it is about you, baby. You make me so fucking turned on." With one hand, he yanked her panties down her legs, still holding her dress up with his other hand. "You always look so . . ."

"What?" she whispered. How did he see her?

"Ready for me. Like you want me to take you."

"I do. Take me." She couldn't believe the words coming out of her mouth. She'd never talked like this, never been so demanding. But with Ash she felt safe. *Maybe too safe,* a little voice whispered in the back of her head, and she ignored it.

"Spread your legs."

She stepped her legs farther apart, as wide as she could go. With both his hands, he kept her dress up around her hips and pushed her ass back against the wall. Rope hung to her left and to her right, above her. Binding her. Surrounding her. She shuddered.

"Taste me, Ash. Fuck me."

"How did you know dirty talk turns me on?" he asked with a wicked grin.

"I want to feel your mouth on my pussy."

"That's my girl," he said, and then he was licking her, spreading her with his thumbs, spreading her wide so he could use his mouth to sweetly torment her, and she heard herself moaning, pleading.

"Oh, God," she said, pressing hard against him, pulling

at her bindings. "Yes, oh my God. I'm going to come, Ash. . . ."

He looked up. "Do it. Come for me, right here against my face. And then I'm going to fuck you, and you're going to come again."

"Yes," was all she managed. "I want that. . . ."

Slowly, tortuously, he licked her, from as deep as he could reach to her throbbing clit: licking, sucking, tugging. She threw her head back against the wall, feeling her hair tangle as she thrashed her head from side to side. When she came against his face, it was like lightning shooting through her, and she screamed his name, crying out over and over as he sucked every last tremble out of her body.

Finally, when she stilled, he stood. His gaze raked over her, and she imagined what she must look like. Arms tied overhead, her dress wrinkled and hanging around her waist. Her hair a rat's nest. In total disarray, the exact opposite of everything she'd come to know about Ash.

But he smiled at her and brushed a strand of hair off her face. "You're a mess."

She felt the blush starting at her neck.

"I like it. I don't know why, but I do. You're so different, Joy. Different from any woman I've been with."

She lifted her chin. "Is that good or bad?"

"Good." He kissed her, and she tasted herself on his lips, acidic and erotic. "Right now it feels really good."

"You know what would feel even better?" she asked against his mouth, licking at his lips and tasting herself and him, while a fresh wave of lust washed over her.

"What's that, baby?"

"If you did as you promised and fucked me."

Reaching into the neckline of her dress, he slid his hand beneath her bra and took her nipple between his fingertips. She gasped as pleasure bolted through her. "I intend to," he said, kissing her again. He beaded her nipple and pinched, the sharp sting heightening the powerful sensations already pulsing through her, and her sex clenched with need.

"You like that, baby?"

"I think so." He pinched again, harder, and pure bliss rushed through her. "Yes."

"Good. Now tell me what you want. Exactly what you want."

"I want to feel you inside me. I want you to fuck me right here, against this wall."

"Goddamn, Joy." He kicked off his boots and pulled his shirt over his head. Her gaze landed on his exposed upper body with appreciation. She'd thought him thin, but he was all muscle. Sinewy elegance, almost feline. So unlike her own curvaceous body.

Don't think about it. In any other circumstance, she would have probably run away, her insecurities taking over as she looked at a man so hard, lean, and powerful. But she was too turned on; her body needed him, and as he pulled off his jeans and boxers, she could see he needed her, too.

He glanced down at the erection standing straight up, long and hard and male. "You do this to me, Joy." He took his hard penis in his hand, starting at the base, and stroked up to the head and back again. She licked her lips as a drop of come leaked from the engorged head.

"Is this what you want? It will be, sweetheart. Hard and rough. I bet that's how you like it."

She swallowed. "Yes." She could feel her body

secreting her arousal, knew she'd be so wet and slick for him. "Hurry."

He had a condom in his hand, and he tore open the packaging and rolled the rubber onto his cock. Wide-eyed and panting, she watched him as he came for her. This time when he kissed her, it was rough, forceful. She moaned deep in her throat as she met him full-on, pulling on the rope binding her, encouraging him to take her as he wanted.

His hands on her thighs were also rough as he lifted her and pushed her body against the wall. He picked her up as if she weighed only as much as a feather, and a wonderful sense of femininity settled inside her. She wrapped her legs around him as he drove into her, filled her.

"Yes, Ash. Like that." Talking like this, telling him what she wanted, felt so right.

"Like this?"

He pulled out and fucked her again, his hands on her body rough and bruising. He kissed her once more, trailing his fingers up her arm until he was touching the rope around her wrists.

"God, yes."

"You like giving yourself to me, don't you, baby?"

"Yes," she admitted, and the word was raspy, dry. Her mouth felt like a desert.

Every time he drove into her, it seemed harder and deeper than the last time, and that was exactly what she wanted; she wanted to be taken like this, by him. Hard, reckless, wild.

"You're so hot and wet for me," he said, driving into her with such force she felt the wall scratching at her back. "I want you to come now, Joy."

She was already on the edge, and those words were all

it took as he buried himself into her one more time, and she exploded, screaming, shaking, mindless.

"Fuck, yes, that's my girl." Every muscle in his body seemed to go even tighter as he stiffened, pressing his entire lean form against her, and she felt him ejaculate, pulsing hotly inside her.

She wasn't sure how much time passed, but as the endorphins of sex with Ash began to fade, Joy became hyperaware of everything else: a car whizzing by outside, the orderliness of his loft, their bodies sticky against each other. She squirmed against him as a flush began to creep up her neck.

What had made her feel sexy only minutes before now caused her to burn with shame. Her makeup was probably smeared; her hair was a mess. Her skirt was hiked up nearly to her breasts, and the curve of her stomach felt soft against Ash's rigid, solid abdomen.

Beyond Ash's shoulder, she took in the photograph of the model with the perfect body, and Joy's skin began to crawl. Had Ash ever been with a woman as curvy as Joy?

What must he be thinking of her now? That he'd made a big mistake?

She tugged on the ropes. "Let me down. *Please.* Ash."

Within seconds she was free, and he was carrying her in his arms.

"You can put me down. Seriously, I'm way too heavy for this."

He looked at her as if she were crazy. "What are you talking about? You weigh nothing."

"I mean it, Ash. You don't have to do this."

But he was already climbing the stairs, at an impressive

clip, she had to note. He must be freakishly strong to carry her so effortlessly.

When they reached the top floor, he walked straight to his bedroom. Like the rest of the house, it was spotless with nary a stray sock in sight. He rested her on a bed made so tight she could have bounced a quarter off it.

She went to pull her dress down, but he prevented her from doing so with a firm touch. "Stop. How do you feel?" He massaged the places on her skin where the rope had been tied.

Embarrassed, awkward, anxious. She tried to smile. "Fine."

He continued to massage her flesh, and she felt her pulse relax a little. Then he kissed her wrists, softly, and smiled at her. "I want you to stay here tonight."

She tried to push herself up onto her elbows, but he urged her back down until she was flat on the bed, flat on her back. He slid one long leg between her thighs and leaned his chest against hers. He kissed her.

She resisted for a second, but then she was reaching up to hold his head to her, to run her fingers along the muscles of his neck. She wasn't sure how much time passed with the easy way they kissed and touched, but by the time he pulled back, she knew he'd done it again. Made her his. What she wasn't sure of was why.

And at the moment, it didn't matter.

She thought of all the reasons she'd come here, to lure him to the gallery, to tell him about the sculpture. But this was too good to mess up with that kind of talk. It felt too good when he pulled her to his body and tucked her under his arm. She sank into him, into the bed, and eventually into sleep.

Chapter Five

"Still no answer?"

Shaking her head, Erica flipped her cell phone shut with a frustrated click. "No, and now I'm really getting worried. It's 1:00 a.m." It was, in fact, so late that Erica and Blaine were the only people in the building using the student kitchen.

Fellow culinary student Blaine Prescott looked up from the pan of onions he was sautéing. "Do you always look out for Joy like this?" he asked in his annoyingly precise voice. It reminded her of those overeducated students she used to serve, and she clenched her teeth. She'd heard a rumor that he was on a break from his überlawyer job because he wanted to learn how to cook. Must be nice.

She gave him her dirtiest look. "I can't help it if I have friends I care about." For the millionth time, Erica cursed her instructor for pairing her with the stuck-up chef-to-be for the entire semester. The man was always questioning everything Erica did. And making suggestions when she hadn't asked for any. His only redeeming quality was that Blaine did possess an impressive palate. Annoyingly impressive, but she supposed that was to be expected. He'd probably grown up with a chef trained by Julia Child.

And she had to admit he had some other qualities that didn't suck. Such as his nice ass, his chocolaty brown eyes, his solid-looking shoulders . . .

Ack! What was she thinking? Instead she reminded herself that Blaine epitomized all the things she'd come to detest in a person. He was a conceited, upper-class, rich yuppie. The first time they'd met, he'd just stared at her tattooed arms as if they were overcooked slabs of meat. So she made sure to wear tank tops whenever she knew she was going to see him.

"I have friends I care about, too, Erica. Doesn't mean I stalk them all night long."

She hated it when he said her name. It made her stomach do funny things, which she ignored.

"That's because all your friends are probably home in bed by ten, tucked tidily underneath their three-thousand-thread-count Egyptian sheets."

"Actually, seven hundred is the softest. Anything over that is just silly."

"And I'm sure you know all about thread count. Did your nanny teach you? Or were you just born with this amazing knowledge?"

He paused his stirring, pretending to think. "Must have been born with it. I'll ask *Mummy*." He said the last word with a hoity-toity accent. "You're doing it again."

"Doing what?"

"Playing with your necklace."

She yanked her hand away from the amethyst. It had been a sixteenth-birthday present from her mother, and she never took it off. It reminded her of her mother's strength as she'd single-handedly raised four children, even if it took four jobs to do so.

"Anyway," she said. "I'm not stalking. I'm being a *friend*. Joy went over to some strange guy's house, and I haven't heard from her since. I care. It's called compassion; maybe you've heard of it."

He grinned. "Nope." Then he leaned a bit closer to her, and she tried to ignore the way her heart skipped. "And I never donate to any charities, either. Nor do I help old ladies cross the street. Let them hobble on their own, I say."

"Oh, I don't doubt it." Erica put her hands on her hips. "Joy is my best friend. That's what friends do; they look out for each other."

"Uh-huh." He tossed some chopped fresh sage into the pan.

She held her breath, counted to ten, but in the end she couldn't stop herself. "What do you mean, *uh-huh*?"

He didn't glance up. "I mean *uh-huh*."

Why was she even talking to him? "What the heck do you mean, Prescott?"

"I guess I just don't understand why a beautiful girl such as yourself spends all her time either here or with her best friend or worrying about her best friend. Surely you have other things to occupy your time? A boyfriend? A cat? A body part to pierce?"

Blood beginning to boil, she stepped forward. "Listen, unlike you, I'm here because I want a good job. Not all of us have a fancy degree and can afford to take months off at a time to go to cooking school simply for fun." Erica yanked on her white apron ties, making it tighter, but despite how irritating he was, she couldn't help the little thrill that shot through her at his words. He'd called her beautiful.

Yeah, right. He was just being a sarcastic jerkwad.

"*I* need a good job after I finish school."

"And you'll get one. You're one of the best students here. Not as good as me, of course. But a close second." His grin softened the words into a joke.

But Erica wasn't laughing. "Blaine. Why are you always giving me such a hard time?"

He stared at her, seeming to think about the question, and each second that passed had her pulse racing faster and faster. Finally he said, "I don't know. You're just so uptight. I can't help myself."

A loud guffaw erupted from her throat. "I'm uptight? Me? You're the one with the frat-boy haircut, the perfectly pressed trousers, and the uppity speech pattern."

"So? I could be covered in tattoos and have hidden piercings for all you know."

"Right. I bet this preppy look is just a ruse for your hidden wild nature. I bet you even leave the Beamer at home and take public transportation sometimes!"

He just shrugged. "Actually, I have a Ducati motorcycle. Whatever. Let's just hurry up and finish. Your being overly distracted with your girlfriend is what's keeping us here so late."

Erica ignored the truth of the accusation. "I like things to be perfect; that's the reason I keep starting over. Deal with it."

"I am dealing with it. That's why I'm still here in the student kitchen when I should be tucked under my goose-down comforter."

"You're really irritating, ya know that?"

"So are you."

But he was staring at her, his striking, mocha-colored eyes holding Erica's gaze until she shifted, her black comfort shoes squishing on the rubber floor. *Stop looking at me like that!*

Taking a deep, deep breath, she straightened her apron. Again. It had to be the straightest apron in history. She wasn't going to stop calling Joy until she heard for herself that her friend was okay, but she'd let it rest until they finished in the kitchen and cleaned up. She didn't want to hear any more bitching from Blaine.

"You should add some brandy to that pan," Erica said, just to annoy her partner.

"Oh, shit!" Joy tossed Ash's watch back onto the nightstand. "I have to go!"

A sleeping Ash had bolted upright at her exclamation and was now looking at her with eyes that shouldn't be so awake and alert so fast. "What's wrong?"

Joy went to slide out of bed but realized she was naked. "Where did my clothes go?"

"I took them off when you were sleeping."

"You what . . . ?"

"Took them off while you were sleeping," he said slowly, as if speaking to a person of limited intelligence.

"Great. So you saw me naked."

"Um, yeah. Don't you remember last night?"

"Well, I was awake then! Anyway, where are they?"

"What?" he asked, looking very confused.

"My clothes!" No way was she prancing around in front of Ash in the buff, not with the morning sun glaring through the window, ready and able to showcase each minor imperfection of her body. She pulled off the comforter and wrapped it around her before scooting off the bed.

"Where did you put them?" she said, scanning the floor; that was usually where all Joy's possessions ended up. "Damn, my grandmother's going to kill me." She pictured her wrinkled dress and knew she was going to have to run home and change so she didn't show up at her grandmother's house in a soiled and crumpled garment.

Ash ran a hand over his hair. "It's only nine. Where do you have to be so early on a Sunday? Church?"

"Worse. Every Sunday I go to brunch at my grandmother's house on the peninsula. If I don't show up at ten on the dot, she gets . . . upset." And mean, but Joy kept that part to herself. "Now, where are my clothes?"

Ash got out of bed, clearly having none of the self-conscious issues Joy possessed. Why did men always seem to feel comfortable buck-naked? He strolled over to Joy, gave her a kiss on the head, and headed to the bathroom. "They're in the closet. I washed them."

Joy stared after him, her heart pounding. In the dim light of the previous night, she hadn't noticed the scars on Ash's body. About six inches of skin on his right shoulder looked mottled and uneven, as if he'd been burned. What had happened to him? Then she recalled the way he'd teased her the other night about her slamming into him, and she wondered how much he'd been kidding.

Some instinct told her it wasn't the time to ask. Despite his sexual advances, she realized Ash rarely talked about himself, and she knew she'd have to tread gently if she wanted to know more about him.

With a start, she realized she did. Badly.

Clothes. That's what she needed now. Nearly tripping on the edge of the comforter, Joy padded to the closet. When she opened the door, she nearly dropped the bed-covering altogether because Ash hadn't been joking. Her dress hung, smartly washed and pressed, next to one of Ash's shirts. Her bra and panties were draped neatly over the same hanger.

"Oh my God, when did you do this?" she shouted over her shoulder.

"Last night, while you were sleeping. I had some work to do, anyway." She jumped; he was suddenly standing right behind her. He pressed his body against her back, and she felt his erection through the thick comforter. "You're so cute when you're all frazzled, Joy."

"I'm always frazzled."

"I know."

Her eyes drifted closed as she leaned back against him as he kissed her neck. "I have to go . . . ," she said.

"Mmm. You can. Just give me one kiss first."

She slanted her head back against his shoulder, and just when his lips almost touched hers, she jerked away. "No! Really, you don't understand. I can't be late!" If she started kissing Ash, she'd be unable to stop. Then she'd be really late, and her grandmother would blow a gasket. That was never a pretty sight.

"Fine. Okay." Grinning, he stepped back.

"Thank you for washing this dress. I think I can go straight from here now. Would you do me a huge favor and bring up my bag?"

Still naked, he trotted off, and she couldn't help but pause to admire his firm, naked ass. A wave of desire washed over her, but it was quickly quenched by the fear of being late for her grandmother's brunch.

When he returned, she took her bag and her clothes and disappeared into the bathroom. Like the rest of the house, Ash's master bath was big, modern, and elegant. A huge, square, Zen-looking bathtub took up one side of the room, and on a long walnut counter there were side-by-side white-porcelain-vessel sinks. Lush towels were folded neatly in an open cabinet, and Joy would have given anything to spend the morning pampering herself in the spa-like room.

Instead she quickly rinsed off and put on her bra and panties. Then she turned over her bag and dumped the contents onto Ash Hunter's floor. Smiling, she picked up a linty toothbrush and a free sample of moisturizer. *And this is why I love my purse,* she thought, and was suddenly glad she wasn't the kind of girl who went out at night with only a tiny clutch. If any of those women at the museum fund-raiser had gone home for a one-night stand, they would have been woefully ill-prepared for a brunch date the next morning.

The minute Joy pulled onto the long, tree-lined road leading to her grandmother's house, her palms started to sweat. Even though she was wearing the brown dress from the night before, the cut made it suitable for daytime, and on her feet were the tan flats she always wore. She'd pulled her hair back into a ponytail she hoped would stay put and had applied a little bit of makeup—not too much. She'd even put on some lipstick when she'd found her favorite shade after she'd gone through the contents of her purse. It had rolled behind the toilet (an area, she noted, that had been spotless), but she'd retrieved the tube and now a neutral shade of peach coated her lips.

Grandmother shouldn't have much to pick on.

Now if only Joy could stop thinking about the mind-blowing good-bye kiss Ash had given her just before she left. She could have stayed in his doorway all day, simply kissing him. As she pulled into the gravel driveway and slowly rolled her 1975 Mercedes to a stop, her toes curled as she remembered the way he tasted, the way he'd held her shoulders tightly as he'd slowly licked his way around her mouth.

Heaven.

But she pushed the lovely memory aside as she paused to prepare herself for brunch. Calling her grandmother's residence a house was a slight understatement. It was more like a mansion, and in Atherton, California, a place like this was worth many millions of dollars. Her grandmother owned one of the most expensive pieces of property in the Bay Area.

Built like an English manor, the exterior of the Tudor-style house was covered in ivy, and several huge oak trees dotted the property. Joy had parked in the back, and as she looked around the separate garage area, she tried not to be disappointed.

She had hoped to find at least one of her brothers' cars parked there, but no such luck. With a deep breath, she opened the door and went inside the house, using the kitchen entrance.

"Hi, Grandma." Joy found her grandmother setting bread on the dining table.

"Good morning, Joy," she said, not very surreptitiously glancing at her watch.

It seemed every week she visited her grandmother, the elderly woman became smaller and smaller. As she approached Joy, her back was stooped in her white sweater and her navy slacks seemed loose. When Joy hugged her, she felt the bones of her grandmother's shoulders.

"What can I do to help?" Joy shrugged off her jacket and purse and dropped them onto a side chair.

"It's all done, dear." She gave Joy the weekly once-over and shook her head. "A girl with your figure shouldn't wear that fabric, Joy. It does nothing to hide that tummy." She touched her own trim waist. "I always had the opposite problem. I was so skinny I couldn't find anything to fit properly."

Joy never had that particular problem. Instead she could never find pants that accommodated her curvy hips. "Yes," she said. "That must have been very hard for you."

Grandmother's face was tight as she picked up Joy's discarded items and disappeared through the kitchen door. Joy glared after her, wondering what Ash thought of her midsection, and immediately pictured the superthin model in the photo hanging over his sofa.

She should probably start another diet, but instead she suddenly wanted to eat everything on the table. For some reason, she always ate until she felt sick every Sunday morning she spent in Atherton.

Grandmother came back a few seconds later carrying a plate of smoked salmon and placed it on the table.

"I could have gotten that, Grandma! Why don't you sit down?" *And why are you so freakin' stubborn?*

"Tell me how your week was, Joy." Grandmother took

a seat at the head of the oversized dining table and placed a linen napkin on her lap.

Well, I think I'm getting fired from yet another job, I committed a felony, and I let a playboy artist tie me to a wall and fuck me last night.

She helped herself to a bagel, slathered it with cream cheese, and took a big bite. "You know, Grandma. The usual."

Grandmother eyed the bagel with a frown.

Joy slowly put the bagel on her plate. "Why do you always put them out if you don't want me to eat them?"

"David said he might come to brunch."

Of course, it was okay for one of her brothers to eat as much as they wanted, but not Joy. She laughed harshly. "David always says that, and David never shows up." None of her brothers ever showed up.

Which was why Joy always did.

"He's a busy man. A wife, two kids, and he just was made partner in the firm."

Joy scooped up a large piece of frittata and slid it onto her plate. "That's wonderful."

"Yes, it is." Grandma daintily ate the tiniest piece of smoked salmon. "David made partner in his law firm, Samuel just got the job at Stanford as their newest heart surgeon, and another one of Campbell's companies has gone public. All the boys are doing so well." The words hung heavy in the air, suffocating Joy with insinuation.

"That's just great." She forked in some more frittata. "Good for them."

"You must get your appetite from your father. Your mother was always a dainty eater. Like me."

Joy's mouth was full, so she couldn't answer verbally.

Instead she nodded her assent. Plus, Joy knew where this conversation was headed, and there was no point in arguing. Since Grandmother hit her mid-eighties, she tended to repeat herself, and it was the same story every week.

"It was just awful when your parents died in that plane crash. I *told* them to never fly private in Spain!" Her blue eyes went watery, and Joy never knew if the tears were real or good acting on her grandmother's part. "It's a horrible thing to lose your daughter, Joy. A horrible thing."

Joy thought it had been pretty horrible to lose her parents, too, but she refrained from saying so.

"You were sixteen, and the boys had just gone off to college. I was so proud of the way they handled everything. So proud." She looked at Joy, who was helping herself to another piece of frittata. "Well, an art history degree is great, too."

"The PhD program at Stanford was pretty difficult, Grandma," Joy couldn't help but say.

"Oh, I'm sure. And living in Paris, and traveling, looking at art all day long. Studying." She said the last part with a chuckle. "I can imagine it was just lovely. Girls your age have so many options, don't they? Why, when I was twenty-nine, I already had three children to raise."

And Joy didn't. No children, no husband, and a career that seemed frivolous to the rest of her family.

But she had learned long ago not to argue or defend herself. Nearly fourteen years of experience had taught her it wouldn't do any good. The fact was, Grandmother had taken Joy in when she was a teenager. It was Grandmother who'd come to her high school graduation, who never forgot her birthday, who always made sure she had what she needed. Besides her brothers, the older woman was the only family Joy had. Despite her faults, she loved her grandmother.

"Do we have any champagne?" Joy asked, pushing out of her chair.

"Why, yes. But are you sure you want the extra calories, dear?"

"Oh, I'm sure," Joy said with a sweet smile. "I'm really, really sure."

Chapter Six

After Joy left, Ash stood in his bathroom, gazing sightlessly around him. For the first time in months, he wanted to take photographs, and he wasn't sure if it was his mind's way of rebelling against a job he said he'd never do again, or because of Joy and his desire to see her on film. He wanted to see her through his lens. He wanted to capture the mischievousness that sparkled in her hazel eyes.

And part of him just wanted to capture *her*.

He wanted to see her bound. Last night was a crude tease for him; he needed to explore her body, to decorate her form with rope until she was completely his. Just the thought made him hard. With his models, he rarely became aroused. They were simply objects to help him carry out his vision.

Joy was different, in every way. She was so open; he thought he could tell her anything and she wouldn't judge him. Somehow, he trusted her completely, and in his experience, that was a quality that couldn't be taken lightly.

He twisted the hair tie he'd found on his bathroom floor and smiled. He sniffed it, and it smelled like Joy, like vanilla. His cock twitched. Already, he wanted to see her again.

And he wanted to photograph her. Maybe even do another sculpture; maybe he'd do one just for her. A gift.

Pushing the thoughts aside, he went downstairs to his computer. He couldn't think like that. Hell, maybe he wasn't thinking at all; as Joy slept, he'd been up all night researching navigation routes for a transport that was scheduled in a few hours.

He'd committed to be part of a team, and even if he was doing it from home, he had to put the job first. This was partially why he'd stopped doing art in the first place. He couldn't afford to be frivolous. He needed a steady income, and no matter how much money he had in the bank, it wasn't ever enough. He never felt confident that his mom and sister would be secure if something happened to him.

And yet Romero had called it. Ash couldn't deny the antsy feeling in the pit of his stomach. He knew that feeling, knew it would grow and grow until he was bouncing off the walls. The need to go. To flee.

But he couldn't just pick up and go, not anymore.

He was going to deposit every paycheck from this job directly into his mother's account. His sister's wheelchair was nearly two years old. She could use a new one—and the things weren't cheap. He had responsibilities. He couldn't be distracted by Joy, by art, or by anything else.

That afternoon, Joy was recovering from brunch with Grandmother by reading the latest *Art News* when the doorbell rang. She went to the call box and pushed a button. "Yes?"

"Joy! Where the heck have you been?" Erica's voice asked in a high, shrill tone.

"Hang on." She buzzed her in, and a minute later, Erica was stomping through the door, her red peep-toe pumps clicking on the hardwood floor.

"I've been worried sick, Joy!" But despite her harsh tone, she grabbed Joy in a tight bear hug.

After Erica released her, Joy removed a pile of art books from a kitchen chair and plopped down. Her entire body slumped with weariness, and suddenly the thought of a long, hot bath sounded like heaven.

That would have to wait. "Why were you so worried about me? You know I see my grandmother every Sunday."

Her friend crossed her arms in front of her chest. "I've been calling you since last night!"

"Oh, crap. I think my phone battery died sometime yesterday."

Erica just stared at her for a minute before lifting a basket of fruit off another chair and sitting across from Joy. "Listen, next time you go to some guy's house and disappear, do me a favor and keep your phone on, will you?"

Guilt flooded her. "I'm sorry, Erica. I wasn't thinking about that, I guess. I wasn't planning on spending the night."

Erica leaned across the table, her eyes wide. "You spent the night? Details! Now!"

An unwanted hot flush crept over Joy's skin as she remembered waking up in Ash's arms. "Yeah."

"Did you . . ." Erica made a circle with one hand and moved her other index finger in an in-and-out motion.

"Um, yes. We did." Joy arranged a stack of bills on the table. For some reason, she wasn't ready to talk about the details of her experience with Ash, not yet. She was still relishing the new feelings of being bound by him, still processing the whole thing in her head. It was like a little treat just for her, and she wanted to savor the feelings.

It was a first. She'd met Erica over ten years ago. Unlike most college students who preferred partying on weekends, Joy had spent her Friday nights going to the small but trendy café in Palo Alto for their amazing crème brûlée. Joy normally confided everything to Erica, including her feelings of animosity toward her grandmother. And including details of her sex life.

Joy always thought it strange that, despite her beauty, Erica never seemed interested in any of the many men who courted her. The girl had a wall around her heart two feet deep.

Now Erica's gaze sparkled. "Are you going to see him again?"

"I have no idea. I had to leave in a hurry this morning to get to my grandmother's in Atherton. He didn't mention it, and neither did I." She shook her head at herself, wondering if that phenomenal kiss had been a long kiss good-bye. "But I never did get around to discussing business with him."

"You were there all night, and you never discussed the gallery?" Erica asked incredulously. "What were you doing?" She held up her hand, palm out. "Wait. I don't want to know."

Silence stretched on for a few minutes before Erica spoke. "I don't want you to get hurt again, Joy."

Joy blinked. "Why do you say that?"

"It's just that you always go for these guys who are players, like Cartwright."

"You haven't even met Ash. He's nothing like Cartwright." And yet she'd thought the same thing when she met him.

Now, just the thought of the dashing Englishman sent a rancid churn through her stomach. He truly was an entirely different breed from Ash; she knew it in her heart. Everything about Ash was open, honest. Even though she sometimes caught a glimpse of something dark in his eyes, she trusted him to at least tell her the truth.

And she'd stolen from him.

She pinched the bridge of her nose. "Erica, I appreciate your concern, I really do, and I'm sorry I made you worry. But I've had a long couple of days, and I just want to take a bath and have a glass of wine."

Erica's eyes went soft. "I'm sorry I freaked out on you. I just worry, you know? You're my best friend. I don't want you to get hurt."

Standing, Joy went to her friend and gave her a tight hug. "I know you do. That's why I love you."

Erica squeezed her before breaking away. "Go take your bath. I'll run to the market and get something to make us for dinner. How does coq au vin and roasted potatoes sound?"

Joy beamed. "That would be divine. Thanks, Erica. You're the best."

After Erica had left, Joy took what remained of her glass of wine, cleared some room on the sofa, and plopped down. Her hair was still wet. She'd waited to take her bath until after Erica had gone, and now that she was alone, her thoughts drifted to Ash. The knowledge that she'd stolen from him went from a niggling doubt at the back of her mind to full-on, raging guilt. She had to tell him. Now that she knew him so intimately, she realized she couldn't live with this between them. Even if she never saw him again, it was eating her up inside.

Tomorrow; she'd tell him tomorrow.

She sat there a second longer, staring into space, before she realized she couldn't wait even one more day. "Shit," she muttered, picking up the cell phone off the coffee table. Fully charged now, she had no excuse not to call him.

She had to call Ruby to get his home number, which fortunately her friend gave her without asking any questions. Then, with trembling fingers, she dialed Ash's number.

He picked up after two rings.

"Ash, it's Joy."

"Joy," he said, and she couldn't tell if he was happy or not to hear from her. "How was brunch at Grandma's?"

"Fine. Listen, I need you—I mean, there's something I need to talk to you about. Like, now."

"I'll be right there."

"N-no, that's not necessary." She really did not want to have this conversation in person.

"See you in twenty minutes." And then he hung up.

"Damn," she said, and downed the rest of her wine. Not only did she prefer to tell Ash she was a thief over the phone, but she was also in her grungiest sweatpants and tank top, she hadn't gotten around to blow-drying her hair, and she wore no makeup.

Looking around, she wasn't sure what was worse, the

appallingly unkempt state of her apartment or her own appearance. It was a close call. She bit her lip; her place was even messier than it usually was.

She loved her Victorian apartment, and she wished she was naturally more organized, but it just wasn't in her nature. Her living room was set up comfortably, with an overstuffed sofa and two well-loved chairs arranged around a coffee table. But one chair was filled with a basket of yarn, knitting needles, and a book titled *Stitch and Bitch*. She really needed to finish that scarf one day. . . .

The sofa was where she lived, so it was strewn with blankets, pillows, and books. And some slippers. She had a fireplace, but she used it mainly for storing magazines.

Shit. The neat-freak Ash was going to shit a brick when he saw this mess.

Still, she was a girl, so vanity won.

She dashed to the bathroom to at least comb her still-damp hair and put on a bit of makeup. She'd barely gotten on the tiniest bit of lip gloss when the call bell rang. She didn't even have to look at the clock to know twenty minutes exactly had passed since he'd hung up.

Slowly, she approached her front door as if it were a guillotine. Crap, she really did not want to have this discussion. But she buzzed him in, and seconds later he was coming through the door, carrying a square black bag.

Pausing, he seemed to take in the state of her apartment in silent shock. But he just shook his head and brushed a lock of blond hair behind one ear. Everything in her went hot and alive. Being in the same room with him was enough to shoot up her heart rate, to make her want to throw herself into his arms.

A moment's pause and then he was coming at her,

focused on her lips. She welcomed him, let him back her against the door as he pushed his way inside her mouth, as he kissed her until she couldn't think about anything except his body solid against hers, his rock-hard erection pressing against her pelvis.

He picked her up, and she wrapped her legs around him, knowing she shouldn't be allowing this to happen but unable to stop it. He put her down in front of the kitchen table and yanked off her shirt, her bra. She tried to cover herself, but he pushed her hands aside, cupping one breast as he bent to lick around her other nipple, teasing her until she leaned back against the table. He pulled her nipple into his mouth, across his teeth, biting and licking and sucking until she moaned aloud.

"Spread for me, Joy."

She felt his other hand moving to cup her between her legs, his hand warm through the fabric of her sweats. His palm pressed against her clit as his long fingers reached to firmly grasp her until she was rubbing against his hand, getting wet for him. Ready.

"Turn around."

Slowly, she turned to face the kitchen table. With a sweep of his arm, he flung the piles of books and papers onto the floor. She felt his hand on her upper back, urging her body to rest against the warm wood. Wasn't she supposed to be talking to him about something? Oh, right, her latest hobby, thievery.

But then he was tugging her sweats and panties down her legs, and she kicked them off. She was naked, bent over, exposed.

Sex now. Talk later.

His hands were on her, rubbing her shoulders, her arms,

her back; such calming hands. She felt his long fingers on her ass, his hand warm as he ran his palm over the curve of her body, from her lower back to the fleshy part at the bottom.

"You have a beautiful ass, Joy."

Normally she'd protest the compliment, but now she was so far gone she just smiled.

Then she felt a light slap on her bottom; he'd spanked her. She paused for a second, but when he massaged the area he'd just spanked, she sighed, comforted.

"Did you like that, Joy?"

"Yes. Do it again." She couldn't help but think of Cartwright. With him she'd been passive, timid even. Now, a pleasurable tingle surged through her, making her brave enough to ask for what she wanted.

He slapped her harder, and the sting, surprisingly, melted her even more. She seemed to sink into the kitchen table, and when he took her arms and stretched them to the side, she held on to the edges, bracing herself.

Again he slapped her, and she felt her pussy go a little wetter, loving the way the pain quickly turned into delicious pleasure. She closed her eyes, let him spank her again and again, loving the sound of his palm slapping her skin. Each time his hand struck her, she clenched her fists around the table and inhaled sharply. It hurt. She loved it.

"Ash . . . it feels so . . ."

"Good?"

"Yes." Her pussy was dripping, throbbing. Need rushed through her veins, filling her everywhere.

Slap, slap, slap . . . every smack was a bit harder than the last, and she was squirming, lost in sensation.

"Do you want to be fucked now?"

"Yes. I need to be fucked now. By you."

"Spread your legs wide for me, Joy. I want to see you. I want to see how wet you are."

Her legs trembled as she moved her legs as far apart as she could.

He leaned across her back, and she felt his breath near her ear. "You're a bad girl, aren't you, Joy? You deserved that spanking."

You have no idea, she thought, picturing the stolen sculpture.

He took her hair in his hand, twisting it firmly in his fist and pulling until her head lifted off the table, and she gasped.

Her hair still tight in his hand, he stepped behind her, between her legs. She wasn't aware of when he'd taken off his pants, but he was naked, his legs strong and solid between her own. His cock hard as he slid it into the crack of her ass and lower, using the juice from her pussy to coat his erection, already sheathed in a condom.

"Goddamn, Joy. You're so wet. So gorgeous."

"Mmm," was all she could manage, nearly coming from the feel of him, and he hadn't even entered her yet.

Then he yanked her hair one sharp time and thrust into her. Her head thrown back, she cried out.

"That's right, let me have you, baby. You want it rough and hard, don't you?"

"Yes," she said through gritted teeth, trying not to come, not yet.

But he was fucking her, fast and deep and steady. She'd never felt like this before, like she could scream as loud as she wanted, ask for whatever she wanted. Behave as naughty as she wanted to.

"Harder, Ash. Fuck me harder. Pull my hair."

His fist tightened and with his other hand he reached around her body to cup her pussy from the front. He fingered her clit, grinding into her until arousal overwhelmed her. She climaxed, one long scream ripping from deep in her throat.

Releasing her hair, he gripped her hips as he stilled and she felt him ejaculating into her body, his cock pulsing steadily as his grip clasped her hips, holding her still.

She waited for the same embarrassment to attack her as it had the last time they'd had sex, but somehow the spanking had numbed her to those feelings; maybe the endorphins, those morphine-like hormones, muted more than the pain; maybe they dulled her brain as well. She knew she should get up, should cover herself, but she was too comfortable where she was.

"Don't move." He pulled out of her, and she heard him disposing of the condom and rummaging around.

"I can't move. My legs feel like jelly." She closed her eyes and waited for her limbs to regain some sort of strength.

Click.

A bright light caused her eyes to pop open. "What was that?"

"I said, don't move."

Ash had a camera in his hand and was circling her, snapping quickly, repeatedly.

"Stop," she said, trying to push up, but he was there, stopping her.

"Do what I say."

His tone left no room for argument, and she admitted a part of her liked the fact that he wanted to photograph her. So she kept still, closing her eyes and listening to the rhythmic click of the shutter.

She was half asleep when he finally stopped. With a gentle hand, he tugged her to her feet and, like last night, carried her to bed.

"Holy shit," he said when they got to her room.

"What?"

"Um. By any chance have you been burglarized today?"

She looked around at the unmade bed, the half-open dresser drawers with clothes spilling out of them, the piles of books scattered on every surface.

"I was going to clean up today, but . . ."

He tossed aside a pile of clean clothes she'd been meaning to fold for more than a week and placed her on the bed. Imagining his spotless house, she asked, "Does it totally turn you off?"

After a few seconds, he shook his head. "No. Normally it would, but with you . . ." He blinked. "Nothing seems to turn me off with you. It's the exact opposite, in fact."

"Don't look so shocked," she said, pulling a blanket over her naked body.

He smiled. "So, was there something you wanted to talk with me about?"

Her stomach turned with nerves. She wanted—*needed*—to tell him. But she was fuzzy-headed and so very satisfied. Would one more day really make a difference?

"It can wait until tomorrow," she said, feeling too good and pushing away the guilt.

Leaning down, he kissed her forehead. "Then would it be okay if I went home and developed the shots I took? I won't rest until I get that film into the darkroom." He ran his fingers through his hair. "I need . . . to see what I captured."

What *had* he captured? She couldn't help but wonder. Every time she was with him, she seemed to give him a little more, seemed to feel him a little more. And she couldn't help but think he was capturing more than her image on film. Suddenly it wasn't her naked picture she was worried about him taking. It was her heart.

She nodded. "Fine. But tomorrow. We have to talk tomorrow."

"Okay. Come by after you get off work." He kissed her once again. "Have a good sleep."

But later, when she was alone in her room, alone in her head, her thoughts began spinning out of control, her heart pounding too hard to let her sleep. A wave of nausea rushed over her.

What had she gotten herself into?

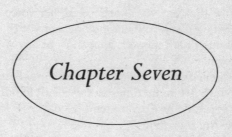

Chapter Seven

For the first time in her job history, Joy arrived at work early. Two hours early, in fact. But it wasn't her buried overachiever that had driven her to work at the crack of dawn; it was guilt.

All night she'd been tossing and turning, the thought of the sculpture haunting her, shame eating at her like a gangrenous disease. She wasn't going to show it to her boss; she was going to return it and hope Ash didn't kill her.

If she hurried, she could get the sculpture, return it to Ash, and, providing he let her live, be back in time to start her day.

After she'd flipped on the lights, she marched straight to her desk and yanked open the bottom file-cabinet drawer.

And her heart stopped.

It wasn't there.

"What the hell?" she muttered, pulling open all her drawers and pawing through the disorganized contents.

"Where the fuck are you?" she asked, her voice echoing in the empty gallery. "Where the *fuck* are you?"

The statue didn't answer, appear, or in any way make itself known.

Joy searched the reception area, the storage room, and her own desk five more times and was still looking when Andrew appeared just before ten o'clock.

"Wow. Are pigs flying?"

"What?" she demanded, looking up from the garbage can she was currently picking through.

"You're here before me. It's some kind of miracle."

Desperate, Joy blurted out, "Andrew, have you seen a marble sculpture, about this high?" She measured about twelve inches between her hands.

Andrew dropped his messenger bag into the reception desk. "Yeah."

"What? You have? Tell me where it is!"

"A really sexy piece, right?"

Joy stood and stalked across the room. "Where *is* it?" she demanded, unable to keep the shrill tone out of her voice.

Andrew raised one brow at her tone. "Panos sold it yesterday."

"What!" Panic washed over her body in a nauseating wave. "I don't understand. How? Why? *Fuck!*"

Andrew eyed her with a puzzled expression. "What's the big deal? You should be happy we made a sale."

"But he doesn't even know the artist; how did he sell it?"

"Um, it had *Ash Hunter* carved on the bottom?"

"Shit. I never looked at the bottom."

"Well, congratulations; your job's safe at least. Panos freakin' loves you right now."

Just then the boss himself strolled through the door. Joy rushed up to him and clutched his shoulders in a death grip. "Why were you going through my desk?" She clutched harder. "And why did you sell that sculpture?"

"It was an odd chain of events, actually." He unpeeled Joy's fingers from his body and stepped back.

"Of course it was." Joy went to her desk and fell into her chair, unsure if her legs would hold her up much longer. She barely held back a grimace as she took her seat, her ass still sore from last night with Ash.

Oh, God, he was going to do more than spank her when he found out what she'd done. He really was going to murder her. She should just start planning her own funeral now.

Fighting down her panic, she asked, "So what was this amazing chain of events?"

Panos came over and lifted a hefty thigh to half sit on the surface of her desk. "An older couple came in and showed some interest in one of our pieces. So I went to pull a brochure out of your drawer and instead I found this sculpture. I set it on your desk, and this couple goes crazy, asking me who the artist is, blah-blah-blah. Lo and behold, I look on the bottom and it's signed *Ash Hunter*."

"Right." She dropped her forehead into her palm.

"Turns out, they've been wanting an Ash Hunter photograph for over a year and couldn't find one anywhere. But they seemed even more happy about the sculpture."

"Of course they were."

"They want more, and I told them you were the girl!"

"Of course you did."

Lifting her head, she picked up a pencil and began to doodle. *Shit, fuck, asswipe, grrrr!*

She took a deep breath and exhaled. "Mr. Panos, I

didn't have permission to sell that sculpture. That's why it was in my desk."

Panos's beady eyes went cold. "You didn't have permission."

Slowly, Joy shook her head.

"Then get permission." He pushed off her desk and loomed over her. "Or you're fired." Then he stalked to his office and slammed the door.

"Why are we here again?" Erica followed Blaine into San Francisco's latest hot spot, a French fusion restaurant located a few blocks from the culinary school. The entire back wall was lined with racks of wine bottles, and Erica didn't need a menu to tell her this place was a budget-breaker.

"Two, please," Blaine said to the hostess.

Erica jerked his arm, tugging him away from the hostess. "I asked you a question. Why are we here? I thought we were going on a quick run to the Asian market. We need bok choy, remember?"

He looked as laid-back as ever. Did anything faze the guy? "This joint is getting write-ups all over the place. Don't you want to see what the latest trends are?"

"No. I don't care about trends. I care about getting to the store and back." That wasn't one hundred percent true, but she wasn't about to tell Blaine the Preppy that she couldn't afford a high-priced lunch.

Annoyingly, he grinned down at her. "It must be hard being you."

"I have no idea what you mean." She crossed her arms in front of her chest.

"Would you like me to pull it out for you?"

She blinked. "What? Pull what out?"

"That stick up your ass."

She gasped. "I don't have a—" She lowered her voice to a whisper. "A stick up my you-know-what."

"Good. Then it won't be a problem to get a quick bite." He turned and motioned for the hostess to seat them.

She stared after him. She could leave. She could walk out the door and go to the store on her own. But as she watched him walk away, his posture perfect and his head high and confident, Erica couldn't make herself break away. That would be a small victory in his overly confident mind, and she didn't want to give him even that much. Hands clenched, she followed after him.

After the hostess had seated them, Blaine looked over the menu at her. "What do you think of the ambience?"

The place was exactly the opposite of how she pictured her own restaurant would be one day. Polished concrete floors, a stainless-steel bar, and white pendant lighting gave the place a stylish, vogue feel, but it left her cold.

She shrugged. "Honestly, it doesn't do much for me."

"Yeah, me neither."

"Really?"

"You seem surprised."

"I am. This place is stylish, trendy, and full of wealthy patrons. You fit right in."

He leaned forward. "Yeah, well, maybe you don't know as much about me as you like to think."

A little rush went through her at his words, at the way he looked at her with those chocolaty eyes, and she quickly raised her menu to hide herself from his gaze.

Why? Why did she always feel all funny around him?

She didn't even like him, yet he got under her skin. And not always in an unpleasant way.

"The crab and bacon sandwich looks interesting."

She scanned the menu. Nineteen dollars for a glorified BLT? No effing way.

"What?" he asked.

"What, what?" she said, peering over the menu.

"You grunted."

"I did not."

"Yes. You did. Why? You frown upon bacon?"

"No. I frown upon pretentious food, but I suppose you wouldn't understand. You probably have French fusion for breakfast."

"Actually"—he pulled down the menu in her hands, exposing her face fully—"if you must know, I prefer traditional, slow-cooked food. Classic dishes like coq au vin and roast pork loin. The simpler the better."

"I don't believe you."

He shrugged. "Okay."

If she had been standing, she would have stomped her foot. He was doing it again, getting under her skin. And the worst part? She was starting to think he was right. Maybe she didn't know him as well as she thought.

A very disconcerting thought. She remained silent, only speaking after he'd ordered—the sandwich and a bottle of wine. She ordered some lobster bisque and pan-seared duck breast, knowing she'd be living on carrots the rest of the month.

But she refused to order like the pauper she was. Not in front of Blaine.

"Prescott?"

She looked up to see a group of three men surrounding

them. With their expensive suits and similar builds, they looked interchangeable. Even their gold wedding bands looked alike.

Blaine looked up and smiled, but Erica noticed his mouth was tight. She'd never seen him look edgy, didn't think he had it in him. But as he greeted his friends, she saw his shoulders tense. Interesting.

"Chip, Walker, Amherst. Good to see you." She sat there, silent as he talked with his friends. Deducing they were some of his lawyer buddies, she waited patiently as they chatted. Every so often they'd glance her way, and she felt their gazes on her like boiling water, running over her tattooed arms, her nose ring, her pink hair. The silent question burned her ears: What's a guy like Prescott doing with a girl like her?

Eventually one of them, distinguishable by being practically bald and wearing thick glasses, leered her way. "So, do you have any tattoos we can't see?"

It was like being thrown back to high school, and she repressed the knot of anxiety that had settled in her belly. She was about to retort, but Blaine cut her off.

"So, Chip. How's the *Tyler versus Amherst* case going?"

Blaine succeeded in distracting the conversation from her invisible tattoos, and, sipping her chardonnay, she waited until they'd made ambiguous promises to get together. Eventually they left, and Blaine watched them go, his tense body visibly relaxing as they exited. Then he turned to her. "Sorry about that."

"You mean about not introducing me?" she said flippantly.

He looked taken aback. "I meant about Chip. Did you want me to introduce you?"

"It's the polite thing to do."

"You wouldn't have wanted to meet them."

"How do you know?"

"Just trust me," he said.

"You mean you didn't want to explain to them who I am."

The waiter placed their appetizers on the table, and Erica immediately slurped up a big spoonful of the bisque.

"That's totally wrong."

"That you didn't want to explain who I am? Or this bisque? Because you're right about the soup. It's totally wrong to charge this much for anything this salty. I'll be bloated like a puffer fish tomorrow."

"You know what I mean."

"It doesn't matter," she said between slurps. "I really couldn't care less what your lawyer friends think." Even if her heart hurt a little because he was ashamed of her, she wasn't about to admit it.

The moments stretched as they ate. Finally he put down his fork and lifted her free hand. Her pulse caught at the contact, and she went to jerk her hand back. But he held her firmly in his grasp. "They're idiots. I just wanted them to go."

She met his stare. "You didn't hear me. It really doesn't matter what they think. Or what you think."

He held her gaze a few seconds longer before dropping her hand and shoving a bite of salad into his mouth. They ate the rest of the meal in awkward silence. When the bill came, he tried to pay, but she shoved her credit card across the table.

"I'm getting my share."

"No, I'm the one who chose this overpriced place."

"I chose to eat here with you."

"Hey, I know you—" He stopped himself, and she saw his cheeks were actually tinged the slightest shade of pink.

"You know what?" she demanded, frustration coursing through her. Too many emotions in too short a time. "What do you think you know?"

"That you're struggling."

The words were like a slap in the face and she recoiled. "Don't you ever presume something like that. I'm paying my share of this stupid lunch."

"Erica—"

"Stop."

Finally he released her gaze and asked the waiter to split the bill on both cards. Good. The last thing she wanted was a handout from Preppy Boy. In fact, she didn't want anything from him. Ever.

When Ash emerged from his darkroom, the sunlight was like a sucker punch in the eyes. When had it become morning? As usual, he'd totally lost track of time when he was printing photographs, but he'd had no idea the entire night had passed since he'd descended into the garage-turned-darkroom after he'd returned from Joy's last night. He'd checked a few things online and answered his cell, but overall he'd been obsessed with a subject that wasn't related to work at all.

Joy. He'd been staring at the postsex photographs he'd taken of her for hours, printing her, dodging and burning the images to catch the highlights of her flawless skin, to showcase the messy tangle of her hair and to emphasize the deep, dark satiated look in her eyes.

He'd given her that look.

Rubbing a hand over his face, stubbly after two days' growth because he'd forgotten to shave, he went upstairs, hoping a shower would wake his brain-dead ass up. Because it didn't matter if he hadn't slept last night; it was Monday, and he had work to do. He needed to be online by eight to chat with some of Juan's guys overseas, and he wouldn't let them down.

You never do, Hunter; you never do. Romero's words floated through his foggy head. But Romero was so wrong. He'd let plenty of people down in his life, mainly his mother and sister. While he'd been off on missions, his sister's condition had gotten worse and worse, and Ash hadn't done a goddamn thing about it. He'd been so busy saving strangers' lives, he'd neglected his own family.

The thought made his gut clench. He'd never forgive himself for abandoning his mom and sister to join the military. His dad had died of cancer when Ash was just thirteen. But at eighteen he'd been restless, ready for action. He'd loved the excitement of the military, and when he'd made it into special ops, he'd been more than ready. So ready, in fact, he'd barely made it home those first few years and hadn't made any great effort to communicate with his family.

He'd let his family down.

He was going to make up for it, though. After the incident in the Middle East, he'd come home and been hit with reality. The silver lining to the recent national security crisis was that his high-tech skills were much in demand in the private sector, and he'd simply picked the highest-paying job and made sure to get stock options. He'd made a promise to himself to always make sure his mother never had to worry about money or caring for his sister. His mother had refused a nurse, but he'd remodeled their house, now outfitted for his sister's special needs. He'd done the best he could.

But it never felt like enough.

When the company he'd worked for had gone public, he'd made enough money to feel secure, at least temporarily. And, for the first time in many years, he'd found he had some spare time on his hands. He'd dug out his old camera from when he'd taken photography in high school and had immediately become obsessed with combining two of his hobbies: bondage and photography. They were the only things in life that allowed him to totally lose himself, to forget the dark places his mind tended to roam.

And Joy . . . he could lose himself just from being in the same room with her.

Now, as he stepped into the shower and stood under the powerful warm spray, just the thought of her got him hard, throbbing. Unlike any other girl he'd met before, he never knew what was going to come out of her mouth. Usually something foul; the girl cussed like a sailor.

He smiled. She looked so innocent, and he could see everything in her eyes. He doubted the girl could tell a lie to save her life, and he appreciated that. More and more, Ash learned that trust was a hard trait to come by, but Joy was different. So open, so honest.

Something about Joy brought out his dominant tendencies like no girl ever had. He wondered if her ass was red today, sore from his hand. His cock twitched at the thought as he remembered what her skin had felt like when he'd spanked her, what her cries of pleasure had sounded like. Joy held nothing back. And he found that, when he was with her, he didn't, either.

He palmed his cock, feeling how hard he was. He wanted to do more than spank her. He wanted to see her bound, for him. He wanted to tie her to the bed, to a chair—anything. And then he wanted to fuck her as hard as he knew she wanted it.

Stroking his cock, he flipped the showerhead to pummel mode and turned to let the water pound his shoulders, his back. He cupped his balls and stroked himself, remembering what it had felt like to be inside Joy last night, what she looked like bent over her kitchen table, her pussy dripping with want, spread open and waiting for him. When he'd yanked her hair, she'd tightened around him, her pussy clenching with need.

His erection swelled in his palm as he pumped himself, holding his fist tightly around his dick. He wanted to feel Joy's mouth on him, wanted to see her on her knees before him, maybe with her hands tied behind her back. He hitched a breath, the erotic image making his blood pound.

He stroked himself faster, tighter, his thighs tensing as he turned to lean back against the tiled wall of the shower, putting his dick right in the intense spray of the water. Images flashed through his mind . . .

Joy, on her knees before him.

Joy, tied, spread-eagled on his bed.

Joy's breasts with his cock right in the middle of the two luscious mounds, fucking her, fucking her everywhere . . .

His climax pounded through him, and he came in a series of hot spurts, his come disappearing in the solid hammer of the shower jet's spray.

He stayed that way for several minutes, leaning against the wet tile, panting. *Get a grip, Hunter!* This was not the time to be starting a relationship. Just the word sent a shiver of fear through him. Ash had only had one so-called *relationship,* and he'd fucked that up. Not in the way Ruby thought, but still. He'd never felt the way he knew he should have, the way she wanted him to, and he'd let it go on way too long.

He liked Joy. He wanted to bind her. But he refused to let it get serious. He didn't have the time or the energy to do his job, support his family, and start a new relationship. His family had to come first, and that meant his job needed to be the priority. That also meant he couldn't stay up all night in a darkroom and expect to still competently do his job.

He'd already let people down, and that was something he couldn't allow to happen. Ever again.

Joy was locking up the gallery when she felt her cell phone vibrating in her purse. "Crap." Dropping the bag onto the ground, she began pawing through the contents and finally dug out the phone just one ring before it went to voice mail.

"Hi, Erica," she said, standing.

"Hey. Just wanted to say we're meeting for Monday night cocktails at the Zone instead of the usual bar. I guess there's some bartender Scott is crushin' on."

Joy closed her eyes momentarily. "Oh, crap."

"What?" Erica asked, her voice curious. After all, Joy had never missed one evening of Monday night cocktails.

"I can't go." Joy stepped onto the street and closed the door behind her, locking it. The sky was a gloomy gray, and it felt like rain would fall any second. The first rain of the season; it was early this year. "I have to see Ash tonight," Joy said.

There was a long pause before Erica spoke. "Ash? Didn't you just see him two nights ago?"

"And last night," she said before thinking.

"Wait. I was at your house last night. Did he come over after I made dinner?" Erica asked incredulously.

"Yeah. I needed to talk to him about . . . something."

There was a long pause; Joy knew Erica was waiting for her to explain. When she didn't, Erica said, "So he showed up at what? Ten? Eleven?"

Joy paused at a crosswalk, waiting for the light to turn. "Around ten thirty. Why do you sound so shocked?"

"Joy. That was a booty call."

"What? No. I asked him over because I needed to discuss business with him." The light turned green, and she stepped into the street.

"And did you?"

"Um . . . not really?"

"Did you do it?"

"Um, by 'it,' do you mean sex?" Why was Joy blushing at the memory of being spanked over her kitchen table?

"Of course I mean sex! Well, did you?"

"Listen, I'm going into the garage to get my car. I'm going to lose my signal in a minute."

"So you're flaking us off to go see Ash?"

Joy did feel guilty about that. Every Monday for nearly two years she'd been meeting the same group of three of her closest friends for drinks and dinner. Under any other circumstances, she wouldn't have flaked off her friends, but she had to see Ash. She had to tell him about the sculpture, and she couldn't wait one second longer than necessary. She'd been sick to her stomach all day thinking about it, but it had to be done.

"Listen, I'm sorry. Tell the gang I'm sorry, too. If my talk with Ash goes fast, maybe I'll catch you later."

"Yeah. Right. Somehow I have a feeling that won't be happening."

"Erica, don't worry." A few drops of rain hit her head, and Joy picked up the pace. The last thing she needed was to show up at Ash's with damp, frizzy hair. She nearly laughed at the thought—frizzy hair was the least of her worries.

The phone was silent for a long minute and then Erica spoke, this time in a softer tone. "You're right; I'm being overprotective." Joy heard voices in the background, and Erica lowered her voice. "I just don't want you to get hurt, Joy. I—"

But Joy had entered the parking garage and her signal dropped. "Crap," she muttered as she unlocked the Mercedes and got inside. There had definitely been a strange undercurrent between her and Erica over the last few days, ever since she'd met Ash. But she couldn't worry about it now, and anyway, it was probably going to be a moot point after Ash found out about the sculpture.

She pulled out of the garage and immediately had to turn on her wipers as rain assaulted her windshield in hard, steady drops. The streets were full of drivers honking and generally driving crazy, as they tended to do each year during the first rain. Driving only made her more nervous, and as she made her way to Ash's place, her stomach felt sicker than ever. Yeah, Erica had nothing to worry about. After tonight, she doubted Ash would ever want to see Joy again.

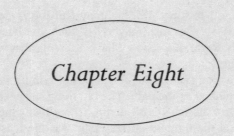

Chapter Eight

Standing in the corner of the student kitchen, Erica stared at her cell phone. Joy had never missed Monday night with the gang, and now she was doing so for some guy she'd just met?

Something wasn't right.

Ash Hunter. He was obviously using her; why else would he show up for sex late at night? And Joy, so sweet and so naive, was totally clueless. Just like she had been with Cartwright.

"Your girlfriend acting up again?"

Erica jerked her gaze up to see Blaine staring at her with a raised brow and a smirk.

"Don't you have some bread to burn?"

Blaine took a step closer, and damn if her heart didn't skip a beat.

"So sassy."

Taken aback by something in Blaine's eyes, Erica shook her head, for once in her life having a hard time finding words to make a retort. "Stop it." *Yeah. Real cool, lady.*

Blaine's expression changed, softened, and he took a step closer—too close—and reached up to softly graze Erica's cheekbone. Her breath caught as Blaine ran his finger down the side of her face, her throat, to skim the V-shaped neckline of her short-sleeved dress. "I think you need to find some other ways to expel all that energy of yours," Blaine whispered before turning on his heel and walking away.

Exhaling, Erica stared after him, her heart beating a mile a minute. What had that been about? She wasn't exactly sure.

And she wasn't sure she wanted to know.

There wasn't any parking in front of Ash's building, of course, so Joy had to run two blocks in the pouring rain before he let her into his apartment. Shivering, she stood in the entry and knew she probably looked even more of a mess than usual.

Ash took her bag and coat and hung them on the coat-rack. "You're soaked through."

"N-no. I'm fine." She brushed a dripping-wet lock of hair out of her eye.

"Come on. Let me make you some coffee."

She followed him toward the kitchen. "How about some whiskey instead?"

Glancing over his shoulder, he raised a brow in question. "Long day?"

She pictured Panos's beady eyes as he'd yelled at her earlier. "You could say that."

Ash went to a cabinet and pulled down a bottle of Bushmills. "On the rocks?"

"Neat."

Ash poured some of Ireland's finest into a tumbler and handed it to her. She tilted the glass and poured the potent liquid down her throat. Swallowing, she gasped as the whiskey burned its way into her gut. She held out the glass. "More, please."

"That must have been some day." Ash poured another two inches into the tumbler.

"It's about to get even better." This time she took a smaller sip instead of drinking the entire contents in one swallow. She met his gaze. "Ash, there's something I have to tell you. It's important, and I'm afraid it may affect your feelings for me."

But he was just staring at her again. "Okay, but first I want to show you something."

"But—"

He took her free hand. "It will only take a second." Leaning in, he kissed her ear and gave the lobe a sharp nip. A shudder went through her, but this time it was Ash-induced instead of alcohol.

Oh, but the exquisite whiskey was hitting her blood now, and a warm glow was spreading over her. "Fine. But don't distract me for long. I want to talk to you about something significant."

"Scout's honor." And then he kissed her like no Scout should know how to kiss.

When he released her, her eyes drifted open lazily. "Damn, you're good," she said, drawing out the last word. And that whiskey was lovely.

"Come on." He led her to a door and stepped through.

"The garage? You want to show me your garage? Hell,

if I knew you had a flippin' garage, I would have parked in it instead of a mile away in the rain."

Laughing, he said, "Watch your step; it's narrow. And this was a garage, but now it's my darkroom."

As she followed him down the steps, the acrid smell of chemicals hit her. "You want to show me your darkroom?"

He paused in front of a table of plastic trays but nodded to his left. "No, I want to show you these."

A clothesline stretched across a twelve-foot space, and pinned to it were several black-and-white images. She slowly walked toward the photographs, her eyes widening as she got a closer look.

"These are . . . Is that . . . *me*?"

He was behind her now, and she felt the warmth of his body, felt him breathing as he tucked a lock of hair behind her ear. Every time he did that, it melted her just a little.

"But, how did you do this?" Logically, she knew the images were of her—he'd taken them last night, but the woman in the photographs was someone else entirely. That woman looked Brigitte Bardot–sexy, with her wild hair and sex-glazed eyes, her curvy form stretched across the table.

"How did you do that?" she whispered.

"What?"

"Make me look . . ."

"What, baby?"

"Not fat," she whispered, and her face burned at her own words.

She felt his hand on her side, palming her rib cage. She could see her ribs in the photograph, and it shocked her.

That girl in the picture wasn't nearly as big as Joy knew she was.

"Don't you ever look in the mirror?"

She actually avoided full-length mirrors whenever possible, but she didn't tell Ash that now.

Ash reached into the waistband of her jeans, his hand sliding in easily to span her pelvis. "You should wear tighter clothes, Joy. You have a body that should be shown off."

Her chest gave a nervous clench, and she tugged at her loose shirt. She remembered the knit dress she'd worn last week and how her grandmother had told her girls with her figure shouldn't wear things like that. "No," she said.

"Look at the woman in those photographs. Is she unattractive?"

Slowly, she shook her head. "You're just a talented photographer."

"Hey, I don't mess with the photographs by using any of that digital shit. It's simple. You're a beautiful woman, Joy. And it shows."

She didn't believe him, but she wasn't going to argue with him anymore. And then he turned her around and started kissing her. "I tried not to think about you today."

"Gee, thanks," she said against his mouth.

"I didn't succeed. I thought about you all day. I thought about you all night, when I was printing these. My mind was going crazy with ideas."

"What kind of ideas?" she whispered, her heart hammering.

He brought her wrists behind her back. Settling her

hands against the base of her spine, he pressed her to his body, his erection hard beneath his jeans. He pulled her arms back, gently, until her chest arched forward.

He ran his tongue along her bottom lip. "Naughty ideas. Perverted ideas. Things I want to do to you, what I want you to do to me."

Her nipples swelled inside her bra, but she said, "We need to talk. . . ."

"I *am* talking. I'm telling you exactly what I want you to do." He reached to the side, and she saw a length of clothesline in his hand. He grinned. "Never thought I'd use anything but nylon or hemp, but right now I just want to bind you, and I don't want to wait."

She didn't want him to wait.

So weak. With him, her body's response always won, and she knew, once again, she was going to delay the little talk she'd been putting off for too long already. Just a bit longer . . .

Along with being a disorganized, tardy mess, she also had the lovely character trait of being a big procrastinator.

"I'm going to tie your wrists behind your back."

"Yes." *Please.*

He spun her around, and seconds later she felt the scratchy rope around her wrists. When he was done, he turned her back to face him.

Just the act of him binding her made her pussy throb and dampen. Just knowing he wanted to own her, knowing he wanted to use her, made her insides flutter.

He unbuttoned her blouse, the backs of his knuckles warm against her skin. When it was undone, he pulled one of her breasts out of her bra and squeezed her flesh, tightly. She gasped as desire washed over her, landing in a hot pool right between her legs.

"Yes," she hissed.

He undid the front of her jeans and slid his hand beneath her panties to slip a finger into her moist folds.

"You're wet for me." His fingers were long and warm as he reached deeper, and she bucked against his hand. "Fuck my hand, Joy. Show me how much you want to be fucked."

Even as her skin burned with embarrassment, she began to move her hips against his hand, back and forth, rubbing her slick skin until her pussy felt swollen, wanting. He beaded her nipple between the fingertips of his other hand and pulled; she cried out as the sharp pain shot straight to her sex.

"Yes, that's my girl. Beautiful girl." He slapped her breast, lightly, and she felt her flesh bounce when he did it again harder.

"Ash . . ." She couldn't believe what he was doing to her, what she was letting him do. Letting go, giving him total power over her. Using her.

She continued moving against his hand, let him slap her breasts. Her arms clenched behind her back, her wrists strained against the twine. Her thigh muscles tensed as she moved her hips, back and forth, trying to hold off her orgasm, just a minute longer. . . .

"No, not yet." He released her pussy and then brought the finger that he'd used to fuck her to her lips. He ran his fingertip over her mouth, pushed inside, forced her to taste herself.

"I want you on your knees."

Nodding, she sank before him. The concrete ground

was hard through her jeans, hard on her knees, but she didn't care; every little discomfort only heightened the arousal coursing through her. It seemed the more disheveled she felt, the more Ash liked it. And, bizarrely, the more confident she became.

She looked up, waiting. He took her head in his hands and stepped forward. Rubbing her face against his denim-clad erection, she felt the abrasion of the fabric on her cheek and welcomed it.

"Feel that? Feel how fucking hard you make me?"

"Yes," she said, her voice husky. She nuzzled him more, wanting to feel every inch of him.

He unbuttoned his jeans and tugged them and his boxers down his legs. "Open your mouth, Joy."

She did, and he guided himself across her lips, taking his time as he rolled the head of his cock across her teeth, her tongue, the roof of her mouth.

"Lick the head of my cock, Joy."

Every word he uttered made her tremble, made her throbbing pussy wetter. Wanting to please him, she licked around his engorged head, swallowing the drip of come that leaked out of the tip. When she swallowed, he jerked in her mouth so she did it again. Lick, swallow, suck; she found a rhythm and he was moving, too, moving with her.

"Go on, Joy. I want you to take me as deep as you can."

She glanced up, saw the sweat beading on his brow and the way his hair hung in his face. Despite his controlled words, his face was tender; his eyes were dark and affectionate. Her heart swelled, and she took him deeper into her mouth, as deep as she could, until she nearly gagged, but he held back with perfect timing.

His hands were on her head, holding her steady, pushing her to the very edge, like he knew exactly how deep she could take him. "That's right, Joy. Your mouth feels so fucking good. You take it so fucking deep."

Her eyes were watering, but she didn't care. Her pussy was aching, and she felt her own hips bucking, needing to feel something between her legs, anything at all.

"I'm so close to coming, Joy. I want to come on you; I want to see it on your body."

A shudder went through her at the thought, at the thought of him using her like that, and her sex clenched tightly, dripping. He slowly pulled out of her mouth, and then she was looking up at him, her lips swollen and raw from sucking his cock.

Reaching low, he pushed her blouse and bra as far down as her shoulders and bound wrists allowed. Then he stood before her, stroking himself, and she licked her lips, wanting to taste him again.

"Oh, Joy." He pumped himself smoothly, his fist clenched so hard she could see every sinewy muscle in his arm. Her entire body shook as she watched his cock, watched as he stroked himself, all the while staring at her. At some point, he'd removed his shirt, and now she watched every inch of his taut body as his abdomen tensed, every solid muscle visibly clenching.

He ejaculated his hot liquid onto her naked skin. It hit her breasts, and she moaned aloud, clenching her legs to keep upright. Her arms strained against the bindings as she continued to watch, felt it as semen continued to stream onto her body in smaller and smaller drops, until her breasts were dripping with his warm come.

She knelt before him, tearstained and trembling with

want, her chest covered with his come, her hands tied behind her back. She wanted to be fucked more than she'd ever wanted to be fucked in her entire life. Wanted to be fucked by one man only, the man standing before her.

Joy knelt before him, her shirt and bra pushed back, her jeans undone, her hair a mess and her breasts covered with his ejaculate, her chest rising and falling with short, sharp breaths. Her eyes were wide and glossy. She'd submitted to him so fully, and she hadn't even known it.

His cock was already twitching for her again.

Wait.

He went to the sink and dampened a cloth with warm water. When he turned back to her, the muted illumination of the safelight cast her in an amber glow, making her red hair stand out like wildfire. He was struck by her beauty and wondered how she could ever doubt that about herself.

He kicked off his boots and jeans, and, kneeling across from her, he gently touched the damp cloth to her chest, cleaning her skin. She trembled as he grazed the valley between her breasts, her chest, her nipples, which looked tight and hard. He bent and took one in his mouth, sucked and bit. She just slightly sighed, but he felt it everywhere.

Gently, he leaned her back, laying her limp body on the floor. He kissed her lips, her throat, her breasts. Kissed the soft mound of her belly and the sharp curve of her hip bone. He pulled off her shoes, jeans, and panties and spread her legs to kneel between them. She watched him, her gaze roaming over his chest, his arms, his now-rigid cock.

Her arms were still tied behind her back, and she arched slightly against him. "I need you. Now."

"I know. I need you, too." Impatient, he rolled a condom onto his erection. He was already so hard for her; he wanted to bury himself inside her again and again.

His eyes locked on hers as he slid into her pussy in one strong thrust, so deep it scooted her a few inches across the floor. The floor was hard, and her arms were underneath her. Not exactly satin sheets, but he knew what she wanted; she wanted it hard, raw. And he was more than ready to give her what she wanted.

She was so warm, so tight, and so his. He pumped again, and she cried out, bowing her neck as he lowered his head to kiss her and then bit her skin lightly. She moaned, wrapping her legs around his hips.

"Yes . . . bite . . ."

He did. He moved to her breast and bit the soft flesh just above her nipple, biting as he fucked her, again and again, sliding across the floor, wild.

"Yes! Just fuck me, Ash; fuck me so hard. Take me . . ."

"I will," he said. "You're mine to use right now, aren't you?" He had no idea where the words were coming from, but he couldn't stop them. "Right this minute, you belong to me."

She thrashed her head from side to side. "Yes. Yours. Use me, Ash."

"I will." He bit her nipple, his teeth clamping onto her as she bucked against him. "I am."

He couldn't stop himself, and she seemed to respond to his loss of control. For the first time he could ever remember, he made love to a woman and didn't worry about restraining his own pleasure. Because this was what turned Joy on, feeling him fuck her. Use her.

She was beautiful beneath him.

"Joy, I want you to come. Now." He bit, drove in deep, moved her body a few more inches across the floor. She screamed, and he felt her clench around his cock, pulling another climax out of him. "Mine, Joy." He heard the words coming from his own mouth as he pumped his seed into her, couldn't stop the words. "Right now, Joy. Mine. You're fucking mine."

Chapter Nine

Joy was shaking.

Wearing one of Ash's beat-up Navy sweatshirts and wrapped in a blanket, she sat on a stool at his sleek kitchen counter, her limbs trembling. But, despite the rain hammering against the building, she wasn't cold.

She didn't know what the hell she was.

Mine, Joy. You're fucking mine.

Surely those were words said during a moment of passion, yet she couldn't get them out of her head; couldn't get any of it out of her head. Suddenly she realized that she'd made love to Ash three times in the last four days and barely knew anything about him.

And he hadn't asked much about her, either.

Maybe Erica was right. Maybe he did just want her for a booty call. Never mind if it was a damn good booty call, the best she'd ever had, in fact.

After they'd caught their breath, he'd climbed off her, silent. He helped her upstairs, gave her his sweatshirt to wear. Waited while she cleaned up. But since having sex they'd barely spoken. Now silence filled the air, heavy with awkwardness. She couldn't even fathom talking about the sculpture now.

"Maybe I should go," she said.

"No." He cleared his throat. "You want some tea? Coffee?"

"I'll have some more of that Bushmills if you don't mind."

Grinning, he pulled two tumblers out of the cupboard this time. "Not at all. I think I'll join you."

He poured two neat glasses, slid one across the table, and lifted his, nodding once at her. "Cheers."

"Cheers." She gulped down half the contents, and this time when it hit her stomach, she felt it rumbling around. She realized she was starving; she'd had a small salad for lunch and nothing since. Now, lunch seemed so very long ago.

But she was too embarrassed to say anything about being hungry; her grandmother had made sure she never felt comfortable eating in front of a man. Erica and the gang were the only ones who really knew about Joy's overzealous love of food. Her grandmother had hammered the "eat like a lady" mantra into her for years.

At the moment, after what she'd just done with Ash, she felt very unladylike. And, she realized, she liked it.

"So," Ash said, staring at her from the other side of the kitchen table.

"So." She took another large swallow of whiskey and chased it with a deep breath. Fuck it. No time like the present. "So, Ash. I have something I want to tell you."

Leaning forward slightly, his green eyes nailed her with his sharp gaze. "That's one of the things I like most about you, Joy. Your honesty. You're so open. . . ." He shook his head. "You don't know how rare that is."

She laughed nervously and gulped down the rest of her whiskey. "Yeah. About that."

Reaching across the table, he took her hand and rubbed his thumb across her knuckles. "What is it? You can trust me."

But you can't trust me. "Um. Well. Can I have another shot, please?"

"Yeah. Sure." Just as he stood, his phone rang. "Hello?" he said, cradling the receiver to his neck while he poured her some whiskey. Whoever was on the line must have distracted him, because he poured the alcohol until she had to motion for him to stop.

"Yeah," he said, his brow creasing. When he was silent, the sound of rain pounded against the window in the quiet loft. "Right. Okay, I'm leaving now. I'll be there as soon as I can. Right. Bye."

When he looked at her, his expression had changed completely. He was frowning, and his eyes were dark, shut down. "Listen, I'm sorry, but I have to go. My family needs me. They live in Palo Alto."

She looked down at her bare legs. *Booty call.* "Oh. Okay, right." Erica was right. Joy tilted the glass to her lips and swallowed a deep gulp.

Mmm. She liked whiskey.

Glass in hand, she pushed herself out of the chair. "Right. I'll just get dres-s-s-ed. And go." She looked around the immaculate loft. "Where are my bag? I mean, where *is* my bag and purse? Huh. That didn't sound right, either." The room tilted, and she reached for the chair to steady herself.

Ash ran a hand through his hair. "Fuck. You can't drive. And I don't want to take you home in the rain on my bike."

"Bike?"

"My Ducati. My truck's in the shop."

"Palo Alto is a good thirty-minute freeway drive away. You can't do that on a motorcycle, not in this downpour." She turned, splashing whiskey on the spotless floor. "I have a car. I'll drive you."

Ash gently removed the drink from her hand. "No way, baby. You're not driving anywhere."

"And I'm not letting you drive in this weather on your motorcycle." As if to emphasize her point, lightning flared outside, flashing through the loft in a bright blaze. A second or two later, thunder shook the walls and floor.

She shook her head. "No way, Jose."

"Pardon me?" He looked incredulous that she was arguing with him.

"I'm huuungry." She put her hand over her mouth. "Oops! I didn't mean to say that."

He immediately looked concerned. "When did you eat last?"

"Um, I had a salad for lunch. I'm on a diet."

"For 'effen sake, and you just drank all that whiskey?"

"Maybe?"

He looked so distressed she held out a hand and put it on his shoulder. Surprisingly, he looked up and didn't remove it. "Ash, listen. I'll go with you to your family's. You can drive my car, and we'll stop and grab some drive-through on the way, eat in the car. It's okay."

He looked unsure. "You don't understand. When my mom's like this, it's . . . not pretty."

"I don't mind."

"And my sister . . ." He shook his head, and he looked so distraught she wanted to go with him, wanted to comfort him.

"Ash. Really, I can handle it. Let's go."

"Are you sure you want to do this?" he asked.

She didn't know what *this* was, but she wanted to do it. She nodded. "Yup, I'm sure."

"Okay. But we're going to In-N-Out on the way to Palo Alto. You're eating before we do anything."

She beamed at him. "That sounds wonderful. Do you think I can put on my pants first?"

As if he'd forgotten she wasn't dressed, he glanced down in surprise. "Yeah. Pants, then cheeseburgers."

"Ash?"

"Yeah?"

"You're the best."

Ash had no fucking idea what he was doing bringing Joy to his family's place. He'd never brought a girl home, especially not one he'd known for less than a week. Not that he was bringing her home per se; she was just helping him out. He never could have made it to Palo Alto on his bike.

"It's really pouring," Joy said between bites of her Double-Double.

"I know. Storms came early this year. I had my truck in for a tune-up, thinking I had a few weeks of good weather left."

"I love the rain." She slurped deeply from her root beer. Ash loved that Joy ate like a woman and not a bird. So many of the girls he'd been with ate nothing but rabbit food. Then again, he did tend to date model-types, so he supposed their rabbit-food diet was to be expected. Joy wasn't a model, but she became more and more beautiful to him each second he spent with her.

And she was a wildcat in bed.

His cock stirred whenever he thought about sex with her, which was all the fucking time. Gripping the steering wheel, he focused on the road.

Joy patted the dashboard. "Don't worry. She may not have much horsepower, but she'll get us there safe and sound."

No horsepower was the understatement of the night. The old diesel went from zero to sixty in about ten minutes. But he had to admit that once they got cruising, the old car ran smooth and steady.

The wipers swished across the windshield, barely able to keep up with the torrent of rain. He glanced sideways. "So, I guess I should warn you about my family."

"Oh?" She tossed a napkin over her shoulder. Joy's car may have run clean, but the interior was anything but. Books were piled between them on the bench seat, he'd had to move a pile of sweaters off the driver's-side seat in order to get behind the wheel, and he could have sworn there was a wayward bra strewn across the backseat.

He tried not to think about that.

"They can't be any worse than my family," she said.

Ash sighed. "My sister's a paraplegic."

Out of the corner of his eye, he saw her go still. "Oh. Oh, I'm sorry."

He swallowed. "It was a random burglary. I was overseas." Every time he told the story, a knot of anxiety tightened in his gut. He would never stop feeling like it was his fault. "My sister was shot. She lived, but she needs care. Full-time care. My mother quit her job, and it's been . . . rough on her."

"I can imagine."

Ash's palms were damp on the steering wheel. "Mom's great—amazing, actually. But sometimes it gets to be too much for her, and my sister senses when she needs a break."

"Is that what happened tonight?"

"Yeah. My sister called and asked if I could take over until Mom went to bed. I want to hire a nurse, but Mom adamantly refuses, says she can do it all herself." He shook his head. "I don't know what I was thinking bringing you. Must have been the whiskey."

Reaching between them, she touched his shoulder gently. "Maybe you wanted some support."

"No, I'm used to taking care of this by myself."

"What about you?" she asked softly.

"What do you mean?"

"Who takes care of you?"

Gaze focused on the road, he answered, "No one. It's *my* job."

She gave his shoulder a soft squeeze. "You carry a lot of responsibility, don't you, Ash?"

He shrugged. "It's my duty."

"Is that why you joined the military? You felt it was your duty?"

He paused, unsure how to answer. But then he admitted something he never had before, not out loud. "No. I wanted out."

"Out of your house?"

"Yeah. Even before the accident, I always felt responsible, ever since my dad died when I was thirteen. One day when I was a senior, I saw the recruitment station set up at my high school. I signed up and never looked back."

"Did you enjoy it?"

"Loved it."

"Why'd you leave?"

He shifted in his seat, his shoulder suddenly tingling as he remembered exactly why. "Helicopter accident. We were shot down. I was discharged."

Joy didn't ask for details, and he was glad because he didn't want to give any.

"My sister had been paralyzed a few months before that, so it was good timing. I needed to come home and take care of things here."

"Your being shot out of the sky was good timing?" she asked incredulously.

"Yes." He was dead serious. He'd needed to come home, and that was the only way to do it honorably. Seven years later, his shoulder still gave him trouble. "Rotator cuff injury. You can't be a SEAL if you can't swim. So I came home, got a real job, and started supporting my family. I want my sister to have the best care possible."

"Are you like some kind of saint?"

"Did I seem like a saint earlier, when I had you on your knees?" he asked, ready to change the subject. Sex was always a good distraction.

She got the hint, and when he glanced at her, she was smiling. "You definitely didn't act like a saint earlier. But, you can be the devil with Miss Joy anytime you like."

Chapter Ten

Joy tried not to be nervous when they pulled up to a cottage-style house near downtown Palo Alto. Everything was familiar to her; Ash's family lived only a few blocks away from the restaurant where she'd met Erica. But this was new, meeting his family. She had no idea what to expect.

He pulled to a stop in the driveway. Silently, they both looked at the front of the house. It was quaint and charming, the kind of house Joy loved, with big trees dropping colorful leaves onto the lawn and lots of foliage growing around the exterior. Modest yet lush.

"Ready?"

Joy nodded. Ash's back was straight as a ruler as he approached the front door. He knocked softly and entered, not waiting for an answer. "Hello? Ma?"

"In her room," came a soft, feminine voice.

Joy followed Ash through a hallway to a living room. It was decorated in bright colors, with two comfy-looking sofas and a coffee table stacked high with books and magazines. Next to one of the sofas was a woman—she looked like a girl, really—in a wheelchair. She was beautiful, a feminine version of Ash. Her blond hair was pulled into a ponytail, emphasizing her striking cheekbones. Though her legs were disproportionately thin, it was obvious she was tall. She could have been a model.

Ash went to her, bent and kissed her on the cheek. "Pretending to be fine. She's in her room, supposedly reading, but I heard her crying earlier."

She looked over Ash's shoulder with surprise. "Who's your friend?"

Ash stood quickly. "Oh, this is Joy. She's an art curator. Joy, this is Violet."

Unsure, Joy approached Ash's beautiful sister, who graciously smiled and held out her hand. "It's okay. I have full use of my arms."

Joy shook her hand. "Nice to meet you."

Ash shifted awkwardly. "I'm going to go check on her. Then I'll be back to help you get ready for bed."

"Thanks, Ash," Violet said, and Joy saw concern in the young woman's eyes.

Ash left, leaving Joy alone with his sister. Smiling, Joy sat across from her on the yellow sofa.

"So, how did you meet Ash?" Violet asked.

"I first bumped into him—literally—when he was visiting my neighbor about six months ago. Then he was a guest at a museum gala last week, and we, um, got to talking about . . . art and things." She hoped Violet didn't notice Joy's blushing face. "He said he's giving up art, which I admit I find a shame. He's very talented."

Violet nodded. "I know. But he also gets restless. He's

always loved to be in the heart of things, especially when he was in the military. But he worries about me and Mom, even though I wish he wouldn't." She waved a hand as if to dismiss the subject. "Anyway, Ash and his security. He's a bit obsessed with it."

"Oh?" The only thing she'd seen Ash obsess over was photography.

"Yeah. After this happened"—Violet motioned to her legs—"I think he thought it was his duty to secure the entire world."

Joy must have looked confused, because Violet asked, "Did he tell you what happened?"

"That you were . . ."

"Shot. Eight years ago, when I was seventeen." She smiled gently. "Don't worry, it's not a secret."

"He did mention it."

"Did he tell you what happened?"

Joy shook her head. "Not really."

"We were robbed. Right here in this house. I was a stupid teenager, tried to stop them from taking the television. One of the guys was trigger-happy. Happened to pierce my spinal cord. Lost all use of my lower body. Major recovery time; took years, but now I can at least take a shower with minimal help, be more independent."

The bravery in Violet's eyes nearly made Joy tear up. "It must have been hard." She thought of Ash. "On everyone."

"It was. Is. Mom had a successful landscape company but gave up everything to care for me. She's been amazing, but she doesn't take care of herself like she should. She always puts my needs before her own, and sometimes I know it's overwhelming for her."

"I'm sure," Joy murmured, her heart aching for Ash's family.

"I was wondering how long he'd stay away from doing what he loves. He's forever trying to catch the bad guys."

"Oh?"

"Yeah. I think he has some unresolved issues, because the police never caught who broke in that night."

The blood drained from Joy's face. "You mean the thieves?"

Violet nodded.

"Right. Makes sense." Joy tried to remain calm, but every nerve in her body felt like it was twitching. What the hell had she gotten herself into? She wanted the ground to open up and swallow her. How could she possibly tell Ash about what she'd done?

He was going to hate her, which, she realized, was way worse than killing her.

"I'm writing about it."

"Pardon me?" Joy asked, drawing her attention back to Ash's sister.

"That's the silver lining. I'm writing my autobiography. I never enjoyed writing before, but it's been very rewarding, very therapeutic. Not that anyone will ever read it." She laughed, a light tinkling sound that warmed Joy's heart. "Ash says it's a good thing I'm writing because otherwise I never stop talking!"

Reaching out, Joy took Violet's hand. No matter what Joy had done, Violet was a good, sweet girl. "If you ever need someone to talk too much to, call me."

Violet gave her a wide smile. "Thanks, Joy. I just might do that."

"She's in bed. I got her to agree to let me take care of you tonight."

The girls looked up to see Ash standing in the hallway. "I'm sorry, Ash," Violet said.

Ash came into the room and stood before his sister. "I've told you a million times, never apologize to me."

"I know, but—"

"Do you need me to spend the night?"

Violet shook her head. "You've spent all this money making this place accessible for me. I'll be fine, I promise. Can you just help me change for bed?"

"Definitely." He looked at Joy. "Do you mind waiting a bit?"

She shook her head. "No, of course not."

Violet moved a control on the right armrest of her wheelchair and backed up a few inches. "It was lovely to meet you, Joy."

"Hang on!" Joy dug into her bag, produced a pen and paper, and scribbled her number on it. "Remember what I said. Call me anytime."

Violet smiled, her blue eyes warm. "I will. Definitely."

Ash followed his sister out of the room, but not before something flashed across his face, something Joy swore could have been admiration.

And it tore her apart inside.

The rain had faded to a light patter on the windshield as they drove north, back toward San Francisco. So much had happened that day: discovering Panos had sold the sculpture, the mind-blowing sex in the darkroom, the trip to Ash's family home, meeting his sister.

Finding out that Ash had a personal vendetta against thieves.

She felt like there was a twisting, turning ball of anxiety in her core, tearing her insides apart like jagged wire.

She had to tell him. And it wasn't the fact that she was developing feelings for him that made her so afraid to do so; it was the fact that he seemed to trust her, and she was going to break that trust. She had the distinct feeling Ash didn't trust easily.

He was going to hate her. And because she was selfish, she also couldn't help but think that she was about to lose her job. All because of one stupid, impetuous impulse. *You never think, Joy*.

"Joy, thank you for coming with me tonight. You were . . . very kind." His face was tight, his gaze aimed straight ahead.

"I didn't do anything."

"You didn't freak out when you met my sister."

"Why would I?"

He gave a wry bark of laughter. "You'd be surprised. But somehow I knew you'd be okay. You're a good person."

Stop saying things like that!

"I feel bad."

She twisted to face him. "What? Why do you feel bad?"

"Because you've been trying to talk to me about something for a few days, and I keep cutting you off."

"Oh, it's okay. Really." Joy Procrastination Montgomery. That should be her legal name.

"No, it's not. And I'm pretty sure I know what you want to say."

She froze. "You do?"

"It's about the art, isn't it?"

She thought she might puke up the cheeseburger from earlier. "How did you know?" she whispered.

"It's pretty obvious."

"Are you horribly mad?"

He glanced her way, his brows furrowed. "Of course I'm not mad. It's your job."

"I-it is?"

"Yeah. You work for a gallery. You want my art. It's your job."

She stared at him. "You mean . . . ?"

"Yeah. I'll do a show for you. After tonight, I think it's the least I can do. But I have a stipulation."

She could barely speak, let alone negotiate. "Okay. Right."

"No sculpture; only photographs I already have and any I take of you."

She recoiled. "Me?"

"You got it. Like the ones I took of you the other night, on the table."

Out of nowhere, the memory made her tingle a little bit, everywhere. "Um, Ash. I don't know."

"You want erotic art, right?"

Or I'll be fired. "Yes." They could discuss the sculpture later. She was sure she could persuade him to include those beautiful pieces.

"And, Joy?" He slanted her a look.

"Yes?"

"I plan on taking some more. Pictures of you, that is."

"You do?" she squeaked.

"A lot more."

"Who's going to want to see pictures of me? Naked?"
A shudder of fear went through her. It was like her worst
nightmare coming to life, and yet she was in no position
to argue. He was going to do a show for her!

"Didn't you like the photographs you saw earlier in
my darkroom? You sure seemed to. In fact, I think you
liked everything that happened earlier tonight. You like to
be mine for a little while, don't you?"

She tried to ignore her pulse, now racing from his
words. "I don't think it's a good idea, Ash. Really."

"Are you questioning my artistic vision?"

"No . . . but I just don't think people are going to want
to see that."

"See what?" he asked.

"Me, my body . . ."

"You're crazy."

She lifted her chin; this was ridiculous. "Ash! Come
on. I'm no model!" Her skin burned from humiliation and
shame and frustration. The day had been too long.

She saw his jaw clench, and then he whipped the car to
the right, headed up an off-ramp. They went about a quarter mile in silence before he slowed down. He'd pulled off
on a scenic overlook, and for miles beyond and below, the
lights of the Bay Area stretched before them, dazzling
and blurred through the rainy windshield.

He snapped off his seat belt and faced her. "Who
fucked you up?"

"What?"

"You suffer from a major case of delusion, and I want
to know why."

His words were making the nervous ball in her gut churn
faster. "You have no idea what you're talking about."

"You like my art, right?"

"Yes!"

"Yet you question my judgment when I say I want to showcase you as a model. So, what's the problem?"

Too many years, too many words over time, had been too deeply ingrained inside her head to suddenly become undone just because Ash Hunter said it was so. She knew who she was; she'd lived in her body for twenty-nine years. Was she supposed to change her identity just because he instructed her to?

Leaning her head back against the seat, she closed her eyes. "Listen. It's been a long day. Can we just go home?"

"No."

"No?"

"Now I'm mad at you."

Blinking, she just stared at him. "What?"

"For not believing me when I tell you something. Take off your shirt."

The look in his eyes had changed; gone was the harried expression from earlier, and in its place was something she was beginning to recognize, respond to. Sex: the ultimate way to lose oneself.

He was offering and she couldn't say no. *Girl, you are so messsed up! You need to tell him the truth and be done with it!*

But then he pushed some books aside and scooted over until he sat in the center of the bench seat. He faced her, and she wanted him so much it burned inside her like a wildfire.

"I said, take it off."

Hands trembling, heart racing, she pulled his sweatshirt over her head and threw it in the backseat. It was then that she smelled stale French fries from earlier, and the memory of what she'd eaten in front of him was almost more embarrassing than sitting before him in her jeans and bra. She couldn't look attractive, not after tonight.

"See? There you go again, thinking things that aren't true."

How could he read her mind like that?

He pulled her toward him, and she was surprised when, instead of kissing her, he bent her over his lap. She felt his hand on her back roaming, calming. "Beautiful, pale skin. Were you sore from the spanking I gave you the other night?"

Her skin went hot at the words, and her pussy clenched. The memory made her throb between her legs. "Just for a bit." She was surprised, and surprisingly disappointed, her skin hadn't been red from the spanking he'd given her.

She felt his palm on her bottom, cupping her through her jeans, rubbing her cheeks through the denim.

Glancing over her shoulder, she asked, "Are you going to do it again? Spank me?"

"Definitely. Every time you put yourself down, you get a spanking."

"I'm not sure that's the best incentive."

"I better think of a new one, then, but for now you are definitely going to be disciplined. Now, take off your jeans and panties."

Slowly, Joy lifted her hips to scoot out of her clothing. He pulled off her shoes, slid her jeans, then her panties, down her legs, and tossed them aside. The air was cold on her bare skin, but now that she was naked, she felt his erection pressing against her side and a hot flush went through her.

His hand was on her ass, his palm warm and solid on the skin above her leg. He took his right leg and slung it across the back of her knees, and then, with one hand, he drew her arm behind her back, pinning her to him. The submissive position made her sex start to throb.

"Are you ready, Joy?"

"Yes," she breathed.

Smack, smack. His palm struck her right cheek, then her left. It stung but not as much as that time in the kitchen, and the pain tingled through her.

"Good girl." He smacked her again, right cheek, left cheek, repeating the rhythm over and over, just enough pressure to make her veins run hot with desire, to make her squirm, but not so hard the pain was too much.

"I'm just warming you up, baby. I can barely see the way your ass is turning red. Is it starting to burn?"

"Yes . . ." It was a slow burn, getting hotter and hotter as he continued. *Smack, smack.* He never lost his steady rhythm.

"Oh, please . . ." She tried to move, but he'd immobilized her; she felt her hand clenching behind her back as she writhed on his lap. "It hurts; fuck, it's starting to hurt!"

"I bet. But I also bet you're fucking wet for me. Let me check." He lifted his leg so he could reach between her thighs and slide a finger across her wet folds, and, she cried out in pleasure.

"Yes, you love this, don't you?" he asked, his voice husky.

"Yes," she breathed. "Don't stop, not yet."

"I wasn't going to. I'm not stopping until you beg me to."

He used his fingers to tease her one more second, and

then his leg was clamped down behind her knees again. Then his hand struck her, harder than before.

"Ow!" But it was a good pain, the kind that made everything around her fade away as sensation took over her body, her mind.

"That's right. Tell me how much it hurts." He picked up where he'd left off, switching sides, her ass burning more and more with each slap. She was on fire; it was spreading from her ass to her pussy, to her blood.

"Oh, fuck! That fucking hurts!"

"Good." He tugged her arms tighter behind her so she had to arch slightly back, and he clamped his legs around hers a bit harder. So helpless as he continued to spank her; and she continued to lose herself.

"Let me hear you, Joy. Tell me how much it hurts." *Slap slap slap*.

"Oh my God, it fucking hurts!" She tried to writhe, to ease the ache between her legs, but he had her totally restrained. "Yes, Ash, it hurts so fucking much!" She pressed her legs together. "I'm going to . . ."

But she didn't want to come yet. "Please, Ash," she panted. "Please, stop . . ."

He softly rubbed her burning ass. "Ah, yes, my beautiful girl. You can't take it one more second, can you? You need to come with me inside you, don't you?"

Her heart was in her throat, and her brain was fuzzy. She couldn't think; she was floating.

He lifted her until she straddled him, and she dropped onto his body like a useless heap, nestling her face next to his. But between her legs, she felt his erection through his jeans, felt the hard surface of the button-fly against her pussy. "Fuck me," she whispered into his ear.

He brushed a wild strand of hair off her face. "Oh, Joy. Beautiful girl."

She smiled against his ear. When he said it like that, she nearly believed him. It was such a strange feeling, so unfamiliar, it would have frightened her in any other situation, but she was too far out of her head right then to fight it, to fight anything. When she felt like this, it was so easy to forget everything else, and she welcomed it.

He lifted his hips, sliding his jeans down his legs. Eyes closed, she heard him open a condom and roll it onto his erection. Reaching between their bodies, he took the base of his cock in his hand. She didn't need any instructions; she sank onto him, filled herself as deeply as she could. They both stilled, savoring the moment their bodies joined. Linked, connected. She met his gaze, and his eyes were dark, reflecting the dim glow of the streetlight.

She didn't know what was happening. She felt like an entirely different person than she had just one week ago, like something in the universe had shifted. When she was with Ash, everything felt right. And yet she barely even knew him.

This was the longest booty call in history.

Pushing all other thoughts away, she lifted her hips and sank back down on him. He tilted his head back on the seat, his eyes drifting shut. "That's it, Joy. Fuck me."

His hands gripped her burning ass and sent a new wave of lust over her. She braced her hands on the seat, riding him, using him the way he'd used her. Fucked him until she saw a sheen of sweat on his brow.

"Yeah, baby. Fuck me until you come. I want to feel you come, Joy."

"Yes. Oh, Ash." She sank deeper, closer to his body so

she could rub her clit against his pelvis. Tilted and lifted her body to get it just right.

"Yes, right there, oh my God . . ."

"Touch your breasts, Joy. I want to see you touch yourself." His eyes were half closed, and his voice was throaty.

Taking her nipples in both hands, she pulled and pinched, watching his gaze on her body. His grip on her sore ass went even tighter, sending her over the edge. She climaxed, her breasts in her hands, body clenching around his cock. With a powerful groan, he stilled between her legs, and she felt his own orgasm buried deep inside her.

She wasn't sure how long they stayed that way, but after a while, reality began to set in. The rain had stopped. The air was chilly on her naked skin. The light feeling she'd been enjoying was slowly being replaced by panic at what she needed to tell Ash.

Unless . . .

She climbed off him and gathered her discarded clothing. "Ash?"

He was straightening his pants, buttoning them back up. "Yeah?"

"Are you serious about doing this show?"

"If you let me use you as the model, sure."

"That's . . . wonderful." A plan was starting to form in her head, and as they drove the rest of the way home, she bit her lip, thinking. For the first time, she began to see a way out of this mess, and Ash wouldn't be any the wiser. If she could pull it off, Ash would never need to know she was a thief.

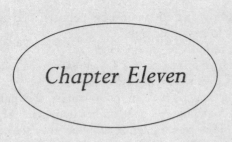

Chapter Eleven

Ash had no idea what he'd been thinking.

He'd driven Joy home, parked her car, and then hopped a cab back to his place and fallen into bed. By then it was dawn, and he'd woken up in time for lunch, starving.

Now it was afternoon; he sat at his computer, waiting for it to boot up. The team was scheduled to do a transport later, and Ash would have to be online much of the night, which left the remainder of the day for printing photographs. For at least the twentieth time, he wondered what the hell had gotten into him. Why had he agreed to put on a show for Joy?

It was, by far, the last thing he needed. But when he was with her, he wanted to please her, wanted her to be happy. Hell, he felt like that even when she wasn't around.

And he needed to capture her: on film, in rope, in his bed. His balls went tight, and he shifted in his chair, pushing the thoughts away.

His computer screen flashed, and his instant-message

window popped up; he already had several messages from the team. They needed him. This and his family, that's what needed to take priority. When he was with Joy, he wasn't himself; he lost track of time; he made crazy promises. And he had no control over his libido.

Things were progressing over there faster than anyone had expected. He'd routed three transfers for American businessmen in the last three days between Baquba and Diyala, two of the most dangerous cities in Iraq. And today the team was escorting a British oil tycoon across the same area. Ash needed to be on top of his game; planning a route free of terrorists, arranging delivery of the appropriate weapons—it was up to him to make sure his team was as safe as possible, and he wasn't about to let them down because he was distracted by a woman and some photographs.

A sudden urge to hop on a plane and join his team in the Middle East rushed through him. He recognized the feeling: Run, flee, go.

But he couldn't, could he? He'd made promises to people, and he never broke his word. But soon the exhibit would be over. And should he decide to go overseas, his income would triple due to the increased safety risk. The extra money would buy his sister a lot of state-of-the-art equipment.

His computer beeped with another message, this one indicating the guys needed to know road conditions on a new route. Apparently there had just been a bombing on the track Ash had planned out for them, and now he needed to find alternative, safe roads for the team to travel. Ash immediately snapped his attention to his job. Now, this had to be the priority.

But he'd made a promise to Joy, and he wouldn't let her down, either.

He'd get it done. He'd get it all done. He didn't know how, but he would.

The first thing Joy did when she woke up was send an e-mail to start her plan of returning the sculpture before Ash could find out what she'd done. Then she called in sick and didn't get out of bed except to eat the only thing she could find in the house—microwave popcorn and chocolate ice cream.

Poor Andrew had to deal with telling Pain-in-the-Ass Panos she wouldn't be in, but Joy simply wasn't up to arguing with her surly boss. She hadn't fallen asleep until dawn, and when the alarm had woken her an hour later, she knew she'd be useless for many hours to come. Her body was sore; her head was sore. . . .

Her ass was really sore.

Yeah, she needed a break.

So much had happened in too short a time period. Had she really only started this thing—whatever it was—with Ash last week? It seemed like months had passed since that night in the museum.

The night she'd stolen from Ash. But all was not lost: She had a plan.

Ash. Her stinging butt reminded her of the spanking he'd given her in the car, and desire washed over her.

Not good. She couldn't let things progress with him until she'd taken care of the little matter of stealing from him.

Not that he'd given her any indication he wanted things to progress. So far he seemed to be interested in one thing only—sex.

She, on the other hand, couldn't stop thinking about him. His heart-stopping smile, the crinkles around his green eyes. The way he made her insides melt with lust.

And his steadfast loyalty and honesty were just the icing on the cake. She already missed him.

So. She could stay inside all night, alone, thinking about Ash and eating the remaining ice cream, or she could go out and try to forget about him for a few hours.

The latter option won.

The bedside clock read 6:00 p.m. Her bag was on the floor next to the bed, and she pulled out her cell phone. "Damn." It was dead, of course. She really needed to be better about charging the thing up. A bit groggy, she climbed out of bed and dug around for her charger. She found it in the kitchen, buried under a stack of dish towels. After a minute, she had the thing plugged in, and as it charged, she dialed Erica's phone number.

"Hey, woman," her friend answered. "Missed you last night."

Tethered to her cell phone charger's wire, Joy leaned her backside against the kitchen counter. "I'm sorry. You think the gang is up for a redo tonight? I could really use a cocktail. Or five."

"I'm supposed to be studying with my partner tonight."

Joy yawned. "Bring him."

"What?" Erica barked.

"I said, bring him. I want to meet this guy who's been 'making your life a living hell.'"

"I don't think that's a good idea."

"Why not? A few cocktails are good for studying, remember? That was our motto at Stanford."

"Joy, I never studied anything at Stanford."

"Well, it must have been my motto, then. Either way, you should ask him. I really want to meet him."

"He's just a rich preppy who thinks he knows much more than a lowly waitress."

"How do you know that?" Joy asked.

"Trust me. I know the type; I've been putting up with their shit my entire life."

Joy knew Erica came from a lower-income family, but she'd never quite figured out why she had such issues with people who had money.

"I'm from a wealthy background and you like me," Joy pointed out.

"I know, but you're different. And no one handed you a gold AmEx when you turned eighteen."

"True. Well, I say invite him, and I'll give you a second opinion."

"Maybe," Erica grunted.

"Great, and would you call the guys? I'm going to hop in the shower."

"Yeah, no problem."

"Mario's at seven?"

"See you there."

Frowning, Joy hung up. Erica had sounded strange, distant. She hoped she wasn't mad about Joy flaking off the previous night. Oh well, she'd get over it. Eventually.

Tugging off her long T-shirt in her bedroom, Joy paused to check out her rear end in the full-length mirror. She bit back a smile. Her ass was bright red on both sides. Why did that send a wave of arousal through her? Her breasts suddenly felt heavy, tingly. She could barely believe he'd taken her over his knee and spanked her like an unruly child, and it was even harder to believe she'd liked it.

But she had. Now, looking in the mirror, she saw her nipples go hard and pointy. She licked two fingers and took a nipple in her hand, imagined it was Ash's mouth tugging, sucking, pulling on her sensitive flesh.

Watching herself, she saw her own cheeks were already flushed from arousal; her hair was a fiery, tangled mess around her head, spilling over her shoulders. She saw her waist, her hips, and her slightly spread legs. If Ash was there, this was what he'd see. He'd see her reach between her legs and slide one, then two fingers into her damp sex.

Pausing, she took in her reflection. Was this the girl in the photographs Ash had taken? She hadn't seen it before, but now, maybe because she was looking through the rose-colored glasses of lust, she saw the similarities. Her hips may not be narrow, but her waist looked smaller than she remembered, and she could count her ribs. When was the last time she'd even looked at herself naked in a mirror?

Using her fingers, she rubbed herself with rapid, even strokes. Simultaneously she tugged on her nipple and watched as her body jerked, stilled. "Ash," she whispered as she climaxed.

Joy was, of course, the last person to arrive at Mario's. She nodded hello at the bartender, passed a pool table, and finally ended up in the very back of the bar where a group of three sat in a large, deep booth. One of the last true dive bars in San Francisco. Joy loved the place.

"Hey," Erica said, sliding over to make room. "I ordered you a lemon drop."

"I knew I loved you for a reason." She smiled at the other two sitting at the table. "Hey, guys, how's it going?" Joy picked up a chilled glass and licked the sugar-coated rim.

"Joy, you got a hot date later?" This was from Scott, a blond with pierced ears and blue eyes that made many a man in San Francisco melt.

"No, why?" Joy asked.

Scott leaned back in the booth. "You're not dressed. . . . How should I say this? As frumpy as usual."

"I don't dress frumpy!" Joy said. "I just like to be comfortable." She adjusted the jeans around her thighs; were they really supposed to be this tight? She was used to looser, less-constricting clothes. But she didn't dress frumpy.

Did she?

"Comfort is as comfort does." This was from Kate. She'd never revealed her exact age, but Joy knew she was in her thirties. Kate, however, was clutching onto her twenties with the tips of her fake-red nails. Her incredibly perky breasts highlighted impressive cleavage in her low-cut blouse, her ebony hair was cut in a modern pageboy, and her makeup displayed bright blue eyes. She managed a chain of junior clothing stores and purchased most of her clothing from her company, despite the fact that the clothes were geared toward women a good ten years younger than she.

Now Kate was practically sparking from excitement. "Does this mean I can finally get you into the store for a makeover?"

"No!" The last thing Joy needed was a wardrobe that was meant for the Paris Hilton wannabes of the world.

"Tell me the truth." She shifted on the seat. "Are these

too tight?" On a whim, she'd dug out a pair of jeans a department store saleswoman had talked her into last year. But the number of the size always seemed too small to Joy, and she'd never been able to wear them out of the house. She wasn't exactly sure why she'd done so tonight.

"Definitely not too tight. You have a great ass, and you should show it off," Scott said.

"Yeah," Kate said, raising her glass. "I wish I had an ass like yours."

Joy scoffed, trying not to think about what the gang would say if they actually saw her ass, red and marked from Ash's hand. "That's ridiculous." She looked at Kate. "I wish I had your tiny waist!"

"Oh my God, you women are ridiculous!" Erica took a dainty sip of her cosmopolitan. "You're both gorgeous; now, would you shut the heck up?"

Scott *rarrred,* trying to imitate a mad cat. "What crawled into your G-string?"

Erica glanced at Joy, and, just for a second, she saw an unfamiliar vulnerability in her friend's eyes. But then it was gone.

"Nothing. I just . . ." She twirled the silver chain at her neck. "I've had a long day."

Joy placed her hand on Erica's leg and was surprised when her friend jumped. "Weren't you going to bring your culinary partner tonight?"

Erica shrugged. "I invited him. I have no idea why; he probably won't show." She glanced around at the bar walls, which were covered in a display of total randomness, from ancient posters to obscure signs to a pair of panties that had been nailed up behind the bartender. "This place is probably way too lowbrow for him, anyway."

"I hope not!" Scott said gleefully. "I really want to meet this person who's making our Erica so insane."

Kate's perfect red lips spread into a teasing grin. "Yeah, the Devil's Spawn, isn't that what you call him?"

"Did I?" Erica muttered, staring intently at her beer.

Silently, Joy watched her best friend. Was it her imagination or was Erica actually blushing?

Scott leaned back, spreading his well-defined arms, showcased in a tight, short-sleeved black T-shirt, across the back of the booth. "Yeah, I believe you said, and I quote, 'He's a scurrilous waste of biological matter.'"

"You must be talking about me."

The group looked up to see a tall man with brown hair standing before them, looking at Erica with amusement in his eyes. He wore khaki pants, a blue button-up shirt, and a smile. Except for the black Doc Martens boots on his feet, Blaine did, in fact, look every inch the preppy boy Erica had described.

He gave a short wave. "I'm Blaine, Erica's culinary partner."

"Hi, Blaine. Please, join us." Joy scooted over to make room. As Scott and Kate introduced themselves, Joy caught sight of Erica doing something that nearly made Joy gasp. There was no doubt about it. Erica was blushing, her cheeks bright as pink rose petals.

What was that about?

The waitress appeared to take Blaine's order, and he asked for a beer.

"Can I see your ID?" she asked.

Kate giggled and then slapped a hand over her mouth.

Sheepishly, Blaine reached into his back pocket,

pulled out his wallet, and handed over his driver's license.

The waitress raised a brow. "Beaumont? Okay, here ya go." She handed him back his ID, then turned and went to get his beer.

Joy had to bite her lip to keep from chuckling out loud, but Erica didn't bother.

"Beaumont?" she said, laughing. "Seriously? I thought your name was Blaine!"

Now it was his turn to have pink cheeks. "I hate that name, so I go by my middle one."

"Beaumont Blaine Prescott?" she said. "Seriously?"

"It's a family name."

"Oh, I bet it is." Erica's tone said the words as if something was being confirmed.

"So," Scott said, obviously trying to change the subject. "Is working with Erica a huge pain in the ass or what?"

"Shut up, Scott." Erica shook her head and dug into a bowl of peanuts that had probably been on the table for at least a year.

But Blaine just leaned back and crossed his arms over his chest. "Not at all. In fact, I find her quite charming."

Erica snorted, but Joy noticed she was really working that necklace now.

"I do," Blaine said. "Her constant abuse and mockery hold a certain . . . je ne sais quoi." He turned to Erica, and Joy saw the teasing gleam in his eye. "That's French."

"You're a jackass," Erica said. And then they glared at each other.

And everyone at the table stared at them silently before Scott broke the silence. "We were just discussing

Joy's wardrobe," he told Blaine, and then lowered his voice and leaned closer. "Or the lack thereof."

"You idiot!" Joy said, and threw a peanut at Scott.

"Joy has a new boyfriend," Kate informed Blaine.

"I do not! I barely know him," Joy said, but the words didn't ring true. She knew how he felt climaxing inside her; she knew he cared for his family more than anything. She knew he liked to tie her up and deliciously torture her.

And she knew he despised thieves.

Throwing back the remainder of her lemon drop, she hoped the alcohol would diffuse the nerves that went crazy in her core whenever she thought about that.

The plan. She had a plan that would fix everything.

"Who wants another round?" she asked.

Everyone raised their hands.

An hour later, they were still at the booth, on their third—or was it fourth?—round. Multiple trips to the bathroom had resulted in musical booth seats, and now Joy sat between Scott and Erica, with Kate and Blaine taking up the ends. Somehow the topic had rolled back to Joy and men, specifically Ash Hunter.

"I don't know . . ." Joy said, her voice loud in her ears. "Guys like that are never interested in me. And look." She began digging things out of her purse and placing items on the table. A brush, an old ticket stub, a belly-dance scarf that jangled loudly as she dropped it on the pile.

Finally she found her cell phone. Squinting, she peered at the blurry screen. "See? No messages." Disappointment settled in her chest in a special drunken way that was extra painful.

"Why do I even care?" she asked her phone. "I barely know you. I mean him."

"But you've done the deed, right?" Scott asked, tipping a beer bottle to his perfectly formed lips. "Danced the horizontal tango? Made sweet, passionate love? Spanked his monkey—"

"Shut up!" Joy said.

"But this is fun."

"*Anyway,* yeah, but we haven't, like, you know. Talked."

She felt Erica stiffen next to her. "Funny. He only calls you at night for sex. There's a name for that, you know."

"Booty call!" Kate said, swigging her cosmo.

"No, no, it's not like that!"

Blaine had been fairly quiet through the discussion, and now Joy turned to him. "What do you think, Pain? I mean Blaine?" His name was darn hard to pronounce after a few drinks.

He glanced at Erica and then back at Joy, lifting his chin just a fraction. "I think you seem like an intelligent adult who can make up your own mind. I'm sure you'll make the right decision."

Silence stretched out before Kate and Scott burst into laughter.

"What?" Joy asked, shaking her head. "Blaine's right. I'm a resssponssible adult."

Scott lifted a lock of her hair and smiled. "It's just that you don't have the best history with men, sweetie."

"Not true . . . There was . . . What about . . . ?" Not Cartwright, he was a philandering charmer. Or that banker, turned out he was married. Or that guy who said he was an organic farmer and then she'd caught him on the news one day being dragged away in handcuffs in one of the biggest marijuana busts in northern California history.

"There has to be one good guy I've dated, right?" she whispered, her voice tiny.

Scott and Kate shook their heads sadly. She turned to Erica, who was just staring at her, her eyes sympathetic. "Joy, I don't want you to get hurt. Again."

Just then her phone started vibrating on the table. Like some kind of alien had just landed, all of the group members stared at the cell in wondering silence.

Five heads leaned to peer closely at the phone. "*Ash*," they all said in unison.

A prisoner in the booth, Joy whipped up the phone and answered, aware of her engrossed audience.

"Joy, we need to talk." His voice sounded strained and tense.

Her heart stopped momentarily as panic set in. Damn. Had he discovered the missing sculpture? She tried to sound casual. "Sure, about what?"

"Listen, can you come over?"

She looked around her, to the four pairs of eyes that were watching, eavesdropping on her every word. *Booty call*. But what if it wasn't just that? What if he knew about the stolen art? What if he was mad at her?

Or what if he did want a booty call?

Her body responded to the sound of his voice, making her blood go hot. Her ass throbbed as a reminder of what they'd done in the car, and she realized she wanted to see him again. Badly.

She nodded.

"Joy, are you still there?" Ash asked.

"Oh, yeah. Sorry. I'll be right over."

Her three "friends" gave exasperated breaths next to her as she ended the call. "Sorry, guys. Gotta go."

"Are you kidding? You're ditching us because some guy calls you and demands it?" Erica asked incredulously.

It was Blaine who put a comforting hand on Erica's arm, but she shook it off.

Joy looked at her friend. "It's not like that, Erica. This is about business."

"At nine o'clock at night?"

Frustrated and guilty and tipsy, Joy nearly told everyone about what she'd done, how she'd stolen the sculpture from the San Francisco Art Museum. She opened her mouth to speak but quickly snapped her lips shut. Yeah, her friends saw her as a bit of a mess, but they also thought she was a good, honest person. Joy wasn't ready to disillusion them yet. And anyway, she had a *plan,* a plan that was going to fix everything.

She shook her head, replacing the contents of her purse she'd excavated while searching for her cell phone. "Please, guys. Don't be mad; it's not like that." Ash wasn't like that, she wanted to add, but knew the statement would only sound patronizing. "Would you please excuse me?"

Erica remained in place, but Scott and Kate scooted out to allow Joy's escape. Digging through her bag, she tossed some money onto the table. "Thanks for understanding, guys."

Avoiding her gaze, Erica just grumbled. Joy would deal with her later, without an audience.

But Scott raised his eyes and smiled. "Use a condom."

Shaking her head, she turned and pushed her way through the now-crowded bar. As she passed the women in their tight jeans, high-heeled boots, and flowing tops,

Joy couldn't help but compare herself to them. Yeah, she was wearing tighter jeans than she usually did, but she still wore an older, loose sweater and her same old flat shoes. Boring.

Ash could have any girl he wanted. If it wasn't about the sculpture (and she prayed that it wasn't), why had he called her? Was she being stupid? Was she simply an easy booty call and he was feeling horny?

As she pushed through the front door of the bar and walked to the corner to catch a cab, she pulled the collar of her jacket tighter around her neck. Winter was on its way, and the streets still smelled like wet asphalt. The scent reminded her of driving to Palo Alto in the rain, of seeing Ash with his family.

He was a good man. He wasn't like the others.

Still, as she climbed into the backseat of a taxi, she couldn't help the little whisper of doubt at the back of her mind. What if she was wrong? And it wasn't as if this was just any old booty call; this was different. Much different. This was new territory, involving rope and domination and submission and a whole bunch of other things she didn't quite understand.

All she knew was that she liked it. A lot. She knew she was starting to crave it, crave Ash. Every time she went to him, it raised the stakes, and she became a bit more vulnerable. He was in charge of so much: her job, her show, her body. Her heart. Yeah, he was slowly growing to hold so much of her life in his hands. The question was, was she ready to give him that much power?

Chapter Twelve

Y ou okay?"

Erica looked up from her beer. Kate and Scott had moved to the bar so Scott could chat up some Goth-looking guy, but Erica wasn't in the mood to talk. With anyone, especially Blaine.

If only he would take the hint.

"Of course I'm okay. Why wouldn't I be?"

Blaine smiled gently, and Erica looked away from those knowing brown eyes. And she also ignored the way her heart beat just a little faster than it should. And why were her nipples getting a little tingly? *Stop that!* They didn't listen.

"Your little friend. You've looked ready to jump out of your skin ever since her boyfriend called."

Erica jerked her head up. "He's not her boyfriend."

"Are you always this involved in her relationships?"

"I told you. She's my best friend, and I care about her. Why is that so hard for you to understand? And why do you care, anyway? Don't you have something better to do? I bet there's a Republican rally or something that could use all this energy of yours."

Blaine just held her gaze for a second before he spoke. "You have a real chip on your shoulder, you know that?"

The alcohol loosened her tongue. "Yeah, well, I know your type, and I don't like them."

He took a slow swig from his beer, and she couldn't help but notice the perfect shape of his lips.

"And what type is that?"

She straightened. "Born with a silver spoon in your mouth. Never had to work a day in your life. Think you're better than everyone because you have money."

"Is that so?" he said slowly. "You think you have me all figured out."

"Yes." But her heart was racing. Suddenly she wasn't sure she knew him at all.

"And how do you know me so well?"

"I . . . I just do."

He encircled her wrist with a firm grasp. "Is that so?"

She couldn't speak, so he jerked a nod.

Scared. That was the only way to describe it when Blaine leaned forward until his face was only inches from Erica's. Her heart pounded, and she couldn't breathe, and every nerve in her body was alive, aware.

And she couldn't move. She couldn't move when she felt Blaine's hand tighten around her wrist, and she couldn't move when she felt his breath on her neck. She couldn't think as Blaine leaned closer, so close she could feel his warm breath on her neck, her ear. Hot, seductive, and male—and sooo not preppy. He smelled like spices and beer, and the scent made something in Erica melt.

"I like you, Erica. You're an irritable, overly confident pain in the ass, but I like you. If you ever get past this hang-up of yours, I'll be here." Releasing her wrist, he trailed his fingers up Erica's arm until goose bumps erupted on her skin. "But I won't wait forever."

Speechless, Erica watched Blaine slide out of the booth and walk away.

Finally, when her breathing returned to normal and her brain started functioning again, anger began manifesting itself in her chest. What did he know? Erica was the one who'd been treated like shit her entire life by the wealthy. Her mother cleaned their toilets, and Erica had served them food for fifteen years. The richer they were, the less tips they left. All the same.

So why was she having this reaction to Preppy Boy?

Temporary insanity. Brought on because when she watched him cook, it was beautiful. The guy could flambé like no one she'd ever seen. . . .

A tiny shiver raced up her back.

I won't wait forever. Blaine's words ran through her mind and were still doing so that night when she got into bed, overriding her worry about Joy.

By the time the taxi dropped Joy off in front of Ash's place, it had started raining again. Obviously, he'd been waiting for her. He was immediately outside, ushering her into his loft under the protection of a big, heavy umbrella.

When he closed the door behind them, she turned to face him with a bit of trepidation, not knowing what to expect. And when she saw the way he was looking at her, her heart skipped.

He looked . . . serious.

Yes, very serious. *Oh, God, does he know about the sculpture? Just put me out of my misery, now!*

He was wearing low-slung jeans, a black T-shirt, and no socks or shoes. Even his feet were sexy: long and lean just like the rest of him. She pulled her gaze away from his feet to catch him running his hand through his hair, which promptly fell back into its disarrayed state. Her own hands curled with a desire to touch him, to hold his head as she kissed him.

Unless, of course, he thought she was a thief, and then there would be no more kissing.

"So, what's up?" she asked, holding her bag close to her body.

He pried the purse out of her fingers and then slipped off her jacket. When his gaze landed on her jeans, his eyes widened. "Wow. You look . . ."

She felt her face go hot. *Fat? Hippy? Plump?*

"Phenomenal." He hung her jacket and purse on the coatrack. "You should wear those jeans more often. Like every day."

Self-consciously, she ran her damp palms over her thighs. "Really?"

Smiling, he tugged her hand and led her to the alcove he used as his studio. On the way, she noticed his dining table held multiple computers and other electronic instruments that hadn't been there before. She didn't even know what half of them were.

She didn't have time to ask him about that, though, because soon he had her placed in front of a camera, and he was standing behind it.

"Ash? What are you doing?"

"Just looking."

"At me? Why?"

"Because I've had this idea in my head, and I can't stop thinking about it."

"But what does that have to do with me?"

"You said you want more pictures for a show, right?"

"Yes, but not of me! I'd planned on talking you out of that part."

He straightened and his green eyes were amused. He knew he had her. "Too bad. That was the deal."

She stared back, something inside her going a bit crazy. Between the lemon drops, her friends' words, and Joy's own wacky feelings, she couldn't keep her mouth shut.

"Ash, what is going on here?"

Pausing from loading some film into his camera, he looked up. "What do you mean?"

"This." She waved her hand back and forth between them. "You and me. You call me up, we have sex. Am I a fuck-buddy, a friend? A business associate? My friends say you're going to hurt me. I don't want to believe them, but frankly this whole thing is fucking with my head, and I don't need another Englishman, banker, or drug dealer!"

"Drug dealer?"

"Long story. Anyway, I need to know something."

"What?"

"Your intentions."

"Intentions?"

She straightened her back. "Yes. I'm not asking for a commitment or anything like that, but is this a booty call?"

"What? No! I just wanted to take your picture."

She gave him a look. "By any chance will I be naked in this picture?"

He had the courtesy to shift on his bare feet, looking slightly uncomfortable. "Underwear?" he asked.

The thing was, she wanted to do it. She couldn't help it; the way he looked at her, the way he photographed her, made her feel beautiful, made her look beautiful. Made her see herself differently.

And yet her self-protective instincts were screaming at her to run for the hills. Well, her instincts and three of her friends.

"Ash, did you call me over here tonight just so you could . . . take a *picture*?"

"I guess I did. Why?"

Anger bubbled inside her. "I thought you had some kind of emergency. I ditched my friends."

She went to walk past him, but he grabbed her arm. "I'm sorry, Joy. I didn't mean for you to do that. For me."

She met his gaze. "Then what did you mean? You call me at nine o'clock at night and tell me you have to talk to me." She shook off his arm and went to snatch up her jacket and bag. "And, of course, I run right over. Just like with the banker."

"Banker? What banker?"

Shrugging on her jacket, she said, "Just another guy who thought I should be so thankful he showed me any attention I had to drop everything I was doing at a moment's notice and run to him. Kind of like you just did."

He opened his mouth to respond, but she held up her hand, stopping him. "I don't want to hear it."

"It's not like that, Joy."

Laughing wryly, she looked around his loft, at all the black-and-white images of female forms, female forms that were tall, skinny, and so unlike her own. She returned her gaze to his. "Then what is it like?" she asked, wondering why her throat felt so tight.

"I'm sorry. It's just when I get an idea, I can't get it out of my head."

She turned away. "So call one of your supermodels." The words sounded bitter, even to her.

Spinning her to face him, he grabbed her shoulders in a tight grip. "I don't want them."

Her throat was now closing down, constricting her voice. "Then what do you want?"

The silence seemed to extend forever, and Joy held her breath. His green eyes roamed over her, taking in her body in one quick glance. "I want you to pose for me."

She tried to jerk out of his grasp, but he held her firmly, and she couldn't move away. "Why me?" she finally whispered.

"Because you're . . . you're . . ."

"I'm . . . ?"

"The most beautiful woman I've ever seen."

She didn't know whether to laugh or cry, but a loud giggle escaped her lips. "What bullshit."

He looked confused and, if she didn't know better, hurt. "What are you talking about?"

"Come on," she said, her gaze darting between photographs. "I'm nothing like what you're used to. *Nothing!*"

"I know."

Still, he held her shoulders, held her gaze. Her giggles

died down until the only sound was the rain pattering against the windows.

He leaned down until his lips were just barely touching hers. "I want to tie you. To my bed. Now."

"I thought you wanted to take my picture."

"I did . . . now I want . . . I just want you."

This was not part of her plan. However, a shudder of arousal went through her, landing right between her legs.

Goddamn motherfucker shitwad. She was weak, couldn't say no, not when his touch was shooting through her like lightning, lighting her up, exciting her. Right then she didn't even care if it was a booty call.

She wanted to call his booty right back.

Kissing her, he pushed his way into her mouth, licking her lips, gently biting her tongue. Her bones went weak, but he was there, holding her, lifting her in his arms.

"I want to please you, Joy."

"I want to please you, too." And she did. The thought of giving herself to him made her breasts heavy, made her sex hot.

"You do, baby, you do." Once again, he carried her upstairs and gently placed her on the bed, following her down and laying his long body across hers, pushing her legs open with one strong thigh. She felt his jeans pressing against her clit, already swollen, throbbing for his touch.

"Will you let me tie you, Joy? And then pleasure you?"

How easily he persuaded her, how easily she melted for him. *So much harder. This one is going to be so much harder when it ends.* Because she'd never felt like this before—so free, so open. She'd never trusted a lover like she trusted Ash, and it made her so very vulnerable.

Which prompted her to ask, "What can you promise me, Ash?"

She saw the unrest in his eyes, saw the turmoil. Everything would depend on this, his answer. Whether she stayed with him, gave herself to him this night, allowed herself to be tied; it all depended on how he answered this one question.

"I can't promise anything, Joy, except what we have tonight. Right now."

She saw the regret in his eyes, and she gave him a watery smile. All she'd wanted was honesty, and that's what he'd given her. All the others . . . they'd made promises, promises they never intended to keep. Now, something inside her swelled at Ash's total honesty, even if it meant a broken heart in the end.

Reaching up, she cupped his face. "Yes. Please, Ash. Do whatever you want. Take me."

Turning his head, he kissed her palm, and she felt his cock pressing between her legs, rubbing the sensitive flesh under her jeans. "Yes," she said again. "Take me."

He pulled off her sweater and tossed it aside. His gaze landed on her breasts, and he leaned down to take a nipple into his mouth, his tongue wet and damp through the red lace.

She arched underneath him as he sucked, tugged, and massaged her breast. Every nerve in her body sprang to life, and she moaned softly as he continued the blissful assault of her nipples and breasts. When he pulled her bra straps down, his gaze was intense on her body, unmistakably full of desire. For her.

A surge of power rushed through her. Somehow, for some reason, this man wanted her. Wanted her to give herself to him, and she wanted it, too. Smiling, she reached behind her back and unhooked her bra to pull it off her body. Taking her own nipples in both her hands, she teased herself, closed her eyes, and moaned. His eyes on her only made her hotter, only made the sensations on her breasts go straight through her to land in her sex. Without conscious thought, her legs opened wider, welcoming him to sink into the center of her.

He kissed her collarbones, her upper chest, paused to suck a nipple in his mouth until she cried out. He made his way down her body, her stomach quivering when he placed a soft kiss on her belly button. She immediately tensed, but he ran a soothing hand over her hip, calming her.

"When are you going to see how beautiful you are?"

When I look in your eyes . . . But she just shook her head, ignoring the question. The last thing she wanted was to feel beautiful only because a man told her it was fact.

He moved down to unbutton her jeans and slide them down her legs, leaving her lying before him in nothing but red panties. Normally this type of situation—lying exposed before a man's gaze—would have made her squirm, beg to have the lights turned off. But this—submitting, giving herself to him—felt too good to stop. It felt too good to be the center of this man's attention.

"Take off your clothes, Ash. I want to see you, too."

He knelt between her legs and tugged his T-shirt over his head. From this angle, she could just barely make out the wounded flesh of his upper shoulder, but now she saw several more scars across his chest, as if he'd had numerous surgeries.

Although she was curious, she didn't ask. Not now.

He climbed off the bed, and when he returned, he was holding four lengths of rope. Just looking at them sent a jolt of lust through her, and she felt her sex pulse.

"Ash . . ."

He stroked her hair off her forehead. "Relax, baby. Trust me."

Nodding, she bit her lip. She did trust him, and she wanted this, wanted it more than anything. She pictured the stolen sculpture, in her mind seeing the erotic pose, the woman's arms bound, her head thrown back, and a shiver tickled over her. She felt like that, like a piece of stone coming alive under Ash's touch.

And right then, that's all she wanted to think about. "Yes, Ash. I trust you."

The thing that was tearing her apart was the fact that she knew he couldn't trust her.

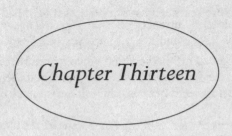

Chapter Thirteen

Joy pushed the thoughts out of her head as Ash took one of her wrists and quickly bound her in the soft nylon. Although he was fast, the pattern of the rope was still beautiful, the knots artistic. After making sure it wasn't too tight or constricting, he gently eased her onto her back and stretched her arm above her head and to the side. A few minutes later, she felt him tie it off to the far edge of the bed.

Leaning over her, he placed a soft kiss on her lips. "How does that feel?"

She gave it a tug, and while the rope wasn't uncomfortable, it definitely felt sturdy and secure. Her heart raced as a slight bite of fear energized her. "It's fine," she said.

He repeated the process on each of her ankles and her other arm, and as he restrained her limbs one by one, her nerves continued to feel as if they'd been electrically charged.

By the time he was done, she was totally bound, totally helpless. Surrendered. Trembling.

He stood back and looked her over, his gaze consuming her nearly naked, restrained form in one all-assessing glance. "Goddamn, Joy." He reached down and spread her hair around her shoulders. "Hang on." She couldn't see what he was doing, but she heard him rummaging around and then the familiar click of his camera.

"Ash, no—" She shook her head, only making her hair more messy.

But he ignored her, circling the bed and snapping away. Despite her awkwardness, she couldn't help but respond to her own exhibitionistic display of being restrained and photographed. Even through her embarrassment, she felt her sex throbbing harder than before, felt her nipples harden under the camera's clicking shutter.

She didn't know how long he photographed her, but eventually he put the camera down and began unbuttoning his pants. Eyes wide, she watched as he kicked off the remainder of his clothes and climbed onto the bed, straddling her chest. Her mouth watered; his cock was close, so close. She wanted to taste him, taste his flesh.

Reaching behind her, she felt him slide a pillow under her head. "You still okay, baby?"

She nodded. She was more than okay; she was high, numb to everything except him, what he was doing to her.

"That's my girl. My beautiful girl." He placed his cock between her breasts. It was then she noticed he held a bottle in his hands, and he poured a generous amount of lubrication into his palm. "It's strawberry flavored," he said with a grin.

"My favorite."

He took his cock in his hands and stroked himself, all the while watching her. Slowly, his long fingers gripping his cock, he stroked from the base to the tip, again and again until she saw the muscles in his lean body tighten.

"I want to feel you, Ash." She pulled at the ropes, but they were secure, on the edge of being too tight; he knew exactly how far to go.

He rubbed his slick erection between her breasts, his flesh sliding smoothly against her skin. The strawberry scent reached her nostrils, mixing with the smell of sex and Ash. She tried to push her thighs together, but her legs were bound wide apart, leaving her aching center open and untouched. Torture.

She watched as he took both her breasts in his hands and began to massage her sensitive flesh.

"Oh, Ash . . ." She felt her arm muscles tensing in their stretched position, and her pussy was getting so damp she could feel her own secretions through her panties.

"Beautiful breasts, Joy; you have such beautiful breasts." He rubbed his cock between the valley of her chest. Side to side, using her skin to pleasure himself. And then he brought the engorged head of his erection to press against her nipples, to rub himself against the sensitive buds, hard and beaded, until she threw her head back, moaning aloud.

"Yes, Ash. Do it. Fuck me there." She bowed under him as desire pooled deep inside her. The feel of his cock, his balls on her chest, made lust rush through her in a hot, raging river.

"Joy, I love tying you, seeing you helpless for me." He took her breasts in his hands and pressed the mounds around his cock. "And you love it, too, don't you, baby?"

"Yes," she breathed as he began moving back and forth, sliding up toward her face and down, just until the tip of him hit the bottom edge of her breasts, and then he moved forward again. Back and forth, thrusting and not gentle. She didn't want gentle.

As he fucked her breasts, his own breathing went harsh and heavy, and his obvious arousal only turned her on more.

"Do you like being bound, Joy? Do you like belonging to me like this?"

More, she thought. *I want more than just this.* "Yes, Ash. It feels so good . . . You feel so good."

He continued to fuck her, his pre-come dripping out of his cock to mix with the strawberry lube. He pressed her breasts more tightly together, making a firm grip for his rock-hard cock. "I can't wait to feel myself inside you, Joy. I can barely wait to fuck you."

"Oh my God, Ash . . ." Her hips bucked up, searching for something, anything. All she knew was that she was aching between her legs, aching for release. For Ash.

He inched up until his cock was right there, a breath from her mouth. "Do you want to suck my cock?"

"Yes."

He gently touched the head of his erection to her lips, and her tongue darted out. She tasted strawberry and his skin mixed with his essence. A shudder of longing vibrated through her as she tried to get more of him; she wanted him to fill her, fill her mouth, fill her everywhere.

But he backed up, climbing down her body until he knelt between her legs, spread wide around him.

"You better not even be thinking of taking a picture right now, Ash."

He grinned. "As much as I'd like to, even I wouldn't push you that far. Yet. Nice panties. I especially like how damp they are—you're so turned on I can see it."

She felt her face burn; it was true. She knew she was wet for him, and in this position she couldn't hide it. She couldn't hide anything. And even as it frightened her, a sense of freedom mixed into that emotion, making her mind feel a bit euphoric and totally unself-conscious. When the option of hiding was taken away, it was as if she had nothing left to do but embrace being exposed.

He went to his dresser and came back with something, but she couldn't see what it was. He held up a pair of small scissors. "I always keep these around, just in case I need to release someone in a hurry." He ran a fingertip along the elastic of her panties, edging around her inner thigh, so close to her pussy. He slid his hand under the lace and immediately plunged two fingers into her.

She screamed out as total pleasure rushed through her. Her body bucked against the rope that held her, constrained her.

"Oh, God . . . Ash . . ."

"That's my girl. Let go. Tell me what you want."

She looked down at him, saw the long sinewy body before her, every muscle visible and taut. His green eyes were so dark, bottomless, like the sea at night.

She took a deep breath. "I want you to do whatever you want to me. Use me." Did she really just say that? Why did she feel this way around him?

"Oh, fuck, baby." With the fabric of her panties moved aside, he placed his thumb on her clit and pushed his fingers inside her again. He brought her to the edge, and she was moaning, crying out for him.

"Three fingers, Joy. I'm fucking you with three fingers, and I don't want you to come, not yet."

"I'm so close, Ash . . . my God, so fucking close . . ."

Just when she thought she would climax, he removed his hand and she lay there, gasping, panting. Watching, she saw him take the scissors, and then she felt the cold metal on her damp pussy. She heard a few snips and then realized he'd cut her underwear off, right at the crotch so the fabric still bunched around her hips.

"Much better. Now I can see you."

Kneeling between her thighs, he took her clit in his mouth, tugged the throbbing flesh with his teeth. She felt his hand sliding through her slick pussy, past her vaginal entrance and then pressing at her anus. She stilled.

"You said use you, right, Joy?"

"Yes," she managed.

He held up a small piece of marble, shaped like a cone with a small base. His smile was wicked. "I'm an artist; I'm obviously into sex. It was only natural that I'd have a few erotic pieces around."

"You made that?"

"Yup."

"What is it?"

"It's for your ass. I'm going to put this in your ass, and then I'm going to fuck you."

Use me. She nodded as her bones melted with desire.

He coated his hands and the marble with lube, and then she felt the sculpture skimming her pussy. Leaning down, he licked her clit again, working her into a frenzy as he pushed the marble inside her, into her ass.

"Oh my God," she cried, straining against the ropes. The marble was solid, filling her, sending a rush of pleasure over her body such as she'd never experienced.

Ash looked up. "How are you doing, babe?"

"Fuck . . ." She couldn't speak, could barely see.

"Hold on for me, Joy. Wait for me." He pushed the marble dildo even deeper, and she screamed as the foreign sensation sent waves of awareness through her.

She'd wanted him to fill her. She'd never thought it would be like this, be this good.

After he'd rolled a condom onto his erection, he climbed on top of her and she met his gaze. "You are such a responsive woman, Joy." He kissed her neck as she lay there for him, her chest heaving as she let him use her.

Then she felt his cock at her pussy; he was guiding himself inside her, and as he buried his erection in one hard, deep thrust, she screamed.

"You like this, Joy?"

"Yeah . . . ," she admitted with a gasp as he withdrew and drove into her again. She felt him everywhere; she could practically feel the marble and his cock touching inside her body. Bliss shot through her as she lost her mind, finally submitted fully to him. She realized that, up until that moment, she'd been holding back, but now, with him filling her everywhere—there was no holding back. The beauty of being restrained was giving up control, giving up all self-consciousness, giving up everything.

Giving Ash everything.

He bent down to take a nipple into his mouth and bit. The pain was exquisite, making every muscle in her body clench as the orgasm thundered through her. She screamed, screamed his name and felt her vagina clenching around him in intense spasms. Seconds later she felt him climax, felt his cock ejaculating into the condom as his entire body tensed and he groaned.

"Joy," he ground out. "My beautiful Joy."

He collapsed on top of her, nestling his head against her neck. They lay like that for a while, waiting as their bodies calmed down, until the euphoria started to wane.

And still Joy thought she heard him whisper once more against her skin, his breath soft and hot, "My beautiful Joy."

And what scared her was that she nearly believed him.

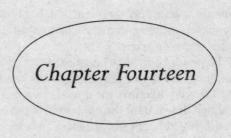

Chapter Fourteen

A sh?"

"Mmm?" They were lying on their sides, and he pulled her closer to his body, tucking her sweet ass against his hips. He couldn't remember the last time he'd felt this relaxed, this calm.

He couldn't remember the last time he'd been satisfied with stillness.

"Do you mind telling me something?" she asked.

"Shoot."

"What happened? I mean your scars . . . How'd you get them? I know it was a helicopter, but do you mind telling me the details?"

He paused. Normally he didn't discuss what happened, but something about Joy made him feel safe, and he found himself wanting to tell her things he rarely talked about.

He trailed a fingertip up her naked arm, her soft, silky skin soothing him somehow. "I was a SEAL, and we were in Afghanistan. I was in the chopper, monitoring the crew. They were militants, came out of nowhere and shot us down."

He felt her sharp intake of breath. "And you were inside the helicopter."

"I jumped, but we were so low to the ground that I was hit by debris when the chopper crashed and exploded."

"Your shoulder was hit."

"It was hit the hardest, yeah."

"How did you escape? Did someone come for you?"

"Eventually." He cleared his throat. Joy didn't need to know about how he'd let his team down by not jumping soon enough, by missing the attack in the first place. He should have picked up the movement with his equipment.

Nope, those were his own special secrets, and he intended to keep it that way.

"It must have been awful. Did anyone . . ."

"Die?"

"Yes," she whispered.

"The pilot. Luckily the ground crew was picked up. Finally."

"And your arm?"

"Nearly lost it." Yeah, a prison cell in enemy territory wasn't exactly the most sanitary of places to be with major injuries. He still woke up dripping in sweat from nightmares of that place. The dirt, the smell, the screaming sounds of inmates being tortured . . .

"That's why your photographs are so moving."

"What do you mean?"

She turned over and faced him, her head resting on the pillow. In the moonlight, her hazel eyes sparkled with amber flecks, and he saw a few freckles scattered across her nose. There was something so innocent about her, so open. He trusted her. He hadn't trusted anyone in a long time.

She brushed some hair away from his forehead. He'd been meaning to get it cut but never seemed to get around to it.

"Your photographs are so deep, moving. I think you channel your pain into them, turn your experiences into something different, something beautiful. Art."

That was the reason he'd gone back to photography and art when he'd quit his last job. He'd needed that escape, and it was easier to look at the world through a camera lens, easier to lose himself in the nontoxic places in his mind. Photographs and sex were the easiest escapes.

"I want to show your sculpture, Ash. In the gallery."

"No, it's not any good. I was just messing around."

"People love it!" She took his hand and kissed his palm. "I love it."

"You're the only one who's seen it, Joy."

Her gaze darted around his face. "Right. Well, I'm sure they would, if, you know, they did ever see it."

"I don't know, Joy. I'm already regretting agreeing to do the photography exhibit."

"What? Why?" She looked truly concerned, and he kissed her furrowed brow. "Is it me?" she whispered.

"No!" He pulled her tightly to his body. "I'm just busy, is all."

"Busy with what? Does it have to do with all those computers I saw on your dining room table?"

Despite Joy's seeming a bit flaky at times, she was

certainly observant. "Yes," he said. "I'm doing some private security work now."

"And that's why you want to give up photography? To work in security?"

Security. He craved it, he worked in it, it was who he was. "In a way. I want security for my family, for my sister and my mother. I never want them to worry . . . As she gets older, Violet's needs will increase. I want to make sure I'm prepared."

"So you're giving up your art for your family?"

"That, and I'm burned out." He traced her bottom lip with his fingertip. "I *was* burned out."

"If we did a show for you, your sculpture would bring in quite a bit."

He chuckled. "You're always thinking, aren't you, little one? You never give up."

"I just hate to see something so beautiful hidden away."

"I do, too." He continued to rub her lip. "Fine, you can have the sculpture pieces. I'll get them from the museum before the show."

She seemed more concerned than happy. "You will?" she asked, and he swore she sounded tense. Did she get nervous before an exhibit, too?

"It'll be fine," he said in what he hoped was a soothing voice. Then he rolled her onto her back and settled between her legs. "I think you could talk me into pretty much anything, Joy."

She wiggled beneath him, and he felt her pussy, warm and wet against his cock. "Anything?"

"What do you have in mind?" She was already ready for him; he felt her slickness against his erection.

Smiling naughtily, she reached for his good shoulder and pulled him lower. "Get a condom," she said against his mouth, "and I'll show you exactly what I have in mind."

Erica dumped yet another custard into the garbage, her third failed attempt at burnt-orange panna cotta that night. She didn't know what was wrong with her, but no matter how many times she tried, she couldn't get the balance right between the orange zest and the sugar. It was either too sweet or too tangy.

It wasn't perfect.

"I knew I'd find you here."

She looked up to see Blaine crossing the student kitchen. Even in his preppy button-up and chinos, Erica couldn't help but scan his solid form. Suddenly her wrist burned from where Blaine had touched her before. And her head burned from his words: *I won't wait forever.*

Fine. Why would she care?

"What are you doing here, Blaine?" she asked, whisking together another batch of sugar, salt, and cream.

"I came to check on you, actually."

Erica jerked her gaze up. "Me?"

"Yes, you. You seemed upset earlier, and I wanted to make sure you're okay."

"I'm fine; thanks for asking. You can go now." God, she sounded like a bitch. But Blaine brought out the worst in her, because he seemed to see things, know things.

And Erica hated the way her body heated just from being around the man. He was everything she despised! He annoyed her so much—how could Erica possibly be having these feelings?

She hated to admit it, but the fact was, she needed to get laid; it had been far too long.

Instead of leaving, Blaine helped himself to a taste of the cream mixture simmering on the stove. "Nice." He tossed in a pinch of orange zest.

Erica dropped the bowl she'd been whisking and pushed Blaine aside. "What are you doing? I've been trying to get the taste right all night! You probably just ruined it!"

Blaine dipped his finger into the warm custard and held it a few inches from Erica's mouth. "Taste it and find out."

Silence stretched between them, and Erica's head spun with so many contradictory feelings: annoyance, resistance, lust. As they stared each other down, Erica's skin heated and her pulse raced. She wanted Blaine, but there was absolutely no logical reason why she should.

Screw it.

Lunging forward, she grabbed Blaine's hand and sucked his finger deep into her mouth, licking and tonguing every last drop of the orange-flavored custard from his skin.

And damn it, the flavor was perfect. So she grabbed him and kissed his mouth, hard, her annoyance fueling the lust coursing through her.

Blaine groaned and Erica yanked him against her body, the kiss deepening. The man who'd been under her skin for so long was kissing her right back and allowing himself to be backed against the butcher-block island. Erica spread Blaine's legs and stepped in close, feeling his strong thighs surrounding her hips.

"Is this what you wanted?" Erica asked.

"No."

Erica blinked up at him; had she made a terrible mistake? Blaine met her gaze, his brown eyes searching, intense.

But then he tugged her closer. "This is what I wanted." He kissed her, kissed her like a man, not like a preppy or a prude or any of the things she'd pegged him for.

When he pulled back, she was breathless, mindless. Her eyes fluttered open. Her heart hammered, and she knew only one thing. "Don't stop," she said.

Turning so Erica was the one backed up to the table, he pushed the dress down her arms and off her body. She stood before him in the practical underwear she wore for work—a cotton bra and unexciting boyshorts. He stepped back to rake his gaze over her, and she wished she had donned sexier panties. She waved a hand across her torso. "I wasn't planning on anyone seeing me . . . like this. . . ."

And he was still staring at her with that look, the one he'd given her when he'd first seen her tattooed arms.

She straightened her spine. "I bet I'm nothing like the girls you usually go out with."

"That's for sure."

His words stung, and she didn't want them to.

"You're a hell of a lot sexier," he said, and came closer. "I hate all that fancy shit girls wear. I like . . ."

"What?" she whispered.

"You."

Her heart was in her throat as he fingered the amethyst at her throat and kissed her. Then his warm fingers went lower, to unclasp her bra and toss it aside. Her breasts were not small, but when he cupped them in his large hands, they fit perfectly. She gasped when he grazed a nipple with his thumb.

She ignored the goose bumps on her arms. "It took me all night, and I still didn't get the orange zest right. And you walk in, and just like that! Perfect."

"I told you. I'm the better chef." But he was smiling, his arms surrounding her as he leaned forward.

"But you're damn good, and now I'm going to reap the reward of your hard work." He reached beside them and lifted a wooden spoonful of the custard out of the saucepan. He then poured the creamy mixture onto Erica's chest, decorating her breasts and her nipples with the sweet yellow sauce.

"Wanna taste?" Without waiting for a reply, Blaine pushed the spoon across Erica's lips. "How is it?"

"Delicious," she breathed.

His gaze focused on Erica as she slowly swept her tongue across the edge of the spoon. When every last bite of custard was gone, she looked into his brown eyes. His intense look sent a fresh wave of desire over her. And then he took the spoon and scooped up more of the sauce, slowly dripping the creamy liquid over Erica's chest before he tossed the spoon aside.

She trembled as he dipped one of her fingers in the sauce and then placed it in her mouth. She sucked her finger as he licked her breasts, cleaning every bit of the creamy sauce off her body. The custard was sweet and tangy, with the perfect amount of citrus. She licked her own finger, pretended it was him, imagining she was swirling her tongue around his cock.

With a groan, she felt Blaine's tongue on her skin, taking his time to explore the curves of her breasts. She saw his gaze fix on her taut nipples, and he whispered, "Perfect."

He sucked and licked every last drop of orange custard off her chest.

It was too much.

Straightening, she pulled his mouth to hers. He pressed back, stepping between her thighs, and she felt his hard erection through his khakis.

Erica shuddered. "Ah . . ."

He reached between her legs and pulled her panties aside. "So tell me, Erica, do preppy boys do this?" He fingered her clit until she felt her own juices coating her sex.

"I don't know," she said, her voice breathy. "I've never let one try before."

"What about this?" He sank his fingers into her sex in a solid thrust that sent her reeling back, moaning aloud. "Oh, God . . ."

Blaine whispered into her ear as he continued, out, in, back and forth, "Admit it."

"No."

Enter, retreat. Hard and deep.

"Admit it, sweetheart. You like me."

"No . . ." Adrenaline pumped through Erica's veins, nearly overpowering the arousal coursing through her. He felt so good, and she was so wet. Even though it was wrong, and she knew she'd hate herself afterward, she couldn't help the words coming from her mouth.

"I'm going to come, Blaine; don't stop, please don't stop."

"I'm not stopping. I'm not going anywhere. I'm right here, sweetheart." He thrust his fingers into her once more, and Erica reached between her legs to hold his hand still, keeping him buried deep inside her sex as she came. Her orgasm nearly overwhelmed her, and when she thought she'd collapse in a heap, he was there to catch her. To hold her.

God, it felt good to be in his arms. To feel his hands on her skin, stroking her arms, her hair.

She jerked back. What the heck had she done?

Her hands shook as she pulled her clothes back on and dressed. Not sure what to do with herself, she went to the sink and washed her hands. The stillness of the empty building seemed to scream between them.

"Erica?"

"I'm sorry, Blaine."

"Why?" He sounded truly confused.

"I shouldn't have let that happen."

"I let it happen, too. I wanted it to happen."

Still facing away, Erica dried her hands. She didn't know why she felt so wrong, so guilty.

Even though she'd just scrubbed her hands, she didn't feel clean enough. She'd succumbed to a man who epitomized everything she hated.

And she hadn't said no. In fact, he'd begged him— *begged him!*

Erica crossed her arms over her chest. "Can we just forget this ever happened?"

"No."

"No?"

Blaine shook his head. "One day you're going to let go of that humongous chip on your shoulder and get to know me. You think you have me all figured out, but I may just surprise you. I'm not pretending this never happened."

Fury boiled up inside her. "I told you. Even if I did find you attractive, which I don't—"

"Right," he said with a smug smile.

"I'm not exactly the type of girl you'd bring home to Mommy."

"Who said anything about bringing you home to my mother? I just want to get to know you better."

"Why?"

"Because I like you. Is that so difficult to understand?"

She thought back to all the rich boys who, over the years, had said the exact same thing. But in the end they just wanted to have fun with the bad girl.

Blaine wasn't any different. She was sure of it.

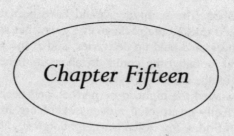

Chapter Fifteen

Needless to say, Panos was thrilled that Joy was curating an exhibit by Ash Hunter. "Good girl," he'd said, and he had actually patted her on the head. But Joy had just smiled patiently at him.

She was too busy to worry much about Panos. She was too busy preparing for the opening-night reception. They'd scheduled it for the first week in December, just in time for some erotic gift-giving.

She'd tracked down the couple who'd purchased Ash's sculpture, and, unbeknownst to Panos, she'd persuaded them to send it back in exchange for a full refund. A refund that would break her bank account, but it was less stressful than the thought of Ash knowing she'd stolen from him and lied to him. Because she was convinced he'd see her little omission as a lie. And wasn't it?

Pulling an antacid tablet out of her purse, she popped it into her mouth. She'd put her plan to get the sculpture back into action, but things weren't going as quickly as she'd hoped. The sculpture should have been back by now. She'd tracked the package every day, but storms in the Midwest had held up deliveries, and at the moment, there was nothing she could do about it. Instead, she focused on the upcoming event.

She wanted the night to be perfect, and because she was perfectly aware of her own lack of organizational skills, on Friday Joy called her neighbor, Ruby the event planner, for help.

The rain had moved on, leaving San Francisco with a clear blue sky and a warm fall day. Telling Panos she needed the rest of the day out of the gallery to plan for the event, she drove across town to meet Ruby at her main place of business, the café called Savor.

The streets were packed, and she ended up parking in a garage a few blocks away. She descended the stairwell and emerged onto a small side street. And when she looked up, she froze.

"Fuck," she whispered. This was the best one yet. The spray-painted mural was an interpretation of van Gogh's sunflowers, a bright, vibrant flash of yellow against a gray brick wall. "Who are you?" she murmured as she taped her card to the building.

She could have stayed much longer staring at the art, but she was already late to meet Ruby. She found her sitting at a table on the sidewalk, peering at the contents of a manila folder through huge Jackie O. sunglasses.

"Joy!" Ruby said with a smile, standing to give her a hug. "I'm so glad you called."

Joy took a seat across from her gorgeous neighbor. As usual, Ruby was impeccably dressed, from her green peep-toe pumps to her sixties-era dress and cardigan draped over her shoulders. Joy immediately felt frumpy in her long skirt, usual flats, and sweater.

After they'd placed their orders, Ruby turned to her. "I've barely seen you around the building lately. What have you been up to?"

"Well, that's one of the reasons I called you. You know Ash Hunter?" Joy laughed a bit nervously. "Of course you do; he was your boyfriend, right?"

"Yes. Good guy. Bad boyfriend." Grinning, Ruby sipped her latte.

But Joy couldn't help but focus on that last part. "Bad boyfriend?"

"I'm sure you know the type, doing what you do. Artists can be a bit . . . distracted."

"I have noticed that. But what about you? Aren't you dating a musician? Isn't he distracted a lot of the time?"

At the mention of her boyfriend, Ruby's entire face brightened. "Yes, definitely. But we laid down some ground rules, and it seems to be working."

"So, it *is* possible to make it work?"

Sliding her sunglasses off her nose, Ruby leaned forward. "Joy, are you thinking of getting involved with Ash?"

"Um . . ." She felt her face heat and took a large sip of ice water.

"It's too late, isn't it?" Ruby stated.

Joy shrugged, wishing she could slide under the table and away from Ruby's knowing stare. Would Ruby be mad that Joy had been getting it on with her ex-boyfriend?

Ruby reached out and touched her hand. "Just be careful, Joy."

"What do you mean?"

"I know what it's like to be with guys like that, guys

who make you feel like you're the center of the universe, like you're the most beautiful creature on the planet."

Joy felt her body heat from the words. That was exactly how Ash made Joy feel.

"I'm not saying Ash can't fall in love," Ruby said. "But he has a short attention span. I don't want you to get hurt like I did."

Joy didn't want to know, but she couldn't help herself. "What happened?"

Sighing, Ruby leaned back in her chair. "We'd been together a year, and I found a pair of underwear in his bedroom. G-string. I don't wear G-strings." She lowered her voice. "Well, I didn't at the time." The server placed two plates of food on the table. "Thanks, Bree."

"So he cheated on you?" Joy asked.

"He denied it, of course. And to be honest, I don't know for sure. One thing about Ash is that he's generally very honest; in fact, he hates liars."

"So I hear," Joy said, taking a big bite of her BLT, hoping it would settle her nervous stomach.

Ruby looked thoughtful. "And to be honest, I wonder if I was relieved to have an excuse to end it. There was always something disconnected about . . . well, about the bondage aspect of our relationship."

Interesting. Joy felt nothing *but* connection when Ash tied her. Still, Ruby's words hit a chord with Joy. He was definitely distracted, and it wasn't as if he'd ever asked her for anything other than sex.

"Anyway, just be careful," Ruby said.

Why did everyone keep saying that to her? Did she really come off as that unable to look after herself?

Shaking her head, Joy watched two smartly dressed

women walking by, carrying large shopping bags. The area was known for the unique boutiques and stylish salons. Unfortunately, every time Joy went into one of the stores, she was overwhelmed by choices and nearly always left without making any purchases.

Ruby moved her hand as if to wave the topic of Ash out of the air. If only it were so easy. "Enough of that. How can I help with your big opening reception?"

Joy paused, taking in Ruby's chic appearance. "Actually, I was wondering if you might help me with something else after lunch. Do you have time?"

Ruby raised a brow. "I could spare an hour or two. What do you have in mind?"

"How does some shopping sound?" Joy asked with a grin.

"Well, shopping always sounds good. In fact, for shopping I can definitely spare an hour . . . or three."

"No, that would look horrible on me!"

Ruby rolled her eyes and thrust the emerald dress onto the pile of clothes Joy already held in her arms. "Joy, you say that about every piece of clothing I pick out. Do you trust my judgment or not?"

"Yes, but—"

"No buts. Now get into that dressing room!"

Biting her lip, Joy went into the dressing room and hung the stack of clothing on the metal hooks attached to the walls. Shopping had sounded like such a good idea at the time, but now that she was actually about to try on clothes, nerves were going crazy in her belly and her palms were damp. Memories of shopping with her grandmother flitted through her head, and she pushed down a wave of nausea.

Girls like you shouldn't wear anything that tight, Joy! Your hips look huge in those jeans, darling! You need to hide your voluptuous breasts, Joy, not wear tops with vulgar, low-cut necklines!

Ultimately, those shopping trips always ended with Joy standing red-faced and embarrassed behind her grandmother as she paid for the clothing the older woman always ended up picking out.

And now Joy held up the green dress Ruby had chosen, hearing her grandmother's voice: *What are you thinking with that color? With that crazy hair of yours, you need to stay with neutrals!*

But Joy liked the color of the dress and decided she was going to trust Ruby's opinion enough to at least try it on.

As she undressed, she avoided looking at her nearly naked form in the mirror, and when the dress was on, she took a deep breath and walked out of the dressing room.

Ruby gasped. "Oh, my God, look at you!"

Joy rubbed the fabric against her thighs. "I'm sure I look ridiculous."

"Well, you're wrong. Turn around and see for yourself."

Slowly Joy turned to face her reflection, staring back at her in all its three-dimensional glory. The stretchy fabric clung to her hips, her waist, and flared out around her knees. It was low-cut enough to show some cleavage, and the color made her hair seem even redder.

Her grandmother would hate it.

But, surprisingly, Joy felt pretty good in the dress, and maybe it was her imagination, but as she gazed in the mirror, she thought she looked pretty good, too.

"Oh, that color is fabulous on you!" the saleswoman

said, approaching with a pair of strappy sandals in her hand. "Size seven, right? Try these on."

Joy looked to Ruby for the go-ahead, to which Ruby nodded vigorously. She was still a bit unsure about the dress, but she sat on a bench and slipped the shoes onto her feet. Standing, she looked in the mirror again.

"I think she needs that dress in a smaller size," the saleswoman said.

"Mmm. Could be." Ruby had her finger to her lips and was studying Joy's form with the eye of an expert. "It does seem a bit big in the waist."

"No," Joy protested. "It's a ten. I'm always a ten."

"Darling, you need to try the eight, or even the six."

"But I've been wearing this size for years!"

"Joy," Ruby said. "When was the last time you went shopping?"

"Um." Joy shifted unsteadily on the wobbly sandals. "I bought a pair of jeans last year?"

Ruby looked horrified. "Oh, dear. Well, I'm glad we're about to put an end to that very disturbing state of affairs." She gave Joy a gentle push toward the dressing room. "Back in you go. I can't wait to see you in that cobalt top. Try it with the black denim skirt, the one with the flare."

Joy went back into the dressing room and removed the dress. Pausing, she said through the curtain, "Ruby?"

"Yeah?"

"How do you know how to pick out clothes so well? I mean, did you learn it or is it instinct?" Joy blushed; she sounded like a total idiot. But she really wanted to know, and it wasn't as if Erica was any help. She shopped only in thrift shops, and Joy never could bring herself to wear used clothing.

But if Ruby thought Joy was lame, she didn't show it. "I've always loved clothes, especially vintage. I tend to shop a lot. Too much, some might say," she added with a laugh.

"Oh, so it is a natural thing." Joy was doomed, she thought as she pulled on the skirt. It was also a size ten, and Joy couldn't help but notice it was big around the waist.

"Not necessarily. You just need to try on things that appeal to you and learn to focus on your assets."

"I don't have any assets," Joy mumbled.

"You have a tiny waist and great tits. That's what you need to emphasize."

Joy thought Ruby was insane; she didn't have a tiny anything. But she continued to try on clothes, trusting Ruby's advice and even learning a few things along the way. Yellow didn't look good on her (which was unfortunate because she had quite a few yellow items already at home), it was okay to buy a V-necked shirt, and A-line skirts made her waist look smaller.

She could remember that.

After she'd tried on what seemed like every item in the store, Joy ended up with quite a large pile of keepers. As she held up her ancient flowery skirt and sweater, she was actually sad to think of putting them back on. They suddenly seemed old, frumpy.

Like something her grandmother would wear.

"Ruby?" she whispered, peering through the curtain. "Would it be horribly tacky for me to wear an outfit out of the store?

Ruby smiled. "No. What do you want to wear?"

Joy looked at the pile of keepers. "Is the green dress okay for daytime?"

"Definitely. Give it to me and I'll have the saleslady remove the tag for you."

Joy gave her the dress, then, on impulse, wrapped Ruby in a tight hug. "Thank you so much, Ruby. This has been really amazing. I could never have done it without you."

Ruby smiled warmly. "Well, I was supposed to meet Mark for coffee, but I just sent him a text to reschedule because something more important came up."

"Oh, I'm sorry! I didn't mean to keep you from your appointments!" Joy said, embarrassed.

"Joy, you are the something more important that came up!"

"No, shopping isn't more important than your boyfriend!"

"Maybe not in the long run, but right now we have more imperative matters to attend to."

"We do?"

Ruby grinned wickedly. "Yup. Next stop, shoes!"

"But I just bought a pair!"

Rolling her eyes, she said, "Girl Rule Number One: You can never, ever have enough shoes! And I know exactly where to take you!"

Joy thought of her already dwindling savings—she still had to buy back Ash's sculpture. But she shrugged the worry aside. She'd deal with that when the time came. After all, wasn't procrastination her middle name?

She stroked the shiny, smooth leather of the pumps she'd just taken off, then poked her head out of the dressing room. "Ruby?"

Her friend turned from the saleslady. "Yes?"

Joy grinned. "I'll wear these out, too."

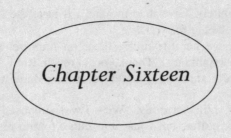

Chapter Sixteen

Later that evening, Joy got lucky. There was a parking spot right in front of the building she and Ruby shared, which made unloading the multiple bags their shopping day had produced much easier. And then Ruby's boyfriend, Mark St. Crow, appeared and refused to let the women unload the car at all. He had to make multiple trips up the stairs to Ruby's apartment, but the guy didn't seem to mind one bit. And when he was done, he gave Ruby a big, wet kiss at the top of the stairs.

Apparently Mark was some hotshot musician, but Joy was totally clueless about contemporary American music. All she knew was, she would love for a man to look at her like Mark looked at Ruby.

One day. Maybe one day.

She immediately thought of Ash, but instinct told her Ash wasn't that man.

Was he?

When Ruby and Mark broke apart, Ruby smiled and

took her hand. "That was so much fun. We have to do it again sometime."

"Definitely. I need your help! I don't think I'll be able to shop alone now."

"Sure you will. But anytime you need a shopping buddy, I'll be here."

"Yes, please," Mark said. "That way I won't have to go."

After she'd said good-bye to the couple, Joy went inside her apartment and closed the door behind her. For some reason, all the shopping had made her restless and a bit energized, and now she wasn't sure what to do with herself.

Digging through her purse, she pulled out her phone, knowing in her heart she wanted to see if Ash had called. But the battery on her phone was dead as usual, so she had to search for the charger—which she found in the bathroom this time—and plug it in.

Had he cheated on Ruby? Despite what everyone said about him, Ruby had a hard time believing Ash would be dishonest about anything.

Staring at the phone, her heart sank. No messages from Ash.

More agitated than ever, she went to her bedroom and shut the drapes. Making sure all the lights were turned low and the door was locked, she got undressed and prepared to do the one thing that was sure to keep her mind off Ash, off the stolen sculpture, off everything.

Pulling on a pair of leggings and a *choli* top that ended just under her bust, she tied a coin-edged hip scarf low on her belly. Then she put on her favorite belly-dance DVD and began to move.

Soon she lost herself in the mesmerizing music. Joy had no mirror to judge herself with. She just followed the

video: snake arms and belly rolls, shimmies and hip circles. The whole thing made her feel sexy, female. The
curves of her body tortured her during the rest of her
existence, but not when she danced.

And, sometimes, not when she was with Ash.

As she went into a backbend, she was happy to see she
could go deeper than ever before, and she smiled.

She wondered what Ash would think if he saw her like
this. When she was dancing, she didn't care if her belly
didn't look flat, and she didn't care if she was exposing
her naked midriff. Would Ash find her dancing sexy?

She would never find out, because no one would ever,
ever see her dance, not in this lifetime. It was her own
thing, her secret. She wished she had the confidence to
dance in public, but that would happen when pigs flew
over the moon. Just the thought made her throat feel tight
with panic, and she pushed the thoughts far, far out of her
mind and continued to dance.

She turned the volume up and played the next set of
routines, the advanced level. She was excited to see she
could easily keep up. A year ago she'd barely been able
to get through the first set.

Over the beat of the drum, she heard a buzzing sound
and realized someone was pressing her doorbell. *Shit.*
Stopping to catch her breath, she paused the DVD, picked
up a towel, and wiped the sweat off her forehead as she
went to the intercom.

"Hello?"

"Joy. It's Ash."

"Fuck!"

"What?"

Nothing appropriate seemed to rhyme with fuck, so

she just said, "Nothing. Hang on a minute." She eyed her jingling outfit. "*Fuck.* What the hell is he doing here?"

"I can still hear you."

She yanked her finger off the box like it had exploded. She *so* did not want Ash to see her like this, a sweaty mess in a half shirt and leggings. Her scarf coins chimed as she ran into her bedroom and yanked an old sweatshirt over her top, throwing the hip scarf to the floor where it landed with a loud clank.

What other evidence could give her away? Finally she calmed down enough to let Ash inside. Smoothing down her ponytail, she pushed the button to open the door.

Then he was there, all long, casual elegance as he entered her place. He eyed her messy appearance. "What were you doing?"

"Um, just finishing a workout. Yoga."

"I thought I heard Middle Eastern music."

Joy swallowed. "R-right. It's a new type where you pose to the music of the yogis."

"The music of the yogis?" he asked with a quirked brow.

She nodded. "So, what brings you here?"

"I came to drop something off at Ruby's."

"Oh?" Joy said, trying to sound casual.

"Yeah, her new boyfriend asked me to make sure I didn't have any photographs of her lying around. Turns out I did, so I brought them by."

"I can't imagine Mark was very happy to see you dropping off nude shots of his ex-girlfriend!"

"Probably not." He shrugged. "Not my problem. So I was thinking you could have dinner with me. Tonight. Now."

Joy stared at him. "Are you serious?"

"Yeah, why wouldn't I be?"

"Because is it possible that I have other plans?"

"Do you?"

"That's not the point. I'm getting kind of tired of you expecting me to be at your beck and call."

He shifted and had the courtesy to actually look uncomfortable. "I guess I wasn't thinking . . . I just wanted to see you."

"Oh, God. Why do you do that?"

He looked confused. "Do what?"

"Piss me off and then make me like you again."

"Um, this is one of those questions women ask that has no right answer, isn't it?"

With a toss of her hair, Joy stomped away. "Give me ten minutes." Pausing, she looked over her shoulder. "I'm only going because I'm hungry, and I'd be eating anyway."

"Fine," he said, his eyes twinkling.

"Fine," she said, her pulse hammering. And that was how Joy found herself on her first official date with Ash.

"What the hell?" As Joy opened her front door, the pounding beat of exotic music blasted through her apartment.

"Get back!" Ash pushed in front of her, scanning her house like a detective out of some kind of action flick.

But Joy knew exactly where the music was coming from and tried to beat him to her room.

He outran her, of course, his legs carrying him in long, quick strides. Now not only was the music louder as they approached her room, but also a voice started speaking: "Now we are going to practice the Hip Bump!"

By the time she caught up with him, he was standing in front of the television, his gaze frozen on the curvaceous woman jerking her hips from side to side in, not surprisingly, a hip-bump move.

Ash looked enthralled.

Joy was mortified.

She moved to turn off the television, which had obviously gone off its pause mode while they'd been drinking wine and eating tandoori chicken at the little Indian restaurant on the corner.

Ash stopped her. "Wait."

She faked a laugh. "Wow, I have no idea how this got on here!"

He simply raised a brow and momentarily glanced at the hip scarf tossed on the floor and then once again faced the TV. "Uh-huh."

The instructor kept bumping her hips, adding a few belly rolls for good measure, and the beat continued.

"Okay, that's enough." She moved out of his reach and turned off the DVD and the television. "Anyway, do you want some coffee? Tea?" *A shot of tequila?*

Turning, he crossed his arms over his chest and raised a brow at her. "You do this?"

She lifted her chin. "No."

"You're a terrible liar."

She bit her lip. "Er, not so much . . ."

Grinning, he sat on her unmade bed. "Show me."

Her entire chest constricted with panic. "No!"

"Yes."

Picking up the hip scarf, she shoved it into a random drawer. "No fucking way am I dancing for anyone—including you!"

"Come on! It's hot," he said, giving her body a once-over.

"No means *no*. Not in a million years."

"How long have you been doing these videos?"

Ignoring his question, she walked into the kitchen and promptly poured herself a shot of tequila. She couldn't believe he'd found out about her belly dancing—even Erica didn't know about that.

He followed her into the kitchen. "Can't you just show me one little move?"

"No. Seriously, I'm not any good, and it would only embarrass me."

He looked at her a second before shrugging. "I bet you're good."

"I'm not." But she liked that he thought that. Let him fantasize about her dancing; it would be much better than the real thing.

He took a step closer, closing in on her, and she quickly downed her tequila with a shudder. Trailing a finger along her jawline, he said, "You have a way about you, Joy. You make everything sexy."

His words sent little tremors through her; she could almost believe him. "I do not."

"Even your apartment is part of your charm."

"What is that supposed to mean?"

"Look at it."

She leaned to the side to glance around his body, which was blocking her view of anything but him. "I guess I haven't cleaned up in a while. . . ."

Which was the understatement of the year. Books were piled everywhere, stacks of unopened mail were scattered all around the kitchen and dining room, and spare blankets littered the sofa, in front of which was a coffee table stacked high with magazines and newspapers. She hadn't wanted to acknowledge how much she'd spent shopping. So receipts were crumpled in an old tea tin.

At least she'd done the dishes earlier.

"You're a mess."

"I take offense to that," she exclaimed, even though she knew it was partly true. Still, she was getting sick of people saying it.

He smiled gently. "I like it. It's who you are."

She couldn't help it; her heart melted a little bit. Her entire life people had been telling her she was a mess, and not in a good way. Now she had this man, this gorgeous, talented man, telling her it was okay. *It's who you are.*

For so long she'd been fighting so many things about herself: her disorganization, her love of a career her entire family thought was frivolous, her body. But Ash seemed not to mind any of that.

In fact, he seemed to like it.

She yanked his head down to hers for a needy kiss. She licked his lower lip, pushed her tongue inside his mouth, taking him, all of him, as their kiss became deeper, more demanding.

All the new shoes she'd bought with Ruby were still in their boxes on the kitchen counter, and he swiped them off with one wave of his arm. Then he lifted her and sat her down, stepping between her legs. She wore the green dress from earlier, and he lifted the hem to spread her thighs wide. Then he yanked her to him, pressing his cock against her pussy, already damp and throbbing.

"Yes," she said. "I want to feel you."

"I want to taste you," he murmured against her lips.

"That's okay, too."

He kissed her neck, her collarbone, and the bit of

cleavage the stretchy dress revealed. She held his head in her hands as he sank to his knees before her, until he was eye-level with her sex.

He pulled her panties down her hips and legs and tossed them aside. Absently, she noted it was the first time she'd ever seen him refrain from putting an item in its proper place.

He was looking at her. "So beautiful," he murmured, and then he kissed her clit, softly at first before darting his tongue out to swirl around the swollen flesh.

"Oh, yes, Ash . . ."

He pulled away to blow softly on her wet clit, and she moaned. He brought his lips to her again, sliding his tongue along her slick folds, tasting, licking, sucking. . . .

He drew her clit into his mouth, at the same time plunging two fingers into her. Her thighs trembled around his head, and she held him to her, bowing her back as a shudder ripped through her, and she came with his face buried deep in her pussy.

He stood. "Stay just like that."

"Mmm," she murmured, too spent to move.

She heard him at the sink, washing his hands and then the now-familiar clicking of his camera. She experienced a moment of hesitation, but it was over in a second. Whatever he did, whatever he turned into art, it came out beautiful. She was beginning to trust him.

And, yes. If she looked closely at the feelings coursing through her as he clicked away, she had to admit she loved the way he saw her, and, even better, she loved the fact that she was beginning to see herself that way, too.

For the first time since he'd started taking photographs

of women, Ash wondered if he'd be able to truly capture his subject's beauty. Because now, as he climbed onto a chair to take a shot of Joy, he saw something in her he couldn't quite express through film.

Because you like this one.

A lot.

With a start, Ash realized he was developing feelings for Joy, feelings he would rather not think about.

He didn't need this.

The very things he adored about her were the very things he didn't want in a relationship. Hell, he didn't need—or want—a relationship at all.

And with Joy? She couldn't even remember to charge her cell phone or fold her laundry. Her place was a wreck (a detail that generally brought Ash's facial tic to the surface), and her car looked like someone had been living out of it.

But as he viewed her now through his camera lens, something in his heart softened. Her red hair was a wild mess, her eyes were heavy-lidded, satiated. Her dress was hiked around her waist, ending just at the tops of her thighs. She had a whimsical, satisfied smile on her face, and he couldn't stop the pure male pride that surged through him.

He'd put that smile on her face.

He could still taste her on his lips, and his cock strained against his jeans. As he circled her, snapping shots, he couldn't stop the images from invading his mind of what he wanted to do to her, the ways he wanted to fuck her.

His balls drew up, and his cock was hard as he zoomed his camera lens to take a close-up of her face. With her petite nose, her mouth that curved up slightly on both sides, and smoky hazel eyes, she was breathtaking.

Suddenly he needed to feel those lips on his. Stepping forward, he kissed her and she sighed against his mouth. "Beautiful girl, I need to see you. All of you." Opening her legs, he took her hand and placed her palm on her sex. "Do you ever touch yourself, Joy?"

She paused and then nodded.

"Do you think of me?"

"Yes, and your . . . your art."

"Show me what you do. Show me how you pleasure yourself." He kissed her again, and after a minute he felt her arm shift as she began to move her hand between them.

"Yes, that's a good girl." He opened her thighs wider, exposing her fully to his gaze. He was so hard, but watching her was exquisite torture. He could not look away.

With one hand, she spread her glistening lips open, and with her other hand she leisurely ran her fingers from her entrance to her clit and back again.

Her eyes sparkled, glossy and hazel, as she watched him. Her movements became faster, and he saw the muscles of her legs tense, saw her toes flex as she stroked herself faster, thrust two fingers deep inside her pussy. "Oh, fuck, Ash . . ."

"Does it feel good, sweetheart?"

"Yes, it feels so good . . . Ah!"

"You like me watching you?" His cock was throbbing with a need to drive into her. She was so gorgeous. . . . It took every ounce of restraint he had in him to stay where he was. And he had to capture her like this; raising the lens to his eye, he began shooting her.

It seemed to turn her on even more. She moaned again and opened her legs so wide her knees touched either side of the counter. Head thrown back, she bucked against her hand, using her fingers to pull her clit.

"I'm going to come, Ash . . ."

"Yes, baby. Come now, for me."

She went still, crying out one last time, and he clicked the shutter, catching her moment of ecstasy on film.

She slumped on the counter, looking exhausted. He put his camera in its case and then lifted her in his arms.

"You . . . ," she murmured against his neck. "I still want to feel you. In me."

"That's convenient because if I don't bury myself in you within minutes, I'm going to fucking explode."

In the bedroom, he stood her on her feet and lifted her dress over her head. He tossed it aside and watched as she did the same with her bra.

Then she was bare before him.

His breath hitched. "You're . . ." He saw vulnerability flash through her eyes, and he was there in an instant, cupping her face in his palm. She seemed so small next to his long limbs. "Stunning."

She bit her lip in a tiny smile. "If you say so."

"I know so." He kissed her, only stopping when he felt her body go slack in his arms. He leaned her back onto the bed until she lay before him.

She watched as he undressed, kicking off his boots, jeans, and T-shirt. When he was naked, her eyes fell on his cock and she licked her lips as he rolled on a condom.

"Turn over," he instructed.

Without hesitation, she flipped onto her stomach, raising her ass in invitation.

"Goddamn, Joy . . ." He climbed onto the bed behind her, spreading her ass cheeks to gaze at her pussy. It was all an invitation for pleasure: her pink lips, her entrance.

He took his cock in his hands and slid between her slick folds, using the tip of his erection to stroke her, gliding his throbbing flesh along hers, from her clit to her anus and back again, stroking until he felt her pussy swell around him, until he felt her slickness coating him.

"Fuck me, Ash!"

"Yes." He thrust inside her, pausing for a moment to feel her clench around him. "Yes, Joy . . . My God, you feel good."

He saw her hands clench at the sheets, saw her shoulders tremble. He pulled out and plunged in again and again, until they both went down flat and he was lying on top of her. She felt her hips moving beneath him, back and forth between his cock and the mattress.

"Ah . . . yes . . . ," she cried. "Ash, I . . ."

Pulling her hair to the side, he leaned down to kiss the nape of her neck as he continued to ride her, driving her deeper and deeper into the bed.

"Bite . . ."

A fresh wave of lust washed over him at her words, and he bent to her shoulder and tasted her salty flesh. He brushed her skin with his teeth and then bit her softly on the shoulder.

"Oh, yes!"

He reached under her body to find her pussy, wet and damp as he cupped her. She responded by spreading her legs wider, sinking into his hand and moaning loudly.

He bit her shoulder again, and she cried out one final time, her inner muscles clenching and spasming around his cock. She'd thrust her ass back against him, and when he came, he was buried in her deep, so deep. . . .

After he'd caught his breath and disposed of the condom, he immediately crawled back into bed and lay on his side. He pulled Joy against him and tucked her ass against his pelvis. He had to admit they fit so damn good like this—like two puzzle pieces.

He gave himself an inward shake. What was he thinking?

Joy wiggled her sweet ass against him, and his cock stirred. He should go. But she felt so damn good next to him. He buried his face in her hair, inhaling the vanilla scent. And there it was again, that feeling of . . . nothing. He wasn't antsy or thinking of where to go next. For once, his mind was still.

This wasn't how he thought it would be. He didn't need any more commitments, and even if he did, he wanted someone who was organized, responsible, and dependable. And neat.

Or so he'd thought.

But he could trust her. Tugging her closer, he kissed her neck, and she rewarded him with one of those soft sighs that made his pulse speed up a notch.

He'd never believed a man like him could ever be happy settling with one woman forever. Giving up field-work forever. But as Joy's breathing turned into the steady, even pattern of sleep, he experienced a strange yearning to be with her. For once the ever-dreaded notion of *settling down* was appealing.

And it scared the shit out of him.

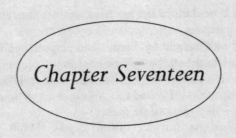

Chapter Seventeen

The door opened, and Joy looked up. Customers! Smiling, she allowed the couple to peruse the collection on their own—she didn't want to seem pushy. Youngish and hip-looking, they actually looked like potential clients. Real ones!

After a few minutes, Joy stood and approached them. "Can I tell you about any piece in particular?" she asked, clasping her hands behind her back.

The woman, a blonde with a bag loudly declaring the designer's expensive logo, turned to her. "Do you have any Kinkade?"

She had beautiful, original pieces on the walls, but no one seemed interested. She smiled tightly. "The Kinkade gallery is just up the street on the right."

They thanked her and left.

Sinking back into her chair, Joy began scribbling on a scrap of paper. *Damn, fuck, shit . . .* She surrounded this tirade in bows before tearing it up and tossing the shreds into the garbage.

Now, with the gallery empty again, her thoughts turned once more to the upcoming opening. Two weeks until the gallery had its reception for *Ash Hunter: Sex in Your City,* and Joy still didn't have the sculpture back. Chewing on her fifth antacid tablet that day, she stared around the empty room, pondering what to do.

Tell him!

He'll kill me!

You deserve it!

She dropped her head into her palms, swallowing down the last of the sickly sweet tablet. It didn't seem to matter how many of the things she popped, she couldn't get rid of the nerves burning a hole in her stomach. She was sure she was getting an ulcer.

Every day she waited for the UPS delivery person to bring her the package so she could sneak back into the museum and replace the sculpture. Her plan was simple. She had friends who worked there; all she had to do was make up a reason to be allowed inside the secure doors, and she'd replace the sculpture where'd she found it. It was a good plan.

If only she had the sculpture to return. The delivery-man had just brought some packages, but there was nothing for her other than some brochures she'd ordered for the upcoming exhibit.

You are so fucked.

Her cell phone rang, and she flipped it open. "Erica, hey."

"Don't sound so happy to hear from me."

"I'm sorry, I'm just having . . ." She chuckled and it sounded a bit frenzied. "One of those days."

"I wanted to know if you're up for Monday night cocktails or if you're busy."

Joy blinked. Erica's tone actually suggested she wouldn't kill her if Joy flaked.

"I'm definitely coming," Joy said. This week's Sunday brunch with Grandmother had been even more stressful than usual, because Joy had made the mistake of wearing one of her new outfits (apparently a girl with Joy's *skin tone* should never wear cobalt blue), she was stressing more than ever over the sculpture, and Ash hadn't called since Saturday.

"Count me in. I could definitely use some inebriation."

"You can tell me all about it at Mario's."

"Can't wait," Joy said, popping another Tums.

"I don't know," Joy muttered later that night at the bar. She swallowed deeply from her margarita glass. "I thought things were going okay, but I haven't heard from him in two days."

Scott raised a brow. "Have you called him?"

"No," Joy muttered.

"Why not?" Kate asked incredulously. "You've been sleeping together. You have every right to call!"

"I know," Joy said. "I just don't want to bother him." The truth was she could barely stand to look at him or hear his voice knowing she was deceiving him.

She wished she had just come out and told him right away; if she had, things probably wouldn't be so bad now. But she'd waited so long, and the more she got to know Ash, the more she couldn't bear to let him down.

Unless that sculpture was delivered while she still had time to replace it, she was going to have to tell him everything. But time was running out all too quickly.

Joy frowned. "Why do we always spend so much time talking about my love life, anyway?"

Scott laughed. "Honey, it's because your love life is such a train wreck! It's like . . . reality TV, right before our very eyes." He waved his hand as if producing a magical television before them.

"It's not a train wreck." *It was sooo a train wreck.* "Very often," she added weakly.

Erica, who'd been strangely silent during all this, looked into the depths of her drink. "Do you like this guy?"

Just the thought of Ash made her hot. All over. "Yeah. I really do."

"He better not hurt you; that's all I can say." *Or I'll kill him.* The words hung in the air, mainly because, after Cartwright, Erica had repeated that phrase about a million times.

Joy took a deep breath. "There's something else I think I neglected to mention." She sucked the straw of her margarita until there was a gurgling sound. "You know the show I have coming up featuring Ash?"

Three heads nodded.

"Well . . . you're all going to find this really funny." She plucked Scott's vodka tonic out of his hand and drank that, too. "You know how it's a show of erotic photographs and some sculpture?"

"What are you trying to say, Joy?" Scott asked, taking back his now-empty drink with a scowl.

"I'm kind of the model in some of the photographs."

Dead silence.

Then Kate finally said, "Oh my God. Are you serious?"

She saw a muscle twitch under Erica's eye. "Are you nude?"

Joy felt her entire face begin to burn. There was nothing more attractive than a redhead blushing—*not!*

She nodded. "Yes, in some."

"But . . . but . . . ," Kate stuttered.

Straightening, Joy clenched her fists. "What? You don't think I'm pretty enough to be featured?"

"No!" Kate said. "That's not it at all."

"Then what is it?" Joy demanded, her voice high.

Scott placed a soft hand on her shoulder. "It's just that you've never been comfortable even being in a bathing suit at the beach, and now you're posing nude for an exhibit to be seen by hundreds—maybe thousands—of people? Your potential clients?"

Joy felt the blood drain from her face. She hadn't really thought about it quite like that. "I've seen the photographs. They're not crude."

Scott squeezed her shoulder. "I'm sure they're not, sweetie. We're just surprised, right, gang?"

Kate nodded.

Erica looked like she was going to rip someone's head off. "Let me get this straight. You're going to be selling naked pictures of *yourself*?"

"I'm not naked in all of them," Joy murmured, sinking down in the booth. In fact, Ash used light and shadow to hide most of her private parts. That was one of the things she found so beautiful about his work. When you looked close, the beauty of his pieces was really in the forms, the shades of gray in the images. "And furthermore, I'm not the only model."

"How did he talk you into this?" Erica demanded.

"He . . . he . . ." She wasn't even sure she knew. "He just did!"

"For heaven's sake, Joy," Erica said.

But Kate looked thoughtful. "I think it's great."

"What?" Joy said, snapping her attention to her friend. Tonight Kate was wearing tight leggings and a fuchsia top that dipped way beyond the curves of her breasts.

"Yeah," Kate said, waving her hand. Joy couldn't help but notice her nails were the exact same color of pink as her shirt. "Let's face it, Joy. You've never realized how pretty you are. Since you've been with Ash, you seem more confident. You're comfortable enough to let him take sexy photos of you." She gave Joy a once-over. "And you even went shopping and bought some clothes that aren't two sizes too big. Yup. I think it's a good thing."

Joy looked over to find Erica staring silently at her. Finally she asked, "So. You really like him?"

Slowly, Joy nodded.

"And he likes you."

"I think he does."

"Well," Erica said after a sip of her drink. "He better be good to you, or like I said, he'll have me to answer to."

Everyone at the table made fake *oooohh, scary,* sounds. But Joy's sound wasn't quite as fake as the others.

"Here comes the rain again . . . ," Andrew hummed absently as he surfed the Internet in the quiet gallery.

Through the large gallery windows, Joy watched people running along the sidewalk, hovering under umbrellas or crouching under wet newspapers if they'd gone out unprepared.

Apathetically, Joy glanced around the gallery, looking for a newspaper.

She heard the sound of her cell phone, its ringtone of the muffled chorus to "Hips Don't Lie" coming from deep inside her purse. "Damn," she muttered when she glanced at the caller ID, but she answered it anyway. "Hi, Grandma."

"Hello, dear. Are you busy?"

Joy started doodling on her scrap paper. "Well, I'm at work, Grandmother, as I usually am on Tuesdays."

"Right," she said, as if Joy was just pretending to have a job. "Well, do you think you could come over and do me a favor?"

Nooooo, Joy doodled and surrounded the word with a rainbow. "Sure, what do you need?" she asked, wishing she'd let the call go to voice mail.

"Well, with all this rain, I'm afraid my patio roses and hanging planters are going to blow away. I need help bringing everything in."

"I'd love to, but I need to have my tires rotated before I drive in this weather. I'm way overdue." Sometimes being irresponsible came in hardy.

"Oh, it's just a sprinkle outside. Besides, that was my car for ten years before I gave it to you, and I never had one problem."

Oh, sure. Remind me that you gave me the car—lay on the guilt, why don't you?

Still, Joy wasn't lying about the tires; she'd already skidded coming down Geary earlier that day. "Can't you call David?" *You know, the brother who lives five instead of forty-five minutes away?*

"He's busy doing an important surgery."

Of course he is, and her other brothers would have similar excuses. "Fine. I'll leave work at four and drive straight there."

"You can't come any earlier?"

"I need to close the gallery, Grandmother."

"Fine," she said with a sigh. "I'll see you later, then. Oh, and I'll make you a lovely dinner for coming. Something low-calorie; I know you're on a diet."

"Gee, thanks, Grandmother."

"You're welcome, dear. See you tonight."

That afternoon, UPS delivered a box from Little Rock, Arkansas, addressed to Joy Montgomery. Her heart thundered in her ears as she realized it was finally here. The sculpture had finally arrived.

Locking herself in the bathroom, her heart leaped as she sat on the toilet and placed the box on her lap. She carefully cut through the tape using a box cutter. At last! Tomorrow she could go to the museum and put it back in that dingy cabinet. Museum personnel were expecting her to come to take pictures of Ash's work for the upcoming exhibit, and while she was there, she would simply return the stolen piece.

"Yes!" The clients had used newspaper to wrap the small sculpture, and now Joy dug through the pages of the *Little Rock Review* until she saw some white marble, the top of the female figure's head. Gently, she lifted the piece out of the box.

And her heart stopped.

It was just as beautiful as she remembered. She ran her fingertips over the smooth form. It was erotic as ever, and a wonderful thrill went through her.

"You okay in there?" Andrew said through the door.

Deep breaths. She said in a high-pitched voice, "Yeah, just um, having some girl issues."

"Say no more," Andrew said quickly, and she heard his boots clicking as he walked away.

Okay. Now she had the sculpture. She could return it, and Ash would be none the wiser. A niggle of guilt reminded her that she was still being slightly dishonest, but it was better than causing unnecessary stress between them, right? Especially when no harm would come of it.

You're so open, Joy. So truthful. He'd said those things and she hadn't denied it. She'd let him believe it.

Shut up.

She looked back at the beautiful sculpture in her hand. Such beauty, so much sexuality. The first time she'd seen it, she hadn't really known what it would be like to feel the energy of being bound. Now that she had experienced such a thing, the piece became even more meaningful, more arousing.

Still, it was stolen. She'd stolen from Ash.

Impulsive, reckless, thoughtless . . .

All those things her grandmother had been saying for all these years . . .

She'd been right.

The rain had started again, and Erica responded by making a big pot of soup. She remembered when she was just a girl and her mother would make this exact recipe: sauté the leeks in butter, then add potatoes and broth. The trick was the spot of cream at the end. Not too much, just a bit to add a hint of richness. Perfect on a night like this. After all the crazy feelings she'd been experiencing lately, nothing sounded better than her mom's soup and some fresh, crunchy bread.

She pushed away the shot of sadness that darted through her when she thought of her mother. The woman had worked three jobs to keep her and her two siblings fed and clothed. They'd lived in a tiny house on the way, way wrong side of the tracks. Due to some ridiculous zoning map, she'd been forced to attend a school whose main population thought a Mercedes was an appropriate sixteenth-birthday present.

Erica's mom had died when she was seventeen. Her brother and sister had been sent into foster families, but Erica was too close to eighteen for the system to fight her on it, so she'd gone to work waiting tables at a local Denny's. And she'd been a waitress ever since.

But not for much longer.

Mom would be proud.

But what would she think of Erica dating a preppy like Blaine? After being treated as second-class citizens, Erica's family held a certain disdain for the upper class. And yet she couldn't get the egotistical chef-to-be out of her head. Even now, the memory of his touch made Erica's bones thrum with unexpected lust. She so did not want to be attracted to the saucy, smug, chef-to-be.

But she was.

How had that happened? She had a long history of not getting along with the wealthy. As the only poor kid in an upper-class school, she knew all about the way lower-class people were treated. And if being shoved into lockers, having her clothes hidden during gym, and being the last one picked during any sports activity wasn't enough to convince her, well, five years of serving stuck-up students surely did: People with money were a different species, one she really didn't want anything to do with.

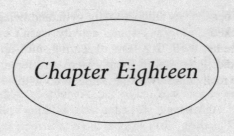

Chapter Eighteen

When Ash returned home later that night, cold and wet and tired, he went straight for the liquor cabinet. His hands shook as he poured a healthy dose of scotch into a glass and gulped half of it down. He felt like the walls were closing in on him, like he couldn't breathe.

It was more than obvious his sister needed a nurse. His mother still refused to admit it, but after seeing her today, Ash knew, without a doubt, that he had no choice. Her overalls had been hanging off her too-skinny frame, and her hair looked as if it hadn't been cut in months. This from a woman who used to dress impeccably each day for the love of her live, the administration of her land-scaping business.

Now she was running herself ragged, looking older every day. Ash had to step in and do something.

His mother could no longer be the sole caregiver for his sister. Ash was going to have to hire full-time care for Violet. But his mom was proud, always needing to prove she could do everything herself. This was going to take some doing.

Guilt was burning a hole in his gut, and he tried to drown it with the rest of the scotch.

"Take care of your mom and your sister," his dad had said when the cancer was really bad. At thirteen, Ash already knew what that meant: He had to take his father's place. And what had he done? Run away at the first chance.

And fuck if he wasn't itching to do it again. He refilled his glass, went to his computer, and booted up.

When Juan had said there wouldn't be any fieldwork, Ash really hadn't believed him. There was always fieldwork, and it was only a matter of time before the e-mail landed in his in-box. That time had come earlier that morning.

Opening up his e-mail program, he stared at the message, rereading it for the umpteenth time. The familiar buzz of excitement started quietly but was beginning to build, thrumming through him, and he tattooed a steady beat with the toe of his boot, the sound a rhythmic clicking on the hardwood.

Ash was tempted. So goddamn tempted.

The team wanted him there, in Iraq. The pussy tech guy they'd hired to switch servers had turned out to be unable to tolerate the communal living conditions and extreme heat. His job as a computer technician was easy—all he needed to do was make sure the servers over in Iraq worked properly. But even the easy job and generous paycheck didn't keep him there. He'd hightailed it back to the States after only a few weeks. Now the guys were stuck with no on-site tech support, which was an element crucial to their operations.

Problem was, if Ash left for the field, he knew he wouldn't be coming back anytime soon, because that antsy feeling was back, stronger than ever, and he wanted to run.

No, you don't run, he told himself.

You escape.

"Shit," he muttered. He couldn't help it, couldn't help the thoughts spinning through his head, no matter how wrong they were. In a way, hiring full-time care would release him, and he couldn't deny there was a part of him that craved that freedom.

Really, the only thing stopping him at this point was Joy. Joy and her show. He couldn't do anything for two more weeks, at least not until the show was over.

Joy. He didn't know what to think about his feelings for her. At the thought of the beautiful woman, of her messy red hair, luscious breasts, and engaging smile, he felt something funny in his gut. And he felt something familiar in his balls, a throbbing lust.

If he left, he'd be leaving her. That had never mattered before; women had never factored into his decisions regarding what he did or where he went. Family and then his job, that was all that mattered. And, for a while, his art.

He looked around his loft. The space was filled with photographs of Joy. He'd been matting them all himself, getting the images ready for the upcoming show. With a start, he realized he'd been so obsessed with the photography, he hadn't actually spoken with his muse in a couple of days. He ran a hand through his hair. This was part of the reason he'd ceased taking pictures. He became so engrossed, so obsessed with getting his vision just perfect, he sometimes dropped out of the world altogether. And he couldn't afford to do that, not with the responsibilities he'd committed himself to.

Responsibilities he could replace with a nurse and a plane ticket.

But what about Joy?

Now, suddenly, he needed to see her, or at least to hear her voice. Something about her grounded him, calmed him. Snatching the cell off the desk, he dialed her number. It went straight to voice mail; she'd probably let the battery die again. He shook his head. That girl needed a caretaker, too, and Ash needed another responsibility like he needed a hole in the head.

Still staring at the phone, he jumped when it began vibrating in his hand. He didn't recognize the number, and he answered cautiously.

"Ash?"

"Joy? Where are you calling from?"

"A nice man's cell phone."

Ash's heart seemed to freeze. "What? And what's all that noise?"

"I'm in—hang on—what's your name again?"

Ash heard a deep voice answer, "Dan."

"I'm in a very nice man named Dan's car, and I was wondering if you could come help me."

Ash was already out of his chair and slipping his leather jacket onto his shoulders. "Wait. Joy, where are you? What's happened?"

"I got a flat tire coming home from Atherton."

"Where are you? Exactly?"

"Um . . . remember that place," she started to whisper, "you and I stopped that time?"

"Yes."

"I'm near there, on the side of the road. My tire blew, and I realized my cell is dead. I don't know what I would have done if Dan hadn't stopped and let me use his phone."

Ash clenched his fist around his keys.

"The auto club said it would be hours before they could get here, and I didn't want to wait alone. Since my phone's dead, I don't know anyone's numbers by heart. I found yours on a piece of paper in my purse. But if you're busy . . ."

"No! Joy, get back in the car. *Your* car. I'll be there as soon as I can."

"Are you sure?" she asked.

"Yes." He said, slamming his apartment door behind him and locking it. "Get back in your car and lock your doors. Wait for me. I'll be right there."

Ash's truck skidded to a stop behind Joy's car twenty minutes later. Wow. That was some kind of record. He must have driven the thirty miles from San Francisco like a bat out of hell.

A second later he was at her window, raindrops hammering down on him, drenching his hair. She rolled the window down. "Hi."

"Are you all right?" He looked inside the car, seemed to assess her appearance in one sweeping glance.

"Yes. It's just a flat tire. Now get in; you're soaked."

He ran around the front of her car and got in on the passenger side. But first he needed to move the plastic jack-o'-lantern full of Halloween candy, leftovers from Joy's favorite holiday. "Want one?" she asked, holding up a tiny Mars bar.

"No!" Turning to the side, he faced her, rain falling off his strong jaw in big drops. "Are you sure you're okay?"

"Yes," she said, brushing a bead of water away from his eye. "It's just a flat tire."

"Don't you have a car charger for your cell phone?" he asked incredulously.

"Yes," she murmured. "But I don't have it with me."

"And that would be because . . . ?"

"I lost it . . . I could have sworn it was in here somewhere," she said, looking around the car as if the charger would just appear.

He ran a hand over his wet hair, and she thought she saw his jaw ticking. "You really do need a handler," he muttered.

"I do not! I can't help it if my grandmother made me come help her move her precious plants off the patio before they blew over."

"Your grandmother made you drive in this weather?"

"She didn't *make* me. Grandmother asked me to." *And made me feel guilty, like always.* Joy lifted her chin. "I was happy to go."

His gaze drifted to her hair, which she knew was a mess, and he plucked a sodden rose petal out of the damp strands. He brought it to his nose and took a deep whiff. "I knew I smelled roses when I got in the car."

She self-consciously tried to smooth down her unruly locks.

Ash reached out and stopped her. "So your grandmother needed you and you went to her."

She nodded, loving the heat from his palm on her hand.

"I admit I understand what that feels like. To feel responsible for someone." And she swore she saw a flicker of admiration in his green eyes. "But promise me you won't do anything like this again without calling me first."

"It's just rain."

"Joy . . . ," he said warningly.

She smiled. "You mean call you before I get a flat tire? It's not like I could have predicted it." Well, not really. She refrained from adding that she knew the tires needed to be rotated.

"Well, I better get to work," he said.

"What do you mean?"

He moved his hand toward the door handle. "Changing your tire."

"No! It's pouring rain, Ash. Just take me home and I'll deal with it in the morning."

"Why? I can have it changed in ten minutes."

"Seriously?" Joy had never changed a tire in her life, and to her the task seemed about as easy as brain surgery. "Still . . . I don't want you to get wet. Er, wetter."

He ignored her. "Is your jack and spare in the trunk?"

"Um . . . ," she said, biting her lip.

"You don't know." It wasn't a question.

Slowly, she shook her head.

He shook his head, too, but in a different kind of way. A way Joy had seen many times in her life and it meant, *Seriously?*

"Flashlight?" he asked.

"Hang on." She dug through her purse; she was sure she had a mini flashlight in there somewhere . . . "Aha!" She pulled a black item out of her bag.

"You actually had a flashlight in there?" he said disbelievingly.

"No, but I found my cell phone charger!" She plugged it in.

"I . . . you . . . Oh, for fuck's sake!"

Silently, she watched him exit the car, and then she saw the beam of a flashlight before she heard him open her trunk. He must have had one in his truck. Of course he did—the man was a freakin' Boy Scout.

He returned minutes later, drenched, and slid back into the passenger side. That nerve in his jaw was jumping as he silently pulled a miniature Snicker's bar out of the jack-o'-lantern. Then he unwrapped it and popped it into his mouth. The entire time he chewed, he stared straight ahead, gazing through the windshield, although it was raining too hard to actually see anything.

After he swallowed, he turned to her. He looked so serious she backed away a few inches.

"Joy. Your tires are totally bald."

"Really?" she said, trying to look innocent.

"Yes." He seemed to be controlling his temper.

She gave a weak chuckle. "Is that really such a big deal?"

"Yes!" he said, and it was the loudest she'd ever heard his voice. "Yes," he repeated, his voice purposefully calm, as if he was trying to contain himself. "It's a fucking big deal when it's pouring rain, the roads are slick, and you're driving seventy miles an hour on the freeway!" By the time he finished the sentence, his voice was loud again.

"Sixty-five," she squeaked. "That's the speed limit."

"Furthermore, even if you weren't driving a deathmobile—"

"Hey! Don't call Bessie names," she said, patting the dashboard.

He ignored her interruption. "—you'd be screwed anyway because you don't even have a spare tire or a jack in your car!"

"Well, why would I? It's not like I'd know what to do with them."

"Woman," Ash said.

"Yes?" she whispered.

"Come here." His voice was flat.

A tiny shiver went through her. "Are you going to spank me again?"

"No." He began rummaging around in her car, twisting to lean over the seat and paw through the disorder in the back. "I knew there'd be something in this damn mess that I could use." He sat back down and ran one of her silk scarves over his palms. It was a colorful silk Hermes, a present from her grandmother. But the pattern had always been a bit stuffy for her, so Joy kept it in the car so she could put it on at the last minute when she visited Atherton.

"Come here."

Not exactly sure why, her body responded with a little pulse in her sex. She scooted closer.

"Lean forward."

She did, and he briskly pulled her hands behind her back. "What are you doing?"

"I have no idea," he said, his voice rough. "I just want to tie you up. I *have* to tie you up."

She felt the silk wrap neatly around her wrists, secure and tight. Then he thrust her back onto the seat, and she sat there, staring at him, her shoulders jutting forward due to the position of her wrists.

"W-what are you going to do?"

"I'll think of something."

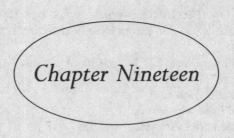

Chapter Nineteen

Come on."

"Where are we going?" Joy stared up at him through the passenger door he held open. The rain had slowed to a drizzle, but it still pattered down upon Ash's wet head. "I'm still tied up."

"I know that." He shrugged off his jacket and held it just outside the car, like a canopy. "I'm driving you home, and in the morning, if the auto club hasn't shown up, I'll call my garage and have them come tow the car."

"But—"

"No." He dipped his head, and when he looked back up, she saw that the wicked man seemed to be biting back a smile. "You're following my orders, Joy. Your hands are tied, so to speak."

"You asshole."

"Ah, I love it when you use special endearments for me. Now, come on."

Scooting across the seat, she glared at him. Her dress

rode up her thighs as she swung her legs out of the car, a fact Ash obviously didn't miss judging by the way he stared at her revealed skin and gave a low whistle.

He took hold of her arm and helped her to her feet. "My purse," she said.

He reached inside and grabbed her big gray bag. *Shit!* The stolen sculpture was in there, and she prayed he didn't notice it. She had an appointment with the curator at ten, and she figured by lunchtime her little snafu would be taken care of.

Now, when he was annoyed and she was tied up, was soooo not the time for him to discover what she'd done.

"What the hell do you have in here?" he asked, holding her purse out. "It weighs a ton."

"You know . . . things. *Female* things." She tipped her head forward. "Lots of them."

At that he seemed to lose interest in the contents of her bag. "Come on," he said.

"Wait!"

He just stared at her.

"My cell phone."

She could have sworn he growled, but he just unplugged her phone and charger, dropped it into her bag, and then led her to his truck. He opened the door and placed her bag on the floorboard. Then he picked her up and sat her on the seat as if she weighed the same as her purse.

"Buckle up."

She just glared at him.

"Oh, right." Grinning evilly, he pulled on the seat belt and leaned across her lap, facing her. He pressed his warm, damp chest to hers as he slid the end into the fastener. Then

he leaned in close but didn't kiss her. She watched, she
waited; he was so near she could feel his heat, smell his
damp skin.

Then he was gone and the door slammed shut. He
hadn't turned off his headlights, and now she watched
him as he ran around the front of the truck, the bright
beams illuminating his long, strong form. She couldn't
help but stare. His damp T-shirt clung to his chest, sticking to every ridge of muscle, and his longish blond hair
hung in damp strands down to his strong jaw. His eyes
seemed to glow as green as one of Monet's water lily
petals.

And she was his prisoner.

A shudder of arousal washed over her, and she realized
she liked it. She wondered why trusting him enough to
give him this control over her turned her on. But it did. A
lot. She leaned back in the seat and prepared to enjoy the
ride.

With one hand on the steering wheel of his fully loaded
Dodge truck, Ash tried to keep his other hand off Joy.

She sat beside him, cozy in her heated seat, looking
totally content to do whatever he wanted, to ride along
wherever he took her. Hands behind her back, she obviously trusted him to take care of her.

Many women had, but for some reason this was different. He liked to control everything, even his environment.
But Joy made him crazy, made him do things he'd never
done—or wanted to do. He'd never even asked if she'd
wanted to be tied, and that was something totally new to
him. But earlier, out of lust or frustration he didn't know,

he'd experienced a sudden, powerful desire to own her. To have her belong to him.

Only him.

During the entire drive to her car, he'd been out of his fucking head with worry. *His* Joy, alone on the side of the road, in the dark with some guy named Dan. If even one hair on her head had been hurt, Ash would have killed him.

Ash had nearly collapsed with relief when he'd discovered her, safe, sound, and alone in her car.

And he'd wanted to kill her as much as he'd wanted to hold her, to reassure himself that she was okay.

Get a grip, Hunter. It was a flat tire, not a rescue mission!

Still, she was lucky she had only blown a tire; something so much worse could have happened. The thought made his chest tighten.

He had to feel her, couldn't wait another second.

Reaching over, he cupped her thigh. He felt her muscles tense under his palm. "Open your legs for me, Joy."

She barely hesitated before spreading her thighs apart, and he slipped his hand up the inside of her leg. Then he was slipping his fingers beyond the elastic band of her panties, and the feel of her, the warm, welcoming feel of her pussy, nearly undid him.

He cleared his throat. "So wet already?"

"You tell me."

He dug deeper, pushing two fingers inside her until she satisfied him with a sharp gasp. His other hand clenched the steering wheel, his knuckles going white. Fuck, he wanted to feel her warm pussy around his cock, not his hand. But not now. Not like this. Now he wanted to pleasure her, and as he continued to work her with his fingers, she arched off the seat, her breasts thrust forward due to her hands being tied behind her back.

"Oh my God, Ash, keep going . . . so close . . ."

He plunged inside her again, and he felt her body slacken around his hand, as if she were sinking into the plush seat.

"That's right, baby. Come for me." *Only me.*

She flung her head back, and he felt her climax as she shuddered, clenching around his hand. He stifled a groan. His cock was so tight, throbbing so hard. . . .

Slowly he pulled out of her, and she collapsed back on the seat, a tiny smile on her pretty little mouth, her lids half lowered. "Mmmm," she murmured.

He brought his fingers to her lips, and her tongue darted out to lick him, suck him. He was about to lose control and pull the car over when he heard a soft rumble.

Joy froze.

Pulling his hand back and steadying the truck, he sighed. "When was the last time you ate, Joy?"

"Um, dinnertime?"

"And when was that?"

"I had a salad with nonfat dressing around six."

He knew Joy well enough to know she needed to eat some real food. "Well, I'm taking you to your favorite place."

"Cha Cha Cha?" she said hopefully.

"Okay, your second-favorite."

"In-N-Out?"

"Yup."

She gave him a brilliant smile. "Ash?"

"Yeah?"

"You really are the best." She winked. "At everything."

He couldn't help it; his male pride swelled. And so did other, more physical parts of his body. But he contained himself.

For now.

At the first big red arrow flashing brightly right off the freeway, Ash pulled the truck onto an off-ramp. Sexual tension hung heavy in the air; Joy was still tied, and she knew he had something up his sleeve. The question was, what?

He pulled into the drive-through and spoke into the fuzzy-sounding speaker. He seemed to remember exactly what she liked, and he didn't even ask her before placing their order. Then they were driving forward to the restaurant window.

"Ash," Joy hissed. "They'll see me." She realized the cashier would have a bird's-eye view into the truck's cab, where she sat with her hands tied behind her back.

"Does that bother you?"

Slowly, she shook her head. It was insane! But somehow she sat there happy as a clam as Ash paid for their food and took the warm bag and set it between them. The teenage boy glanced at her, then not-so-subtly shook his head as he handed over two drinks, which Ash placed in the truck's cup holders.

"Thanks," Ash said, driving away.

"Do you think he saw?" Joy asked, and her voice sounded titillated, even to her.

"Probably."

For some reason the thought of someone knowing what they were up to only turned her on.

What was *wrong* with her?

Well, it didn't matter now. What mattered was her grumbling tummy and the mouthwatering scents coming from the bag of fast food on the seat between them. If only her hands weren't tied, she could steal a French fry.

"Where are we going, anyway?" she asked.

"You'll see."

"So full of secrets."

He slanted a grin at her. "Be patient, little one. All will be revealed."

"Okay, I'll just sit here, starving, with my hands tied behind my back while you travel the backwoods of the Bay Area."

"It's not the backwoods. I know of a lookout up here."

"The last time you stopped at a lookout, my ass was sore for a week."

"And you loved it."

"Maybe."

He just grinned and continued to drive up a winding road surrounded by huge eucalyptus trees. A few minutes later, they crested the hill. The rain had stopped, and the entire Bay Area sparkled before them, the bridges lit and twinkling over the wide, dark expanse of the peninsula. "It's beautiful," Joy said.

"Worth the wait?"

"Definitely."

He backed the truck up and parked so the rear faced the view. "Hang on." He jumped out of the driver's side.

The scent of the food was torture, and just when Joy was considering nudging her face into the bag to pilfer a fry, the passenger door opened and Ash was there, lifting her down. He carried her to the back of the truck, where he placed her on a blanket he'd laid out on the tailgate. The air was damp, but not particularly cold, and she sat cross-legged on the blanket, facing out.

"Be right back."

He darted off again, this time only to return with the bag of food and two drinks. Climbing onto the tailgate, he spread the food out before them on the blanket and settled next to her.

She looked at him. "Aren't you forgetting something?"

He looked thoughtful. "Hmm. Nope, don't think so."

Shrugging her shoulders, she gave him a look. "I'm still tied up. How am I supposed to eat?"

Grinning, he lifted out a tray of French fries. "Do you like ketchup?"

"Yes . . ."

He opened several small packets and made a pile of ketchup next to the fries. "Good." His green eyes sparkled in the moonlight, reflecting the thousands of lights beyond, but she found she'd rather look at him than even the fabulous view.

He dipped the fry into the ketchup and brought it to her mouth. "Open up."

Like a bird she opened her mouth, but he only teased her, taking the French fry, deliciously salty and sweet from the ketchup, and running it over her lips. His eyes missed nothing as he watched her tongue dart out and lick a drop of ketchup off the tip.

Finally he let her eat, pushing the fry into her mouth.

"Mmm. That tastes amazing."

"More?"

"Of course!" She realized she should be totally embarrassed eating this way, being hand-fed fried, greasy fast food. Grandmother would have a fit if she saw her! But Joy just sat there and let Ash bring the cheeseburger to her lips, and she took a big bite. Closing her eyes, she chewed, savoring the wonderful tastes, so much more filling than the chintzy salad her grandmother had served her.

Eyes still closed, she felt Ash lean in closer.

"You have a little something . . . ," he said before she felt his tongue on the side of her mouth, licking off a drop of sauce.

"And here." He kept kissing her, licking her, tasting her.

Who knew fast food could be so sexy?

He continued to feed her, pausing in between to take bites of his own cheeseburger. When they were finished, he took the lid off one of the cups—the chocolate shake—and dipped his finger inside.

"Dessert?" he asked with a sexy grin.

She nodded, and he brought his finger to her lips. She tasted the icy chocolate and drew his finger deeper into her mouth. Hands tied, she watched his face, watched the way his gaze was locked on her mouth. She swirled her tongue around his finger, sucking and licking until she saw his breath hitch.

"You give good finger," he said. "Now come here."

Already her body was thrumming with desire, and a fresh wave washed through her as he took her in his arms and kissed her. She wanted to touch him, to keep him just where he was, but her hands were still bound.

He pulled away and hopped off the tailgate. Then he

grabbed her and set her on her feet, facing the truck. "Ash?"

She felt his hands on the hem of her dress, lifting the fabric high, revealing her ass.

"Wait . . . What if someone drives up?" she asked over her shoulder.

"Don't worry, sweetheart. Right now you're mine. I take care of what's mine. Can you put your trust in me to protect you?"

She paused. Having her hands tied up while going through a drive-through was one thing, but this? Making love in a public parking lot? Granted, it was empty, but still . . . someone could arrive at any time.

But Ash wanted her to trust him. She did trust him—she realized she trusted him more than anyone in her entire life. The realization caused her heart to swell, and she actually felt tears pricking the backs of her eyes.

She blinked them away. "Yes, Ash. I trust you."

"Good girl," he whispered against her ear as he brushed her hair off her neck. A shiver raced up her back as he gently used her hair to push her forward until she was leaning facedown on the blanket-covered tailgate.

Her legs trembled when she felt his hands on her thighs, her ass. He pushed her dress around her waist, and then he pulled her panties down over her legs and feet, making her step out of them.

"Don't worry, sweetheart. No one's going to see you, I promise. I've got you."

"Yes," she whispered, closing her eyes. It was so nice like this, so lovely to let him take control, to let herself swim in the gorgeous emotions coursing through her.

She heard him unzip his jeans and put on a condom.

Seconds later he was entering her from behind, filling her, and when he was buried deeply, she moaned in bliss.

"Yes . . . ," she whispered.

She felt his hand on her wrists, holding on to the scarf that restrained her. Pulling her arms tight, he used his other hand to hold her hips still as he retreated and then entered again. Pleasure arrowed into her sex with every lovely thrust.

"Oh, God. Ah . . ."

"That's right, baby. You love to feel me, don't you?"

"So much." She did love to feel him, everywhere. And she couldn't deny her feelings for Ash had grown so much since that fateful night at the museum. She'd been physically attracted to him then, but now . . . now she felt more. So much more.

And when they were making love, the intensity of this connection—the exchange of power—melted her. Powerful submission; wasn't that what she'd first thought of when she'd seen his sculpture? She'd wanted to experience that feeling but never imagined it would be possible.

He plunged into her again, tugged her arms until her back arched before him.

Yes, she thought. That feeling was possible. And it was sublime.

Chapter Twenty

Erica was finishing up the last of the dishes when a soft knock drew her attention to the door. Wiping her hands on a dish towel, she put her eye to the peephole, half expecting to see Joy in the hallway.

Blaine. Erica's heart skipped, from shock as well as a tinge of excitement she didn't have time to suppress before it shot through her. What was he doing here?

Unsure, Erica opened the door. Why did the man have to be so damn gorgeous? His brown hair was actually a mess, and for once he wasn't wearing a button-up shirt. Instead he wore a long-sleeved black T-shirt that lovingly clung to a ripped torso.

So, Preppy Boy spent a lot of time at the gym.

She cleared her throat. "What are you doing here?"

He held out his hands, in which he held a large white ramekin.

"I brought you something."

She looked at the dish skeptically. "What is it?"

"Rat stew."

She recoiled.

He rolled his eyes. "Crème brûlée. Freshly torched."

Crossing her arms across her chest, she eyed him. "Why?"

"Why not?"

"Because what kind of person shows up at ten o'clock at night with dessert?"

"A smart one?"

She couldn't argue the truth of that. Erica happened to love a late-night treat. Also, she had to admit the man was a god when it came to custard desserts. Especially when he was eating them off her body . . .

Don't even go there!

"I'll get the spoons," she said, spinning on her heel. She heard him following her into the kitchen, and when she grabbed two spoons and faced him, he was there. Too close.

He plucked one of the spoons from her hand and tossed it into the sink. "We only need one of these."

Why was she shaking? Why was her heart racing as he lifted off the foil covering the dish to reveal the amber-coated custard? It was perfect, burnt to the exact shade of ocher that she knew would be neither too bitter nor too soft. Her mouth started to water.

He handed her the spoon. "Would you like to do the honors?"

Breaking the burnt sugar on top of crème brûlée was one of her favorite things in the world, and she gratefully took the spoon.

She tapped it, and a rewarding *crack* sent a little thrill through her.

"Nicely done. Now allow me." He took the spoon and dipped it into the dessert. "Open up."

Feeling self-conscious, she did as he said and allowed him to spoon a velvety bite of the dessert into her mouth. She couldn't help it; she closed her eyes and moaned. Damn, but he was good.

He spooned another bite, but this time teased her, making her move forward, work for it.

"You have the most luscious mouth," he said, and she blushed.

"You have the most luscious everything."

She swallowed. Hard.

"Fuck this, Erica. I need you."

Every nerve in her body was tingling, ready for him. What was it about this guy that set her on fire?

He picked her up and carried her to the kitchen table. Tossing aside a pile of cookbooks, he laid her before him. Then he lifted her skirt and kissed her right between her legs, on her clit, which was already sensitive and needy.

"Yes," she said. "Right there . . ."

"I know, baby. Be patient." Then he stood and slipped out of his T-shirt. Breathing hard, she watched him undress, expecting to see pale, smooth, upper-class skin.

But what she saw instead made her breath catch.

"Oh my God."

"You look surprised."

"I am . . ." His entire upper body was covered in tattoos. Gorgeous artwork, obviously done over many years.

"But . . ."

He grinned. "What? I don't fit into your neat little pretty box?"

She could just shake her head. "Why do you hide them?"

"I don't. I just choose to be judged on who I am, not what I look like." He leaned over her, the muscles of his shoulders solid-looking above her. "Why do you show yours off?"

"I don't." Did she?

"You do. It's your way of telling the world exactly who you are."

"And you?" she asked, searching his eyes. "You hide who you are."

"Not at all. This is who I am. I wear what I feel comfortable in; I do what I want."

She ran a fingertip over the hard ridges of his chest. Dragons, tigers, traditional floral work covered his skin. "It's so beautiful."

"I like beautiful things."

The look in his eyes, the tone of his voice—her stomach flipped deep inside.

Her breath caught. "You even have your nipples pierced."

"You have a problem with that?" he asked.

"No, it's just . . ."

"Maybe you should stop judging people on their looks."

She looked up. "I do do that, don't I?"

"You sure do. But I have a feeling I know why. I remember what it was like when I was in school. What it was like for the kids from the other side of town."

"Does this mean you're not a rich kid?" she asked, smiling.

"I'm filthy rich, actually."

Speechless, she just stared at him.

He brushed a strand of hair off her forehead. "You don't need to think. You just need to let me feel you."

And she couldn't resist him, so she did. She let him pull down her panties and spread her legs. She could see the desire in his eyes, and as he kneeled to kiss the inside of her thigh, she opened for him.

"So pretty, Erica." She could feel the words on her damp sex, and her belly quivered.

"Everywhere."

Then she felt his mouth on her, softly tasting her, using his tongue to lick the moist folds between her legs. A sigh escaped her.

With his teeth he tugged on her clit, biting gently, and the muscles of her thighs tensed. She bit her lip, trying not to cry out.

But then she felt his finger pushing at her entrance, and when he pushed inside her, she moaned. "Blaine . . ."

He continued working her, using his hand and mouth to pleasure her until she couldn't control her own voice.

"Please, Blaine. Yes . . ."

A swirl of lust churned in her core as her climax built. But then he pulled back to stand between her legs.

Panting, she met his gaze.

She couldn't speak. Her stare was riveted on his body, the exquisite tattoo work that covered his taut torso. A fresh wave of lust raged over her.

"Make love to me, Blaine."

He smiled, and it touched her heart. But even now, lost in his touch, she ignored that feeling. Instead, she opened her legs wider in invitation.

She saw his breath hitch as he stared at her sex. Then he was pulling a condom out of his pocket and kicking aside his khakis. He rolled the condom onto his erection and stepped between her legs. With his fingertips, he lightly grazed the inside of her thighs.

"Please," she repeated.

He took his cock in his hand and entered her. Pure bliss exploded inside her, spreading everywhere. She closed her eyes as he pulled out and entered again. Over and over until she was crying out, saying his name.

"Yes, Erica. Come for me."

She did. Her back arched off the table as everything in her constricted in pleasure. She felt him come next, pulsing hotly inside her. "Erica, goddamn." The words shouldn't have made her smile, but they did.

After a minute he pulled away, and then he was beside her on the table, pulling her into his arms. His body was so warm, and she cradled against him.

"Erica, you feel so good here with me."

Silent, she nodded. It did feel good. Too good. She touched the amethyst at her neck, wondering how long the good feeling would last.

"This is nice," Ash said, pulling Joy closer to him. They were sitting on the tailgate, huddled under the wool blanket, gazing at the San Francisco skyline. The rain seemed to have left all the lights brighter and cleaner in the still air.

"Mmm," Joy murmured, then looked up at him. "Wet wipe?"

"Pardon me?"

She scooted away and jumped down. "I need to . . . you know. Freshen up."

He held up his hand, palm out. "Say no more. You . . . do what you need to do."

Smiling, Joy went to the truck's cab and, presumably, dug out her bag and took care of business.

Ash realized he was grinning. She did that to him, made him feel . . .

Happy. Yeah, the sex was great, but he just enjoyed being around her. She was quirky and different and had a zest for life Ash knew he was missing. If he'd ever had it at all.

And yet . . . a part of him was still holding back. Because the last thing he needed was yet one more person to take care of, and Joy definitely needed caring for.

Case in point, he'd had to rescue her tonight.

Of course, if she hadn't called him, he wouldn't be here right now. Wouldn't have made love to Joy outside in the back of his truck.

He shook his head; she had him all messed up.

Frowning, she came back to the truck. Her phone had been charging in the truck, and now she held it to her ear and was silent, as if listening to a message. Finally she flipped her phone shut and bit her lip.

He was beginning to know that look. "What's wrong?" he asked.

"Um . . ."

"Joy," he said warningly.

She laughed nervously. "That was a message from the auto club. It turns out my membership, um, expired."

"Expired?"

She shifted and looked at the ground. "I guess I forgot to pay the bill."

Picturing the stacks of unopened mail lying around her apartment, he wasn't surprised. He shook his head. "How often do you go through your mail?"

"Often."

"How often?"

"As often as you get your hair cut."

"I cut my hair."

"Really? Because that Kurt Cobain look is so 1990s."

"Good Lord. We're talking about you and your money management, or nonmanagement."

"Shut up. Besides, I've only had the electricity turned off once."

"You've had your electricity turned off?"

She met his stare with a raised chin. "So?"

He just stared at her and then, "Joy, I . . . I don't know what to say."

She narrowed her gaze. "Don't go there, Ash."

Jumping off the truck, he closed in on her until she had to raise her chin to meet his gaze. "Damn, woman." Suddenly all his worry from earlier came back in a hot rush, and he stooped until they were face-to-face, equal. "Honey, you're lucky you only suffered a flat tire earlier. You could have gotten into a serious accident with those tires and the road conditions tonight. And then you get into a car with a strange man?" He realized by the end he was shouting, but he couldn't contain himself.

"Oh, relax, Ash."

"Joy . . ."

"It's just tires! Not the end of the fucking world!"

"It's not just tires, Joy. It's your safety at stake! On the side of the freeway, in the middle of the night . . ." He ran a hand over his head, wondering why he was losing it like this. What should he care if Joy was reckless, put herself at risk, and forgot to pay her bills?

Straightening, he took a deep breath and counted to ten. He was losing it; he never lost it.

They stood there in a glare-off until she finally gave her head a small shake and grinned. "Wow," she said. "If I didn't know any better, I'd think you cared about me or something."

"Well, of course I care. I—" He shifted his weight a couple of times. "I . . . like you."

Her expression faded into one of unease, and a little furrow appeared on her brow, which he annoyingly found adorable.

"I think I like you, too," she finally said.

His heart was not beating fast at that. It really wasn't.

"Okay," he said, as much to her as to himself. "So you don't have emergency roadside service. We'll just pay for a tow truck, then."

"Yeah," she said, biting her lip. "About that . . ."

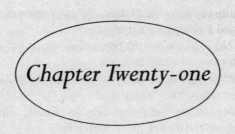

Chapter Twenty-one

This wasn't going to be good.

Joy shuffled and avoided Ash's gaze. "Do you know how much it's going to be?"

"About two hundred dollars. And then you'll need all new tires, so we'll have the tow truck take the car straight to my garage."

"I see," she said, nodding and trying to look thoughtful, but really what she was thinking was:

Shit, shit, shit!

It seemed like an easy solution, right? Just pay for a tow truck. Problem was, Joy had exactly fifty dollars in her bank account, because she'd used every last penny to buy back a sculpture she'd stolen, that had been sold without her knowledge and was now sitting in her purse, which was in the car of the man she'd stolen it from, who was currently staring at her like he was ready to bend her over his knee.

And not in a good way.

"You know," she said, walking around Ash toward the

passenger side of the truck, "I think I'll just have you take me home, and I'll deal with it tomorrow."

"What? No. The car could be vandalized or ticketed. Just call the tow truck and let's go."

Fuck. Stretching her hands over her head, she exaggerated a huge yawn. "I'm really tired, Ash. It's late, and I just want to go home."

"Typical," he muttered.

"What's that supposed to mean?"

"It means," he said, stalking toward her, "that you're irresponsible and take the easy way out."

She started shaking with anger. "That is not true!"

"Really? If it's not true, then why are we even here having this discussion?"

"Listen," she said, getting up in his face. "I'm sorry I'm not an anal, obsessive-compulsive neat-freak who's overly critical of everyone else!"

"What? That's not true!"

"Oh," she said in a low voice meant to be an imitation of him. "Why don't you charge your phone, Joy? Why don't you pay your bills, Joy? Why don't you change your tires, Joy? Why don't you have any money, Joy?"

Pausing, he met her gaze. "I never asked why you don't have any money."

Straightening, she said lightly, "Are you sure?"

"Positive."

"I must have been imagining it, then."

He pinched the bridge of his nose and took several deep breaths. Then, "Joy."

"Yes . . ."

"Do you have the money to pay for a tow truck?"

"Um . . ."

"I take that as a no."

Shame burned her. She hated him having such a bad opinion of her. "You don't understand," she whispered.

"That you don't pay your bills but have no problem going on shopping sprees?"

"It's not like that! And how did you know about my shopping spree?"

"Because you've suddenly been dressing in clothes that get me hard whenever I see you!"

"W-what? Really?"

"And you probably used a credit card. Just charge it, right?"

"I did not!" she protested. "I don't believe in credit cards, so I don't have one."

"You don't have a credit card?"

"My grandmother taught me that if I can't pay cash for something, I don't need it."

"What about emergencies?"

"I've never had one."

"What do you consider this?" he asked.

"An inconvenience?"

"Good. God. Okay, I'll pay for the tow truck. You can reimburse me later."

"No!" She refused to take his money. It would only validate everything he seemed to think about her.

"Joy, you don't have a choice."

"Yes, I do." She stared at him, refusing to back down. "Despite what you think, I can take care of myself. This is my problem, and I'll deal with it. I really appreciate you picking me up, Ash. And, um, dinner. But I refuse to take your money for this. Would you please just take me home?"

He stared silently at her. But, mixed in with all the

frustration she saw there, she could have sworn she saw a flash of something else. Admiration.

"Fine," he said finally. "Get in the truck."

By eight the next morning, Joy was cursing her stubbornness. Which was worse? Asking Ash for money or her grandmother? For a second, she considered just leaving the car there and getting it out of hock when she got paid on Friday, but she just couldn't do that to Bessie.

Sitting at her kitchen counter, she stared at her cell phone. Then, with a big sigh, she dialed.

"Hi, Grandma."

"Joy! This is a nice surprise, hearing from you so early in the morning. I know you usually like to sleep in."

She was about to inform her grandmother yet again that she was always up at eight on workdays but refrained. Now was not the time to bicker with her grandmother.

"Um . . . I need a favor, Grandma."

"Oh?"

"Yes." She closed her eyes. "I need to borrow some money."

She could practically see her grandmother's mouth tighten. "What's wrong, Joy?"

She told her the story of the Mercedes, including the fact that she needed new tires. Ash had stubbornly made her swear on her life not to drive the car until she'd replaced all four tires. A quick search on the Internet had told her that little purchase was going to be an extra $400.

"So the car is still on the side of the freeway?" Grandmother asked in an exaggeratedly patient tone that made Joy's teeth hurt.

"Yes," Joy said, idly picking up an unopened letter. "*Shit.*"

"What?" her grandmother said.

"Nothing." It was the bill for the auto club, postmarked nearly two months ago. She began doodling on the back of the envelope. *Think think think.*

"I'll be able to pay you back when I get paid on Friday, Grandmother."

"Don't you have any money in savings?" her grandmother asked incredulously. Joy knew that, to her grandmother, the meaning of life was to have a huge savings account.

"No," Joy said. "I have no money in savings." *And fifty dollars to my name.*

"Fine, Joy. I'll have my mechanic arrange to pick up the car and tow it to the shop. Then I'll have him bring it here, and you can get it when you come this weekend."

"Thank you, Grandma," Joy bit out.

"I'm planning a special dinner on Saturday, Joy. For your birthday."

"Oh . . ." She'd completely forgotten her birthday was coming up. "Okay." Thirty. When had that happened?

Kill me, she scrawled on the envelope.

"Do you want to bring anyone?" Grandmother asked, which was code for: *Do you have a boyfriend?*

"Um, no. I don't think so." But she couldn't help thinking of Ash. He wasn't her boyfriend, but what was he?

Distracted. Frustrated. Sexy as hell.

She scribbled hearts all over the words on the envelope. "Nope, I think it will just be me." She wondered what buses she would need to take to Atherton. There probably were none.

"Fine, but, Joy?"

"Yes, Grandma?"

"Don't be late."

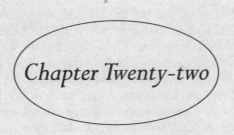

Chapter Twenty-two

Sitting at her desk in an empty gallery, Joy popped another Tums. The museum curator had canceled on her this moring, so she'd had to reschedule returning the sculpture. Time was running out, and her stomach burned with nerves. Maybe she was getting an ulcer. She swallowed the antacid tablet and popped another one, her third that morning. And it was barely eleven o'clock.

Why did she always make such a mess of things? Thinking back, she could recall several instances in which her reckless behavior had ended badly. Like that time in Paris. She'd been strolling the tiny streets in Montmartre when the thumping bass of electronic music had lulled her into a crowded but small bar filled with gay men. That was one of the few times she'd ever danced outside of her house, and she'd gotten sucked onto the packed dance floor. All the men were very nice and bought her drinks. Lots of drinks. By the time she'd finally left the bar, it was nearly 3:00 a.m., the metro had stopped running, and she had no idea where she was; all the streets looked the same. She'd finally hailed a taxi after standing on a corner for an hour, but she wasn't sure where her apartment was so she'd had the driver drop her off at the only place she could pronounce, the Louvre. From there, she knew how to get back to her housing, even though it was another forty-five-minute walk.

She'd had many such incidents while living in France.

Just thinking about it made her skin burn with embarrassment. And to make matters worse, many of the students knew she was saying phrases wrong and had decided it was more entertaining not to fill Joy in on the joke.

Assholes.

As she glanced at her bag, envisioning what was inside, she nearly saw what everyone else saw—a fuckup.

She stared at her purse until her eyes began to burn. Oddly, a tingle of anger started somewhere in her chest and then spread throughout her body, until she realized her hands were shaking from it.

Yeah, she acted impulsively sometimes, but so what? Why did people think that made her stupid? And sometimes it was better not to overthink things. Sometimes going on instinct was for the best.

Sometimes you had to take a risk, and if something went wrong, you just dealt with it, like she dealt with her car situation.

She stood so fast her chair fell behind her in a loud clatter. She didn't bother to right it. Instead she yanked her bag off the floor and made her way toward the door.

"Where are you going?" Andrew said, looking up from his computer.

"I have an important errand to run," she said. "I may not be back today."

"Panos is gonna be *ma-ad,*" he said in a singsong voice.

Before she walked out, she paused with her hand on the door handle. "Tell him it couldn't be avoided. I have to go take care of some business for the show."

Joy didn't stop to think about it; she just went. Clutching her bag tightly to her side, she ran down the street toward the bus stop. Without a car, she had to take the cheapest transport possible until she got paid on Friday. Her fifty dollars had dwindled down a bit too quickly, and now she had only about twenty dollars to make it two more days.

At the corner, she ignored the red light and crossed anyway, nearly getting hit by a speeding taxicab. Jumping onto the opposite sidewalk, she barely noticed him giving her the finger, and anyway, she didn't care. She was going to talk her way into the museum and return the sculpture. She couldn't go one more minute like this.

Passing an alley, a flash of colors caught her eye, colors that hadn't been there just the day before. The colors of the design drew her in a familiar way, and she found herself walking toward it, making her way through the tiny, empty alley.

The buildings on either side of the small street were old and hadn't been kept up, the exteriors painted a dull, peeling gray. She passed a couple of huge garbage bins as she made her way to the mural, and she couldn't help but love the contrast of the beautiful art juxtaposed with the dreary surroundings.

When she reached the mural, she stopped before it and

stared. "Just brilliant," she murmured to herself. It was a modern, urban rendition of Monet's *Water Lilies*. Joy had never seen anything like it, and she knew if she could just nail down the artist, she could get him into a gallery, maybe even some outdoor commissions.

Yeah, if she could nail him down. He was quick and must work at night; she was never going to catch up with him. With a sigh, she pulled out a business card and taped it into a crack in the wall.

Then, for some reason, the hairs on her neck stood on end. The last time she'd felt such a sensation was that time in Barcelona when she'd been robbed. Like now, she'd been alone, in an alley.

She caught a movement out of the corner of her eye and turned. A tall figure, dressed in baggy jeans and a black jacket, was walking toward her. Her instinct told her to get away—fast—but the alley was a dead end. There was only one way out, and it included passing the man walking her way.

Clutching her bag to her side, she kept her head down as she walked briskly toward the street. But, as she approached the man, she wasn't surprised when he stopped in front of her, blocking her way.

"Gimme your purse, lady."

Her heart beat a frightened tempo in her chest. But her purse had everything in it, including the sculpture.

How ironic. Someone wanted to steal the stolen sculpture.

"Come on, bitch!"

He pointed something and her blood froze. He had a gun.

"Here!" Quickly, she dug out her wallet and gave it to

him. Grabbing it, he spit at her feet and ran back the way he'd come.

Shaking, she stared after him, every nerve in her body trembling in fear.

She'd been held up.

Oh, God. Tears sprang to her eyes and rolled down her cheeks. They kept coming and coming, even as she told herself she was fine, that he'd just stolen her wallet and everything could be replaced.

It could have been avoided. She'd gone into an empty alley alone. Stupid! She'd done so many stupid things; she'd made so many poor decisions. Just moments ago, she'd been lost in a beautiful work of art. And now? Now her legs could barely hold her steady because they were shaking like leaves.

He'd had a gun.

She'd given him her wallet.

And now she literally didn't have a penny to her name.

Finally she brushed the tears away, took a deep breath, and walked on. At that moment, there was only one place she wanted to be and one person she wanted to be with.

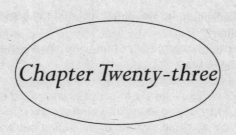

Chapter Twenty-three

Ash. Be reasonable."

Tapping his foot, Ash looked across the kitchen table to where his sister was picking from a bowl of blueberries. She popped one into her mouth and met his gaze.

"Seriously, Ash. You've already done way too much for me, and I don't need a full-time caregiver."

He'd purposely come when he knew his mother would be out grocery shopping, getting ready for Thanksgiving dinner, so he and his sister could talk privately. But his sister was being a lot more resistant than he'd expected.

"Violet, you're the one who called me just a couple of days ago needing help. Remember?"

"I know." She took a deep breath, glanced away briefly and then met his gaze. "I wasn't going to discuss this now, but screw it. I'm moving."

Ash froze. "What? What do you mean, *moving*?"

She lifted a brochure from the table and pushed it toward him. "I want to move here."

Ash picked up the brochure. "Shelter Cove Rehabilitation Center?" Shaking his head, he glanced at his sister. "I don't understand. You've already been through this rehab, years ago."

"I won't go as a patient. I'll be a counselor."

Why did everything seem to be slipping away? His world had been so orderly just last month and now . . . "Start from the beginning."

"Well, over the last year, I've been counseling patients online. And Mom's taken me over to the center a few times to meet with the clients one-on-one. Now they've offered me a position as an in-house counselor—and, Ash?"

"Yeah?"

"I want to do it."

He glanced around the kitchen, at the improvements he'd made to the house to make it accessible. "I thought you were happy here, Violet."

She reached across the table and took his hand. "I am. You've been amazing, the best brother a sister could ever have. But I need more, Ash."

"Like what? You have an equipped house, a special van, the latest technology . . . I don't get it."

"You're right. Thanks to you I have so much, and I appreciate it, more than I could ever say. But I need more."

"What more? You want more money? Because I can give you more, just say the word."

But she was shaking her head, and Ash saw the stubborn look in her eyes, the same look she'd given all her life when her mind was made up. Ash knew from experience that Violet had a mulish streak; it had been apparent since she'd refused to share her piece of chocolate cake with him at her third birthday party.

"I've been putting this off for a while now, Ash, because I knew you'd try to talk me out of it."

"Is it because of Mom?"

"No. It's because of me. Ever since Dad died, you've had this need to take care of us."

Stiffening, he drew his hand back. "I promised Dad."

"Dad never should have put that burden on a thirteen-year-old boy!"

"It wasn't a burden, and anyway, I failed."

"Stop it."

"Stop what?" he snapped.

"Feeling sorry for yourself."

"What are you talking about? That's ridiculous!"

"You didn't fail anyone. This," she said, waving to her legs, "was a random act of violence. When are you going to accept that there was nothing you could have done about it?"

He clenched his jaw. "I could have been here."

"This isn't your fault. And the more you dedicate your life to making up for what you think you did wrong, the worse I feel!"

"Violet, what are you talking about?"

"How do you think I feel being so dependent on you? Knowing you plan your entire life around my needs. And Mom's."

"That's not true."

"It *is* true. Ever since the accident, you've devoted your entire existence to taking care of me, making sure I have the best of everything. But to you, it's never enough."

He clenched his jaw. "I just want to make sure you and Mom have security."

"But where do you draw the line? Listen, Ash, I know you have a lot of money, more than enough to live on— you don't even have to work! And I'm going to get paid for this job. Mom can get back to work, back to her own life. Not to mention, we could easily live off the stocks you put in our names."

He just stared at her. "But . . . I thought you were happy. . . ."

"I am. *We are.* But I think we've all been afraid to move on. Me, Mom. You."

"Move on from what?" He couldn't comprehend what his sister was saying. His family didn't need him anymore? The thought left him cold and anxious, and he eyed the door.

"It's time for us to start a new chapter, Ash. *All* of us."

"And this is what you want? What Mom wants?"

Nodding, she said, "It doesn't mean we still don't need you, Ash."

"Right," he said, pushing out of his chair. "For what?"

"As a brother and a son," she said, her blue eyes watery and shining. "As a friend."

The words echoed in his head after he left, and as he drove home, he expected to feel a sense of loss, a void. After all, hadn't he lived the last ten years with the sole purpose of supporting his family? Hadn't taking care of them been the driving force behind ninety-nine percent of his decisions? But slowly, bit by bit, another emotion crept through him, a feeling he hadn't experienced since . . .

Ever.

Reaching to the radio, he turned up the volume of the AC/DC tune and began tapping his hand on his thigh to the beat of "Highway to Hell." Driving, listening, he couldn't help but feel it. A sense of freedom.

"Joy?" Erica ushered her inside her apartment. "What's wrong?"

Joy lost it.

The tears burst from her eyes as she sank onto the sofa, uttering incoherent things. "The sculpture was just so beautiful . . . in my purse . . . I didn't think—I never think!" She hiccuped. "And then stupid Panos sold it and then I had sex against a wall . . . and I have *no* money, no savings . . ."

Erica gently removed Joy's coat and purse and set them aside. Taking a seat next to her, she silently put her arm around Joy's shoulders. Joy leaned against her friend. Erica was so good; she was always there for her.

"My car's in jail; I had to borrow money from my grandmother . . . no tires . . . Ash thinks I'm irresponsible, and maybe he's right!"

"You're not irresponsible, honey. You're just a bit pre-occupied sometimes."

"I'm a mess!"

"You're not a mess. You have a unique way of doing things that is . . . endearing."

"See?" Joy said with a sniffle. "You get me. Why can't he?"

"Oh, honey." Erica hugged her tighter. "You're too good for him."

Joy shook her head. "No," she whispered. "He's too good for me."

"Bullshit."

Startled by the vehement tone of Erica's voice, Joy glanced up.

Erica gave her shoulder a squeeze. "Sorry, I just hate it when you put yourself down like that."

"Erica, you don't understand. I . . . I . . ." She swallowed. "I stole from him."

"What?"

Joy told her the entire story, from the night she'd stolen the sculpture from the museum to receiving it back. Finally she ended with a "He's been so good to me, and I'm nothing but a thief!" And she promptly burst into tears once again.

"There, there," Erica said, patting her back. "It's going to be okay, I promise."

"No, it's not! Erica, I'm a thief, I'm broke, I can barely afford to fix my car, and I'm going to be th-th-thirteee!"

"Thirty is the new twenty-five."

Joy couldn't help but chuckle through her tears. She hugged Erica tighter, giving her a kiss on the cheek. They stayed like that for a few more minutes, cheek-to-cheek, until finally Joy took a few deep breaths and pulled back. But Erica kept her close, staring at her strangely.

"You love him."

Joy snorted. "What? That's ridiculous!"

Erica just stared at her. "You do. You normally wouldn't care about something like this so much, but with this guy you do."

"Of course I do! I'm not a thief!"

"No, but you usually just accept the outcome of things and move on. You're definitely more upset about this particular shenanigan than usual."

"Maybe," Joy admitted with a pout.

"Uh-huh."

After a few moments of silence, Joy sighed. "We're a mess. I steal from my non-boyfriend, and you hate the first guy you've been attracted to in years."

Erica picked a nonexistent thread off her dress. "Well . . ."

"Well, what?" Joy put a hand over her mouth and gasped. "It's not the rich guy, is it?"

"He's not . . . quite as preppy as I thought."

"So. You misjudged him? The great Erica O'Reily actually got it wrong."

"I'm not saying that. I'm saying I hardly even know him."

"But you had sex with him."

"Maybe."

"How was it?"

There was that blush on her friend's face again. "Freaking phenomenal," she finally admitted. "And . . ."

"And what?" Joy demanded.

Erica squealed as she sat on the sofa. "He's covered in tattoos!"

"Get out!"

"I know!" Erica's eyes glittered. "He looks so preppy, but then he takes off his shirt, and he's totally covered. It's really, really hot!"

Joy nodded. She was well aware of Erica's tattoo fetish.

"And they're good ones," she went on. "Not crappy ones, but very artistic."

"You must have had an orgasm just looking at them."

"I almost did."

Joy was silent for a second. "Yeah, I know how you feel. I get that way sometimes when I see Ash's sculptures."

"So, what's the problem, then?"

"We're total opposites."

Erica looked thoughtful. "Maybe it's true. Maybe opposites attract . . . and then you have to look at the core to see what matches up."

"Are we talking from personal experience, by chance?"

Erica shrugged. "I don't know. All I'm saying is maybe it's a good idea to know all the facts before you make a final decision."

Joy twisted to the side and brought her knees to her chest. "Erica, what's gotten into you?"

Erica twisted the pendant at her neck and gave a nervous laugh. "Um . . . Blaine?"

Joy threw a pillow at her friend. "You tramp!"

"You think so?"

"Yes! And it's about time."

The girls fell into a heap of laughter, just as they'd done a million times before.

Finally Erica pulled away. "You're sure this Ash guy is different?"

Joy paused and then, "Are you sure this Blaine guy is different?"

"No. But I'm willing to take a chance." Her gaze softened. "Are you?"

"Yeah. I think so."

"Now listen. You've been through a lot today. Let me cook you something amazing."

"I thought you'd never ask."

Standing, Erica said, "You just put your feet up and relax for now, okay? I'll bring you a glass of wine."

"Thanks, Erica. I love you, you know."

"I know." Smiling, she turned and went into the kitchen.

Lying back on the sofa, Joy stared at the black-and-white photograph of Erica and her that sat in a frame on a side table. It was from a few years back when they'd gone camping in Mendocino. That was a good trip; they had so many good memories. Joy just wanted her friend to be happy.

And Joy wanted to be happy, too. Erica was finally coming to terms with her working-class roots, but what about her? Why did Joy always pick the wrong guys?

Was Ash wrong?

No, everything about him was right, and just the thought of him made her toes curl and her heart skip as she pictured his teasing grin and electric green eyes. Ruby said he may have cheated, but Joy had a hard time believing that. She just knew he could never do something so dishonest and untrustworthy.

He was different; he was nothing like the usual scammers she picked. She bit her lip. It was Joy who was going to have to prove that she wasn't the unfocused mess he thought she was.

She just wasn't sure exactly how to do that.

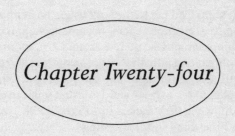

Chapter Twenty-four

You seem jumpy tonight. Anything wrong?" Ash asked as he carried over two tumblers of whiskey.

Just as she was leaving Erica's after a long dinner, Ash had called, inviting her over. She loved that he was thinking of her and had immediately jumped in a cab to his house. Erica had insisted Joy borrow a hundred dollars until she got paid, so at least she had a few bucks to last until Friday.

"Oh. Um." She'd almost forgotten about the events from earlier. "I was mugged today."

"What!" he demanded. Suddenly the easy-mannered blond man she had known turned into something resembling a very angry lion.

She gulped. "Yeah. Earlier. In an alley. I'm okay; they just got my wallet."

He was beside her in an instant, assessing her in one all-encompassing gaze. "Why didn't you tell me earlier? Are you okay? What happened?"

She let him lead her to the sofa where he gently pushed her onto the cushions. She became aware of all the framed photographs scattered around the room, mostly images of her, and a fresh wave of panic washed over her. Guilt still spread through, but she ignored it. She had a plan, a plan to fix everything. Isn't that what responsible people did when they fucked up? Fixed it? She was going to fix it. First thing in the morning.

He took her in his arms, brushing a soothing hand over her hair. "It's okay, baby. I'm here."

She breathed in his scent: whiskey, soap, and him. If he found out what she'd done, would she ever be this close to him again?

"Oh, babe. You're shaking." He scooped her up in his arms and stood.

"What are you doing?"

He kissed her softly on the forehead. "Taking care of you."

Ash lit the last candle. Looking around the bathroom, he thought Joy would be pleased. He'd pilfered about ten big, white candles from his emergency supply and scattered them around, lighting the room in a warm, soft glow. After he'd heard that Joy had been robbed, he thought he was going to lose his head. Pure rage had bolted through him, leaving a white-hot anger pulsing in his veins.

Some fucker had dared to rob his Joy.

His Joy? Where had that thought come from?

Even now, several hours later, he still fought back the anger and fear of what could have happened.

Don't go there, Hunter.

Helpless. He fought that feeling, but he needed to do something for her, anything. Because he couldn't track down and kill the asshole who'd held her up, he decided to take care of her instead.

He was just turning off the bathwater when Joy appeared, looking half awake, her hair still messy from sleeping. His gaze dropped to the pale skin of her thighs, and his body immediately responded with desire.

"What's all this?" she asked, her eyes wide.

He crossed the room and placed his hands on her shoulders. "I thought you could use a nice relaxing bath."

"You didn't have to do this, Ash."

He placed a gentle kiss on her nose. "I wanted to."

She sighed and he could have sworn she looked reluctant for a second. But then she reached up and cupped his head with her palm, pulling him close for a kiss. Holding him, she ran her tongue over his lips, pushed her way inside his mouth.

When she stepped back, his cock was throbbing. Then she pulled the T-shirt over her head and threw it on the ground, and everything in him went tight with lust.

She stood there before him, the candlelight flickering over her pale skin, highlighting the dip of her waist and the beautiful curve of her full breasts. Her nipples were hard, tight points, and he couldn't wait to taste her skin.

She stepped out of her panties and then stepped forward to tug off his shirt and pants. When they were both naked, she got on her tiptoes and kissed him again.

He wasn't sure what had shifted, but her manner was different. He let her lead.

"This was supposed to be for you," he said.

"You deserve a little pampering, too." She glanced around the bathroom, and her gaze landed on some bath items his designer had strategically left near the tub. The bathtub was a huge, square minimalist piece that went with the Zen theme he'd gone for when he remodeled the flat a few years ago. He'd never thought to use any of the props the designer had left, but it looked like Joy had other plans.

She poured a small bottle of some sort of oil into a wooden bowl on the counter, and the scent of lavender wafted through the steam. Then Joy filled it with warm water, submerged a towel into the water, and placed the bowl on the rim of the bathtub.

"Come here, Ash," she said as she climbed into the tub and settled back with a contented sigh.

Even if he'd wanted to deny her, there was no way he could have. Lust pounded through his veins; his cock was throbbing for her. And there was more. . . . He wanted her with more than his prick. The need came from some-where else . . . somewhere in his chest. He didn't stop to examine those feelings.

Sometimes when he looked at her, like now, she took his breath away and he couldn't think about anything except her exceptional, feminine beauty.

Her hair was a brilliant mess, the ends swimming in the water around her shoulders. Her hazel eyes twinkled in the dim light, the candles flickering in their depths. Her skin glowed under the water, her breasts sticking out just enough so he could see her nipples, tight and pink.

"Joy, you're the most beautiful thing I've ever seen."

She opened her legs wide and swam her hand between her knees in the water in a gentle stroke. "Come here, baby."

For some reason, the words sent a shudder through him. No woman had ever referred to him by anything other than his given name.

Joy did everything differently, didn't she?

He climbed into the bathtub, let the warm water swallow him as he settled in front of her, between her legs. Carefully, he settled back against her. He felt the tight curls of her damp pubic hair at the base of his spine, felt the soft curve of her belly touch his lower back . . . her breasts, her nipples wet and slippery against his skin.

His balls were so tight, his cock so hard. But he wasn't in a hurry. Thanks to Joy, the scent of lavender filled the room in a relaxing scent, and the steam rising from the water was like a calming whisper.

He felt her hands on his head as she placed a soft, warm kiss at his ear. "Just relax," she whispered, and he nodded. With Joy he actually could relax and it felt . . .

Damn good.

Her hands were on his face, her fingertips gently grazing his skin. Then she began stroking him in slow, small circles, starting on his chin and around his mouth.

"How does it feel?" she asked in a low voice.

"Amazing."

He sensed her smile. She continued the gentle massage, using those leisurely circles on his cheekbones, his temples, his forehead. He hadn't realized how tight he was until he felt the tension drain out of his body under her touch.

He felt warm water sluice over his hair, and then she drizzled what he suspected was shampoo onto his scalp. Using her palms, she pressed and rubbed her hands over his head, thoroughly massaging his scalp from around his ears, the back of his head, his forehead.

"Oh, yeah . . . just like that, Joy."

"You like it?"

"Fuck yeah," he said.

"I want to please you."

"Oh, sweetheart. You do."

She continued to massage his scalp, working around his hairline. When she reached his ears, she gently kneaded his earlobes, and he was shocked when a fresh wave of arousal washed over him.

"Tilt your head back."

With his eyes closed, he arched slightly and angled his neck so Joy could rinse the shampoo out of his hair. Careful not to get water or soap in his eyes, she used the water that had been in the bowl and poured the warm, lavender-scented liquid over his head in a slow trickle.

His arousal ratcheted up another notch; he was so fucking hard. He groaned out loud from pleasure.

But she wasn't done yet. She wrung out the oil-infused towel and wrapped it around his head. The warmth and scent of the damp towel was like an unknown luxury, and he leaned back once more against Joy.

They stayed like that. Joy traced a lazy pattern around his chest, his nipples, and then her fingers dipped beneath the water to graze his stomach. Softly, she brushed her fingers against the tip of his erection, and he bit back a groan.

She took a washcloth and squeezed some lavender soap onto it. Then she dipped it in the bathwater and began to retrace her path, using the washcloth to rub over his chest, his abdomen, and lower. She wrapped the damp cloth around his penis and stroked him. She paid special attention to the underside, pressing right below the head, and all the muscles in his abs tensed as he gasped.

"Joy, I could get used to this." The sensation of the cloth and warm water, feeling Joy's body slick and wet behind him; add her relaxing treatment from moments ago, and he already wanted to come.

He placed a hand on hers, stopping her. As he turned in the tub to face her, the towel slid off him and into the water. Her eyes were big and dark, her skin slightly flushed. His heart started thumping. With all the women he'd been with, he'd always made sure it was about his partner. He'd never let his own pleasure come first; wasn't that the nature of being dominant? He was the bondage master. He was supposed to be in charge. It went without saying.

But with Joy it was different. When it came to intimacy, things were equal. She asked for what she wanted and had no problem giving him what he wanted in return.

He couldn't name one relationship he'd ever had in which that was the case. And he'd never felt for another woman anything near what he felt now.

Moving to the opposite side of the bathtub, he took one of Joy's feet in his hand. She had beautiful feet, long and narrow, her arch curving as perfectly as Mary's cheek in Michelangelo's *Pieta*.

She shivered under his touch. "Feel good?" he asked.

"Heavenly."

He continued to rub her foot, from her toes to her ankle, which he rotated a few times, and her eyes seemed to roll back in her head. "Mmmm."

He moved to the graceful arch of her foot, using his fingers to rub out the last bits of tension. With slow, firm circles, he worked across the arch, her heel, back over to the ball of her foot. When she looked damn close to a state of ecstasy, he moved on to her other foot.

When he was done, he leaned forward and pulled her toward him. Yeah, judging by her expression, he'd done a good job; she looked ready to sleep, much like she did after they made love. Her nipples hardened once again as she wrapped her legs around his back and settled against him. He groaned; her pussy felt so good against his rock-hard cock. Even through the water he could feel how wet and slick she was.

He fisted her hair and brought her in for a kiss, feeling a shiver run over her when he tugged sharply. He kissed her leisurely, slowly, while tightening his fist in her hair.

He continued his treatment of tender kissing and sharp tugging until she moaned and started rubbing her pussy up and down his cock.

"Yeah . . . beautiful Joy," he murmured, kissing her face, her lips, her nose. She continued to moan, to rub herself against him until it would be easy, too easy, to just slide right into her.

Breathing heavily, he broke away. "Let's get out of here, sweetheart."

Her eyes were wide and deep, and she nodded.

He unplugged the drain and helped her to her feet. Then he turned on the shower and rinsed both of them off quickly before wrapping Joy in a huge towel and taking her to his bed.

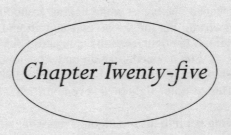

Chapter Twenty-five

As Ash returned from the bathroom, Joy watched him. He was naked and so beautiful he took her breath away. He was so thin and tight she could see the ridges of his abdomen, the muscles visible, and she wanted to touch him there, to taste him everywhere.

A streetlight was the room's only illumination, and it highlighted the blond streaks in his shaggy hair as he came for her. She was lost from the kissing session in the bathtub earlier. She didn't think she'd ever been more relaxed in her life.

"Ash, come here. I want to taste you. I want to suck your cock." She unwrapped the towel and threw it onto the floor.

His eyes bore into hers as he climbed onto the bed. "Jesus Christ, Joy." He climbed on top of her, and she licked her lips, waiting for him to feed her his cock.

But he paused over her, looking at her breasts. "So beautiful . . . ," he murmured, his breath soft on her skin.

He kneaded one breast while licking around her other nipple, swirling his tongue around and around until he finally sucked the tight, sensitive nub across his teeth.

"Oh . . ." She moaned, arching under his touch.

He released her nipple and blew gently onto her damp flesh. Her nipple tightened even further, and she whimpered.

Drawing her into his mouth once more, he bit her sensitized nipple, softly at first and then harder and harder, until she clutched his head and opened her legs around him, inviting him.

But instead of slipping himself inside her, he flipped onto his back, taking her with him.

Straddling him, she looked at him in question.

His emerald eyes were nearly black now, and he said, "Do you want to fuck me, babe?"

A surge of power went through her, and she felt herself get even wetter. Her gaze swept over him, the hard ridges of his body, the dusting of hair below his navel. And his cock, so hard, so gorgeous; it was long and strong, just like the man himself.

She bent to his chest and circled one of his nipples with her tongue. Like he'd done to her, she swirled her tongue around the hard flesh, licking, sucking, tugging. She felt him inhale sharply, and she bit down.

"Joy . . ."

"Mmm." Joy continued to lick his nipples, going back and forth between them. She felt his cock pressing hotly against her pelvis, and after a minute she made her way down, kissing his ribs, his stomach, and finally the head of his cock.

She licked around him, getting it nice and wet. The

surface was smooth and rigid as she kissed and teased him, using her teeth, mouth, and lips to pleasure him. With her tongue, she flicked at the underside of his cock as she slid the head in and out of her mouth.

"Just like that . . . ," he instructed.

She felt his abs clench as she gripped his cock. Sliding her hand down the base, she took him full into her mouth, deep, all the way down until she touched her own hand. She heard his breathing get heavy, and she continued to stroke him as she worked the head of his cock, then moved to the underside of his shaft, kissing and licking him there. She continued down, and then she went farther to curl her tongue around his balls.

"Joy . . . damn, girl. You make me feel so good."

Her own body was responding, her pussy throbbing with want. She felt her own juice on the insides of her thighs. Her nerves were on fire; she wanted to feel something between her legs. As she continued to lick around his balls, she straddled his leg and pressed her aching pussy to his thigh.

"Mmmm," she gasped as she made contact with his skin.

"Go ahead, Joy. Fuck my leg."

She did. She rubbed her wet pussy around his thigh, felt her juices coating him as she pushed her swollen lips to his hard flesh.

Making her way back up to the top of his erection, she took him into her mouth once again. Relaxing her throat, she swallowed him as deep as she could. He groaned, and she looked up to see he was watching her, his eyes dark with desire.

She continued to make eye contact with him as she

went down on him, again and again. As they stared at each other, something electric seemed to pulse between them, a connection pulling them deeper into each other.

And she wanted him to see how much she loved pleasing him, wanted him to see her getting off on his leg. She played it up, moaning and grinding against him.

He was breathing hard, his chest rising and falling in deep, rapid breaths. She was equally as turned on, and her pussy slid easily across the skin of his leg.

"Yeah, sweetheart. Suck me . . ."

"Mmmmm," she said, and he groaned aloud.

Reaching lower, she took his balls in her hand. Using a fingernail, she gently scratched the soft skin until she felt his abs clench again. She drew his balls into her hand and pulled them down, away from the base of his shaft. He groaned aloud, and she saw him fist the sheets.

"You like it when I suck your cock?"

"You're damn good at it, baby."

She blew softly on the damp flesh, and he jerked. "Damn, woman . . . I'm so close . . ."

Smiling, she glanced up at him. "Not yet."

Pleasuring him this way nearly sent her over the edge, and she ground herself even harder against his leg. Close, so close . . .

"I'm going to come, Joy," he ground out.

"Do it." She sucked him as deeply into her throat as she could, splaying her legs around his thigh, straddling him.

She felt him start to pulse, felt his ejaculation beating its way up his cock until it shot into her mouth in hot, wonderful bursts. She swallowed it down, loving the taste of Ash on her lips.

She followed, coming in a rush on his leg, clenching her thighs around his.

"Holy shit," he said.

Smiling, she got up and went into the bathroom to wash up. As she walked across the room, she realized she didn't even feel embarrassed to be prancing around buck-naked in front of him. Strange.

But she was too comfortable to worry about it. Instead she climbed into bed with Ash and nestled into her spot under his shoulder. He lightly brushed her hair off her shoulder and kissed the top of her head. At that moment, she was too exhausted, too satisfied to think anything except how good it felt to fall asleep in Ash's arms.

The next morning as Ash ran in Golden Gate Park, adrenaline rushed through him, and he realized he was taking the course at a much faster pace than usual. But it felt good to run, to be outside. It was foggy but not cold, and the closer he got to the ocean, the heavier the scent of salt water became, pulling him toward it.

He couldn't help but acknowledge the fact that he felt lighter today, like a weight had been lifted. Somehow he'd come to terms with his sister's decision, and even realized it would be good for all of them.

And Joy. She was . . . getting to him. She seemed to be in the back of his head all the time, and now he wasn't even trying to push her out of it.

But Joy wasn't the reason he'd turned down the job in Iraq. She wasn't the reason he felt calmer than he had in a long time. She wasn't the reason that antsy feeling had ebbed somewhat.

Was she?

The thought both frightened and excited him. Joy certainly wasn't the type of woman he'd ever thought he'd settle down with. Hell, he'd wondered if he would ever settle down at all. But, the thought of doing so with Joy wasn't . . . horrible.

He tossed the idea around in his head, let it percolate in his mind. Yeah, the thought of being with Joy wasn't horrible at all.

He rounded a corner and saw as he neared the ocean that the fog had begun to lift, lighting the foliage of the park in vivid hues of green. The damp scent of seawater became heavier, and he sucked in deep lungfuls of it. He wondered if Joy enjoyed the ocean like he did; would she want to go diving with him? He realized he didn't know much about her, not as much as he wanted to know. He realized he wanted—needed—to know everything about Joy Montgomery.

"Well, someone got laid last night."

Joy rolled her eyes at Andrew, but she couldn't help the revealing grin that spread across her face. After they'd fallen asleep, she'd awoken to six foot of man between her thighs. She could wake up that way every morning for the rest of her life.

If the man was Ash.

She shook her head. Where had that thought come from?

You're falling for him, you nitwit!

Was she? Yeah, probably. She never thought a guy like Ash would be interested in her, but the more time she spent with him the less she doubted herself. And, she had to admit, that felt good.

"So who is he?" Andrew asked from his position at the reception desk. She could see today he was watching 1980s videos on YouTube. Currently Wham! was blaring through the tinny computer speakers.

"I never said I got laid," she said.

Today Andrew wore a brown sweater that was supposed to look like it was made in the seventies, and his Mohawk was extra spikey. He raised a perfectly formed eyebrow. "Honey, I know that look. You had it the entire time Cartwright was here last year."

At the mention of his name, Joy recoiled. Just the thought of that man made her feel nauseous. "Don't remind me," she muttered, doodling on a pad of paper.

It was past noon, and although the gallery had had a bit more traffic lately since the invitations for Ash's show had gone out, overall things hadn't picked up much.

She had a feeling that was about to change.

She'd seen most of the pieces Ash was going to include in the collection, and it was turning out better than she'd hoped. She still had some anxiety about having herself featured in the show, but it was too late to do anything about it now.

In fact, she needed to go to Ash's later that afternoon to take some pictures for a client who was interested in a presale. She had expected a lot of interest in the show, but it was shocking just how many e-mails and calls she'd received from people wanting an early viewing. And with the gallery as dead as it was, she wasn't going to make people wait until the night of the reception to make a sale.

But first she had a little errand to run. The museum was expecting her at eleven. All she had to do was take some pictures, do inventory, and slip a little stolen sculpture back into the collection.

Easy-peasy. So why were her palms damp with nerves?

She heard the door to the back office open, and a minute later Panos was standing before her. "How many RSVPs do we have so far, Joy?" he asked for the millionth time.

"About one hundred so far, but I told you most people don't bother responding."

He grunted. "I hope you know what you're doing, Joy."

"Don't worry. It's all under control." Not for the first time, she silently thanked Ruby, who was endlessly patient with Joy's constant questions about event planning.

He gave a look that let her know he doubted anything was under control, grunted again, and made for the front door. "I'm going to the framer's," he said on his way out.

"I hope you know what you're doing, Joy," she said in a mocking tone, all the while wondering the exact same thing.

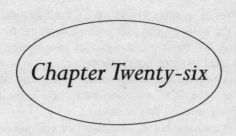

Chapter Twenty-six

Hi. I'm Joy Montgomery. I'm here to inventory Ash Hunter's pieces."

The museum curator looked up from the set of slides he was peering at, his gray eyebrows bushy over a pair of wire-rimmed glasses. "Hunter?"

"Yes. I need to take some photographs for an upcoming exhibit at the Cartwright Gallery. I have an appointment."

He shook his head. "There must have been a misunderstanding. Hunter picked up his work early this morning."

"W-what?" She felt a cold sweat break out under her breasts. "That . . . that's impossible."

"I apologize for the mix-up, but I spoke with him myself. In fact, you just missed him." He stood. "Miss Montgomery? Are you okay?"

She could feel the blood draining out of her face—she must look like a ghost. "Yes." She clutched her bag to her chest. "Yes, I'm fine. Thank you." Turning, she rushed through the hallway, the lobby, and exited the museum.

Pausing on the steps, she sucked in a breath, blew it out, and tried to calm her rising pulse.

Now what was she going to do? She could rush over and try to sneak the sculpture back, but, knowing Ash, he'd already noticed it was missing.

With trembling hands, she dug her cell phone out of her purse and dialed.

"Hey, woman," Erica answered.

"What are you doing right now?"

"I just broke for lunch. Why? What's up?"

Joy moved aside to let a teacher lead a group of elementary school students into the museum. "I need an emergency meeting."

"Where are you?"

"In front of the museum."

"Okay. There's this new place I want to check out that's just a few blocks from where you are. Meet me there in ten?"

"Sure."

Erica gave her the address, and Joy began walking to the restaurant. This wasn't good. No doubt about it, she had to come clean now. She had to tell him what she'd done. Her throat closed down as panic washed over her.

Now she knew exactly what her future held. Hell. Or jail. Or both.

Picking up her pace, she raced toward the address Erica had given her and hoped the place had an extensive cocktail menu.

What had Joy done now?

Standing in the foyer of Z-Café, the latest trendy spot, Erica waited for her friend to arrive. She could tell by her voice that something major was wrong, and Erica had learned that, with Joy, that could really mean anything.

Sighing, she glanced around the newly opened restaurant. Just like all the others, the interior left her cold. But Blaine was right—she needed to be aware of the latest trends so she could graduate with the competitive knowledge that would help her land a good job.

Blaine. Thinking about him sent those little flurries through her stomach. At first the feelings had scared her, but now she was beginning to actually enjoy them. He liked her. He'd been coming over for dinner, calling her, sending her text messages. And now that they were lovers, every time they cooked together, her heart beat faster just knowing he was near.

And knowing what was underneath his long-sleeved shirts didn't help her reaction to him. Those gorgeous tattoos. It was like a little secret, one only she knew, and she liked it.

Just thinking about him caused her to bite back a smile.

What was he doing to her?

She pulled her phone out of her backpack, checking for any messages from him. She hadn't seen or heard from him yet today, and she realized she missed him.

"Erica!" Joy barged through the door. "Thank you so much for meeting me."

"Joy! What's wrong?" Her friend looked pale, and her hands were shaking.

"I'll tell you over lunch. I need a glass of wine."

"Okay." Erica motioned to the hostess, who led them through an alcove toward the dining room.

Just like the foyer, the rest of the restaurant looked like every other "trendy" place in the city. Sheesh. More concrete floors? And the bar had no personality whatsoever. And the male patrons all looked alike, in their business suits and conservative haircuts. Any of them could have been one of those guys she'd seen from Blaine's law firm. In fact, there was one particular man who looked, from the back, a bit too much like Blaine.

For some reason, as she followed the hostess and got closer to that table, the hairs on the back of her neck rose. Yeah, this guy looked a lot like Blaine—he had the same haircut, same solid build, same laugh.

She paused as she rounded the table and saw his face, unable to stop the sharp intake of breath as her fear was confirmed.

He looked up. She saw a flash of pleasure in his eyes, but it quickly turned into something else. Discomfort.

He wore a navy suit, just like the others. And the best part? Sitting a bit too close to him was an impeccable blonde in a red sheath dress. A shiny strand of pearls rested daintily around her long neck.

"Erica? What are you doing here?"

What? She wasn't good enough for one of his fancy restaurants? She touched the amethyst at her throat. "Checking out the competition," she managed.

The blonde took a sip of Blaine's white wine. "Are you another culinary student?"

"Yes. I am."

"We're trying to lure our Blaine back from his little hobby."

She glanced over at the man who'd spoken the words.

She recognized the receding red hairline and thick glasses. Chip, his former partner.

"Right. Well, good luck with that. I better be going." She grabbed Joy's hand and tugged her toward the exit.

"Erica! Wait!"

But she ignored Blaine's call and raced away, through the door and down the block, pausing only when Joy pulled her to a stop.

"Hold it! What's going on?" Joy asked.

"Nothing. I just . . ." What *was* going on? Why had Blaine been dressed like that? Was he going back to his old job? Was chef school really just a hobby? If so, what did that make her?

And, who the heck was that blonde?

"Oh, look," Joy said. "How convenient."

Erica followed Joy's gaze to a sign that read O'DONELL'S PUB.

"Come on." Joy pushed through the heavy wooden door. "I think we could both use a drink."

Numbly, Erica followed her friend inside.

Friday traffic clogged the streets, making the drive to Ash's place take longer than usual. But Joy didn't mind; she wasn't exactly in a hurry to do the deed. Sitting in the back of the taxi, she settled into the backseat.

For some reason she wasn't as nervous as she had been about telling Ash what she'd done. Of course, the three beers she'd had for lunch had helped with that. By the time they were finished, she and Erica had been downright lively about everything.

So a sculpture had fallen into her purse? It was for his

own good. Now he had a big show coming up, and she was responsible for it. He liked her. He'd forgive her.

If he was being difficult, she'd simply use the feminine wiles she'd recently discovered she possessed to distract him.

He'd get over it.

Right?

Definitely. She'd come to realize he was reasonable and good. He'd be mad, that was for sure. But, especially after the night she'd been robbed, she couldn't imagine him hating her over it. And calling the cops? Never, not after the other night.

Just remembering the way he'd kissed her in the bathtub, the way he'd massaged her feet, the way he'd played with her hair with such force while kissing her so gently . . .

God, she was getting turned on just thinking about it. She felt a throbbing between her legs, and when she remembered the look on Ash's face when she'd been sucking his cock, a shiver raced through her.

Stop it! The last thing she needed to do was show up at Ash's door wet and horny. She'd jump his bones and find another reason to procrastinate.

But now that the images were in her head, she couldn't get them out. She kept thinking of the way the candlelight flickered over Ash's taught, golden skin. She kept thinking about the way his cock had felt in her mouth. So smooth, so hard.

She felt her pussy begin to drip with her own arousal.

Goddamn it! Why did she have to start thinking this now?

Because you always think about Ash, and that inevitably leads to thinking about sex.

Scooting to the side of the taxi seat, as close to the side

opposite the driver as she could, she slipped her hand
under her dress.

Just one little touch, she told herself. Opening her legs
a few inches, she slowly, discreetly, ran her fingertips
across her thigh until she touched her pussy, her panties
already damp and warm.

And then it was so easy to slip her fingers under the
fabric and touch her needy flesh. She gasped and then put
a fist to her lips.

Ah, but it felt too good to stop. She leaned back
slightly and parted her legs just a little more. No one
could see. Then she touched her clit, pressing on the sensitive nub, using her own moisture to draw little circles
there, harder and harder, until she had to bite her lip to
keep from crying out.

She couldn't stop then. She slid her hand deeper into
her pussy, rubbed her lips until she was trembling. She
shoved a finger inside her vagina and flung her other hand
against the window, palm out. If the driver suspected anything, she didn't care.

Hell, maybe he was watching her. The thought shouldn't
turn her on, but it did, and she continued to stroke herself,
faster and harder, thinking of Ash's cock, thinking of the
thrill of what she was doing, thinking she was so fucking
close to coming. . . .

A shudder ripped through her, and she barely kept from
screaming Ash's name. Instead, when she came, the word
came out as a whisper and seemed to hang in the air.

When reality returned, she felt herself blushing as she
put herself back together. What had she just done?
Masturbated in the back of a taxicab? What had gotten
into her?

She knew, without a doubt, that she never would have done such a thing before she met Ash. What had changed? What had changed inside that had emboldened her?

She wasn't exactly sure, but she couldn't help but smile; she liked it.

Absently, she pulled a wipe out of her purse and cleaned her hands. Yes, she'd talk to Ash about the sculpture, and then she wanted to talk to him about more. Them. Tomorrow was her birthday, and she wanted Ash to go out with her and her friends.

Her heart fluttered. Was she going to introduce Ash to her friends? It seemed like such a big step but one she wanted to take.

She just hoped he'd forgive her. She'd make him listen, make him understand.

And it wasn't like she'd planned on keeping the sculpture, it just . . .

Happened.

And then the taxi was pulling up in front of Ash's place. As she paid the driver, her hands shook, and she dropped the money twice before finally handing it over.

Getting out of the taxi, she paused on the sidewalk, staring at the door. Deep breath. *Okay. You can do this!*

You will *do this.*

All too soon, she was standing at his front door, knocking. He appeared a moment later, looking surprised to see her.

"Sorry I didn't call. I was just, um, in the neighborhood." Actually, she hadn't called because she'd wanted to leave herself the option of running away if she became overwhelmed by cowardice.

"Can I come in?"

"Oh, yeah. Sure." He stepped aside and she entered his place.

Her heart was hammering in her chest as she made for the living room. And then, when she got there, everything in her froze.

Ash wasn't alone.

A woman stood and held out her hand. "Hi. I'm Heather."

"Joy," she managed, shaking hands.

"Heather models for me sometimes," Ash said, strolling into the room.

Of course she does. Because Heather was everything Joy wasn't. Nearly six feet tall, with perfectly placed blond highlights and the bone structure of a supermodel. Her jeans clung casually to her long legs, stretched tight across a stomach that was flat as a board. Her breasts were petite and perky, mocking Joy from beneath a fitted T-shirt.

This was the kind of woman who epitomized all the things Joy saw missing in herself. This was the kind of woman her grandmother would have loved. This was the kind of woman men like Ash dated.

She swallowed. "Um, I just came by to take a few pictures of some of the pieces." Then she said, trying to sound casual, "I understand you picked up the sculptures. Where would I find them?"

"Still locked in my truck."

"Great! I mean, good. I can take some pictures while you, er, visit with your friend." The supermodel in the tight-fitting jeans.

Today Joy wore a floral skirt, a silky ivory blouse, and a tweed vest. On her feet were brown knee-high boots that she'd purchased that day with Ruby. The outfit had seemed bohemian and cool when she'd put it on, but now she felt frumpy next to Heather's casual elegance.

Ash shifted on the sofa. "Actually, it's all packed up. Come back later tonight?"

"I'm pretty busy later. I'm sure I can manage now. Can I have the keys to your truck?"

He shook his head. "Nah. I need to unpack it myself." Ignoring her statement, he said, "Come around later. I'll be ready for you."

Come by later. She knew what that meant, and damn it to hell, she couldn't repress a jolt of lovely anticipation at the thought.

Focus! "I'm really busy. Can I just do it now?"

"Later." She knew that was the end of the discussion. Damn it! Now what?

He turned to Heather. "Joy works for the Cartwright Gallery and is curating a show for me next week. You should come to the opening reception, Heather." He turned to Joy. "Do you have any postcards with the reception information on you?"

"Um, I think so," she said, digging through her bag. Great. *Heather's* coming to the show. Why doesn't he just bring her as his date? They could be supermodels together—

"Don't bother," Heather said.

Joy looked up to see her lift a tiny clutch off the sofa. She unsnapped it with a click, and her long, dainty fingers reached inside and plucked out a business card.

"Why don't you just e-mail me the information?" Heather said.

"Oh, okay. Thanks." Joy took the card and dropped it

in her bag. She couldn't help but notice the way Heather eyed her purse with a look of anxiety, as if the card would never be seen again.

"So, anyway," Heather said. "I was really hoping you could take some pictures of me for my boyfriend."

"What kind of pictures?" Ash asked.

"Something sexy. Remember that shot of me you did where I was tied in a total-body harness? I think I was wearing the leather bra and panties and those really hot stilettos."

Joy dug her Tums out of her bag and popped one into her mouth.

"Yeah, sure," Ash was saying. "I loved that shot."

"I was thinking something like that, but instead of leather maybe some transparent lingerie. Oh, can we do one with the spreader bar?"

"I need to go to the bathroom," Joy announced.

Ash and Heather just looked at her.

"So . . . I'll go. To the bathroom." She turned and went to the downstairs bathroom. Once inside, she collapsed on the toilet seat and threw her head into her hands. She couldn't help but think about what Ruby had told her, that Ash had cheated on her. If he was taking sexy shots of women like that all the time, if he was tying them, his hands on their perfect bodies, his eyes always staring at submissive, feminine perfection—

Her stomach lurched, and for a second she thought she might be sick.

Shooting to her feet, she blasted into the living room and picked up her giant bag. Plastering a smile on her face, she looked to Ash and Heather. "Okay. I guess I'll just be going."

Ash stood. "Are you sure?"

Joy started backing toward the door. "Mmm. Yeah, I gotta . . . go."

Ash started after her, catching her at the door. "What's going on?"

Glancing over her shoulder, she saw Heather watching them as she crossed her spidery legs.

"I just . . . I have some work to do tonight." She laughed nervously. "You know, for the show. Busy, busy. That's me."

He didn't look like he was buying it, but he let it go. "Okay. Is your phone charged?"

"I think so."

"Good. I'll call you later."

She kissed him quickly on the cheek and left.

"I don't know why I freaked out like that." Joy tilted the margarita to her lips and took another gulp. "I mean, he's a bondage artist . . . I know that, but oh my God. You should have seen her."

Kate rolled her eyes, her heavy eye makeup exaggerating the look. After Joy had run away from Ash's place, she'd rounded up the group for an emergency drinking session. Now she sat in a booth at Mario's, surrounded by Kate, Scott, and Erica.

"I bet she was tall," Kate said scornfully.

"Of course," Joy said. "And gorgeous."

"You're gorgeous, too, Joy," Erica said.

"But not in *that* way. I'm cute," she said, wrinkling her nose.

"Nothing wrong with being cute, Joy," Scott said.

"Anyway." Joy drained the rest of her margarita. "I don't know why I felt so threatened."

"Well, you don't always have the best luck with men, sweetie," Kate said gently. "Maybe it's your self-protection instincts kicking in."

"Maybe . . . but the thing is, Ash hasn't done anything that would make me doubt him."

"Yet."

Everyone turned to Erica. She shrugged. "I'm just saying he hasn't done anything yet. But come on. He's known as this big erotic artist; it's what he lives for. Do you think a guy like that could be happy with a 'normal' life?"

"Hey," Joy said. "I can be freaky!" In fact, her friends would probably be shocked if they knew how freaky she actually could be.

"I'm sure you can, honey," Scott said with a grin that implied he didn't believe it for a minute.

"The thing is . . ." Joy swirled her straw in the icy remains of her drink. She was almost afraid to admit it, but alcohol had loosened her tongue. "The reason Ruby broke up with him was because he cheated on her."

Erica raised her glass. "Men suck."

"Even though," Joy went on, "he never admitted that he had been unfaithful."

Kate snorted.

"I don't know . . ." Her gaze drifted through the crowd and through the front window. The bar was located on a small side street in North Beach. The street twisted up a steep hill, and Joy's eyes were drawn by a movement just near the edge of her view. It was a person dressed in black baggy pants and a black hoodie. He had a backpack. He placed it on the ground and, after he'd looked around a moment, pulled something out of the pack.

Something that looked like a can.

She froze. Could it be her phantom artist? But it didn't make sense. This was a more public street than he usually tagged. If it was him, he was getting braver, bolder. And as she watched him outline what could only be Picasso's *Blue Guitar,* she whipped her head to Scott. "Move!"

"What?"

She gave him a hard nudge. "I said, move, you big lug! Let me out!"

Looking at her as if she was crazy, he scooted over and let her out of the booth. As she pressed through the crowd, she noticed the bartender eyeing the stranger in the hoodie.

Joy burst through the door and was immediately hit by damp, chilly San Francisco air. She also smelled the mouthwatering aroma of garlic; this neighborhood was known for its amazing Italian restaurants. But Joy ignored her suddenly growling stomach, instead walking slowly toward the figure with the spray-paint can.

He looked over his shoulder, and when he saw her, he jumped back and looked ready to run.

"Wait!" Joy said, trotting toward him. "You know me!"

He paused, and she saw he was young, pale, and very suspicious.

Joy stopped about five feet from him. "I mean, you don't *know me* know me, but have you gotten my cards?"

She saw his interest pique. "You're the one?"

"Why haven't you called?"

"How do I know you're not a cop?"

"I'm not."

He took his time looking her over. Apparently her image reassured him—Joy wasn't sure if that was good or bad—because he relaxed slightly. "Okay. You're not a cop. So what do you want?"

"What's your name?"

"Ben."

She didn't believe him, but she let it go. "Well, I think your work is amazing, Ben. Would you be interested in meeting with me at the gallery? I want to discuss representation."

"Are you serious?"

She nodded. "I've been looking for you for a long time. I think you have major potential." He looked dubious.

"Seriously. How do you think Keith Haring got started?" she asked, meaning the famous artist who did the colorful dancing figures. He'd started out as a graffiti artist in New York, and by the time he died, he was a household name.

"I'll think about it," he said.

"Let me give you another card." She began digging in her bag.

It was then that the police cruiser pulled up.

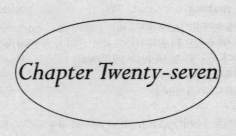

Chapter Twenty-seven

N ot a cop, huh?" Ben said, his voice full of anger.

"I'm not—"

"Shit!" he said, shaking his head as the cruiser stopped in front of them, blue-and-red lights flashing in the night.

"I swear, I didn't call them."

"Right."

Both doors of the cruiser opened, and two men in uniforms emerged. The passenger-side cop was compact with short brown hair; the driver was Asian and looked like he could punch through a door with one of his beefy arms. Joy's palms dampened when she caught sight of the weapons on their belts. Just looking at their guns brought up feelings from when she'd been robbed.

"Identification," the linebacker said.

Ben pulled a ragged-looking ID card out of his back pocket. "I wasn't doing anything," he mumbled.

"That's right," Joy said, the margaritas she'd consumed making her bold. "We were just standing here, minding our own business."

The blond cop turned to Ben and pointed toward his backpack. "I want to look in that bag."

"What?" Joy asked. "Why?" She figured if she argued with the cops a bit, Ben would believe she was the good guy. Plus, she didn't think Ben should be punished for gifting the city with his wonderful pieces.

"Excuse us, miss. We have reason to believe this person is in possession of graffiti materials, which is a misdemeanor."

She drew herself up. "Are you calling art a crime?"

"No, the city of San Francisco calls defacing public property a crime."

She glanced at his nametag. "I'm sorry, Officer Quan, but I certainly don't think anyone would consider beautiful murals that add beauty to our city a crime."

"Lady, I'd advise you to stay out of this."

By now, several people had come out of the bar and were happily regarding the free entertainment. Erica was just shaking her head, Scott was smiling, and Kate was making a signal across her mouth indicating Joy should shut up.

But Joy didn't feel like backing down. She felt like sticking up for Ben's rights as an artist. And she was tipsy.

Blond cop picked up Ben's backpack.

"Wait!" she said, stepping forward.

"Miss, if you don't move aside, I'll book you for obstructing and delaying a peace officer's duties."

"It's your duty to censor people?" She sensed Ben shrinking away from her, as if he wanted it known they weren't together. But Joy couldn't seem to stop herself.

"Do you really believe art should be illegal?" She sighed. "So, so sad."

Quan frowned. "I'm not kidding, lady. If you say one more thing to me, I'm going to arrest you."

"That won't be necessary."

Everyone turned to see a tall man walking toward them, his expression grim.

Shit. What's Ash doing here?

"I apologize, Officer. My girlfriend is just a bit passionate and forgets herself sometimes."

"She's lucky I didn't throw her in a cell."

Ash had his hand on her shoulder now, his grip firm and unyielding. "Thank you for that, sir. I'll take her back inside now, if you don't mind."

"Ash Hunter?" Ben was moving toward Ash, his eyes wide. "The artist?"

"Yeah," Ash said.

"Man, I love your work. I'm a huge fan."

"Oh." Ash shifted, looking uncomfortable. "Thanks."

"No problem."

"If you don't mind?" This from the brown-haired cop. "I need to have a talk with our little friend here."

"You're not going to arrest him, are you?"

"Not tonight. But I'm taking the graffiti materials and giving him a hard warning."

"Oh, thank you, officers!" Joy said over her shoulder as Ash dragged her back to the lounge.

"Joy," he said in a low voice, "when are you going to learn?"

"When are you going to stop hauling me around and telling me what to do?"

He stopped suddenly and turned to face her. "When you start using your head. So. I guess *never*!"

She sucked in a breath. "I can take care of myself, Ash!"

"You were just nearly arrested back there. If it wasn't for me, you'd be handcuffed, sitting in the back of a police car."

"And it would be fine with me, because I would be there because I was standing up for what I believe in."

They were standing in front of the lounge, and Joy felt her friends' eyes on them, watching and listening. She didn't care.

"Tell me, Joy. How would you make bail? You don't have any money, remember?"

She lifted her chin. "I wouldn't."

"You would stay in jail." It was a question, but he made it into a statement.

"Yes."

"Have you ever been in jail, Joy?"

"No."

He leaned in closer, until they were nearly nose to nose. "Well, you wouldn't like it."

"How do you know?"

"I know *I* sure as hell wouldn't like you in a cell!" he said, and she felt his breath on her face.

"Why do you care what happens to me?"

"I just do!" he shouted.

They stared at each other, panting. Her heart was thudding in her chest, and her pulse raced. Ash looked furious at her; his cheeks were flushed with what she assumed was anger.

And yet, something pulsed between them. Something electric and exciting and active.

He finally seemed to realize they'd become a bit of a performance, so he yanked her hand and dragged her into the lounge. "Where's your giant bag?"

"It's over in the back booth. Why?" she said, trotting behind him.

"We're leaving."

"Where are we going?"

Ignoring her, he led her to the place where her friends had abandoned her purse and jacket in the deserted booth. *Traitors,* Joy thought as Ash picked up her things. He slung the bag over his shoulder and carried her jacket as he led her through a door at the back of the bar. Soon they were in a back alley behind the building.

On one side of the alley was a building, and on the other side wooden trees and fencing lined the uneven pavement. Ash led her about fifty yards away from the bar and then made a quick turn and pulled her into a little alcove, above which a big maple tree blocked the sky.

He pushed her against the fence. She watched him begin to pace, looking a bit ridiculous, because he still carried her purse and coat.

He froze. "Are you laughing?"

"No." She put a hand to her mouth but giggled anyway.

He just stared at her, and even in the dim light, she saw a vein pulsing in his neck. Interesting. She'd never noticed that before.

"You're not going to be laughing in a minute, woman."

And just like that, a shot of lust darted through her. "Why do you say that?" she asked, trying to sound coy.

"Because you're going to be too busy begging me to fuck you."

His crude words made her breasts tingle. "In a minute? Just one minute?" she taunted.

"Yup." He dropped her bag and coat on the ground, where the items landed in a pile of fallen leaves. Then he came at her.

He took her arms and spread them wide and high. "Hold on to the fence and don't let go."

If she stretched, she could just grip the top of the fence. "When does your minute start?"

"Now." Dropping to his knees in front of her, he lifted her skirt and yanked down her panties until they fell to her ankles, and he tossed them aside. And then his mouth was on her flesh, sucking her clit right over his teeth. She gasped, suddenly glad to be hanging on to the fence; she thought her legs might buckle.

"Yes . . . ," she said as he thrust two fingers into her pussy. Already, she was so wet he slid in easily, deep and hard, in and out.

He ignored her, instead sliding his hand around in her wetness, coating himself before he plunged into her again. She cried out as her body started to tremble. "Yes . . . unh . . ."

He was working her clit hard now, using his tongue to flick at the engorged flesh until she nearly begged, but instead she bit her lip and thrashed her head against the fence.

Was he going to do it? Make her come in a minute? Not that she had any idea of time; all she knew was that he knew exactly what her clit needed; he knew just how to use two fingers to make her insides clench—and then she felt his pinkie finger, slick from her juices, sliding against her ass. He didn't ask; he slid it in, using his hand to fuck both her holes, fast and deep and beautiful.

She came against his face, her body sagging as she clutched at the fence so hard she felt the wood splinter under her palms.

When she finally floated down to reality, he slid his hand out of her pussy. He stood, straightened her dress, and slanted her a grin. Then he said, "Let that be a lesson to you, miss. Don't fight those in authority; they always win."

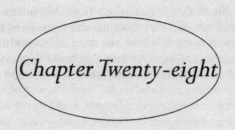

Chapter Twenty-eight

D o you think Joy's okay?"

Erica looked up from her beer to find Kate stumbling into the booth. It was late, nearly midnight, but they were still at Mario's. Scott and Kate were on the train to hangover town, but Erica had been nursing the same drink for nearly an hour.

Slowly, Erica nodded. "Yeah. I do."

"So we finally got a glimpse of Ash Hunter. I gotta say he's fucking hot."

Erica shrugged. "All that matters to me is that he treats her well."

Kate picked up a half-empty glass and gave it a sniff. "After what I saw tonight, I'd say he's perfect for her."

She hated to admit it, but Erica was inclined to agree. The energy between them was obvious, and the way he looked at Joy, like he'd do anything for her, was definitely a good thing. He seemed perfectly able to care for Joy, and more important, he seemed to want to.

Erica wasn't quite sure how she felt about that. All this time she'd been the one to look out for Joy, to help her get out of the messes in which she inevitably seemed to find herself. It felt strange to know that if things continued with Ash and Joy, he'd be that person from now on.

A few weeks ago, she would have been freaking out if Joy disappeared after an argument in the street with some guy Erica didn't know. But somehow she knew that wasn't necessary, not with Ash.

See, she could let go of Joy. Blaine had no idea what he was talking about.

The thought of him made Erica's teeth clench. He'd called and texted her several times that day, but she refused to acknowledge him. She'd known this was going to happen, so why had she let herself fall for him? She was just a diversion, something fun to do before he settled into his predictable upper-class life. Her, the culinary program. It was all fun and games to him. And she'd nearly let herself get caught up in it.

No, this was for the best. Her phone rang again, and she glanced at the display. It was him again. She ignored it. Yes, it was a darn good thing she'd seen the real Blaine while she still had time to get out.

"I have something for you."

They were sitting in Ash's truck, parked in her grandmother's driveway. When she told him she needed to go to Atherton to pick up her car, he'd insisted on driving her there, so she'd invited him to dinner. She really had no choice, as her grandmother was cooking her annual birthday dinner, and now they were staring at the house. It seemed to loom above them.

A wave of exhaustion washed over her. She hadn't been able to get a moment alone with Ash's collection, and now it was Saturday. Her thirtieth birthday. She was entering this phase of her life as she'd entered every other one. A mess.

For some reason, she hadn't been able to actually go inside yet. She just wasn't in the mood to suffer her grandmother's passive-aggressive insults today. Not that she ever was, but with all the stuff that had been going on lately, she was in even less of a mood for the abuse than normal.

Now she turned to Ash, who was pulling something out of his pocket, a small gift box.

"Just driving me here is enough of a birthday present." But, of course, a little feminine thrill shot through her at the thought of Ash giving her something.

He actually looked sheepish. "Here. It's nothing fancy. . . ."

She slowly opened the box and pulled out the item inside. It was a dainty silver chain on which a marble pendant hung. It had been carved into the shape of a delicate sparrow. Her heart beat rapidly in her chest as she looked up and met his gaze. "You made this for me?"

He nodded. "The swallow is a traditional Navy symbol for trust."

"Thank you." Her throat was tight for some strange reason; it was just a little gift, after all! Still, she couldn't believe Ash had made something just for her, that he'd cared that much. And the tiny sculpture was beautiful, its miniature details delicate and smooth. Turning, she pulled her hair aside.

"Would you put it on for me?"

He took the necklace, and she felt his fingers at the back of her neck. Her skin pebbled at the soft, warm feel of his hands on her skin. After he'd fastened the necklace, he leaned forward and placed a kiss next to her ear. But her throat was tight. He'd given her a token of trust.

Finally she turned back to him. "It means so much that you thought of me and made me something so beautiful and unique. Thank you for this, Ash."

He glanced away and then back at her. "Yeah. No problem. I guess we should go in."

"I guess we should." But she didn't want to. She wanted to get away, from her grandmother, from her guilty feelings. But she let Ash lead her out of the truck.

Her pulse quickened as they neared the door. She had no idea how her grandmother was going to behave in front of Ash. She'd never introduced her to a man before and had certainly never brought one to her house for dinner.

Joy led them into the kitchen, where she found her grandmother chopping vegetables, presumably for a salad.

"Hello, dear," Grandmother said, and came to give Joy a tight hug.

"Hi, Grandma. This is Ash Hunter. Ash, my grandmother, Miriam."

Grandmother gave Ash's form a quick scan, and Joy saw her mouth tighten. Ash wore his standard uniform of a leather jacket, T-shirt, faded jeans, and boots. Joy knew her grandmother believed men should "dress for dinner," but there was no way Joy was making Ash dress differently. And Grandmother definitely wouldn't approve of Ash's two-day beard or his longish hair. Oh well.

She pasted on a smile. "Nice to meet you, Ash."

"Likewise," Ash said, shaking her hand.

Grandmother gave Joy's outfit a once-over. "That's an interesting outfit, dear."

"Thanks," Joy answered, as if she didn't know damn well that what her grandmother was really saying was, *A girl with your figure shouldn't wear jeans. Especially not to dinner*.

But Joy didn't care. It was her birthday, and she was sick of worrying about what her grandmother thought or said about her. Tonight she'd worn the jeans Ash seemed so fond of, a colorful silk blouse, and brown riding boots. And, of course, a beautiful necklace made out of marble. She absently touched the little bird at her throat, and a happy buzz of delight went through her. She couldn't believe he'd actually hand-carved a gift for her. Of course, that reminded her of how horrible she was for keeping her secret, but she pushed it aside. It was her birthday, a perfect excuse to ignore her problems.

"Well. Shall we have a drink before dinner? Joy, I know how you like your aperitifs. Just remember, alcohol has a lot of calories."

"Yes, Grandma, I remember." *How could I forget with you constantly reminding me?* Joy was still recovering from the mental beating she'd taken for eating too many mashed potatoes on Thanksgiving.

Her grandmother led them down a hall to a sitting room. The room was painted a light yellow, and on one side an ornately carved marble fireplace took up most of the wall. Joy and Ash took a seat on a floral upholstered love seat, and Grandmother sat across from them in a matching wingback chair. The clock hanging on the far wall ticked loudly.

There were already cheese and crackers on the coffee table as well as a bottle of chilled champagne and two crystal flutes.

"Would you mind opening the champagne, Ash?"

He removed the bottle of Selosse 1999 Millésime from the chiller and expertly popped the cork. Then he filled three glasses.

Grandmother held hers up. "Cheers."

They clinked their glasses. Joy drank half of hers in a single gulp while Grandmother, of course, sipped daintily.

"I'm sorry your brothers couldn't make it tonight, Joy."

I'm not, Joy thought. She really wasn't in the mood to spend her birthday listening to how successful and amazing her siblings were.

"But they're so busy with their careers and families, you know. It's hard for them to take any time away from their obligations." She took another small sip and turned her gaze on Ash.

Joy inwardly cringed; she knew what was coming.

"What do you do for a living, Ash?"

Here we go.

"I'm an artist," he answered casually.

Grandmother's smile went tight around the edges. "An artist? Well, that must be nice."

"It is. In fact, that's how I met Joy. She's curating a show for me next week. You should come."

"Are you a painter?" Grandmother asked, and Joy could practically hear the woman's teeth grinding.

Joy drank down the rest of her champagne and then refilled her glass, hoping that Grandmother would be too disturbed by Ash's occupation to notice Joy topping herself off.

"I'm a photographer. Portraits, mainly."

"Ash is one of San Francisco's leading photographers, Grandmother. He's very much in demand."

"I'm sure he is." Grandmother turned to Joy. "Dear, may I speak with you a moment in private?"

"Um . . ." She glanced at Ash.

"I'll be fine," he said with a smile as he made a sandwich out of cheese and crackers.

Grandmother could barely contain the look of horror on her face as she made her way out of the living room. When they reached the study, Grandmother shut the door. "Joy. Who is that man?"

"I told you. He's Ash Hunter."

"He's an artist," she said with disdain.

Joy plopped into a leather club chair. "Um, I know?"

With a great sigh, Grandmother went to her desk and sat behind it. She clasped her fingers together and laid her hands on the desk. "The last thing you need is a starving artist sniffing around your door."

Joy refrained from telling her grandmother that Ash was anything but a starving artist. For some reason, she was enjoying the woman's discomfort. Besides, Ash's finances were none of her grandmother's business.

Grandmother met her gaze. "Joy, I have something to tell you. To give you."

"Okay . . . so why are we in here?"

"Because it's private and I don't want someone like . . . that man knowing your affairs."

Feeling a bit disturbed by the look in her grandmother's eyes, Joy leaned forward. "What's going on?"

"Well."

Did Grandmother actually look nervous? If so, it was a first.

"As you know, I was the executor of your parents' estate when they died."

"I know."

"What you don't know is that you're due to inherit a trust on your thirtieth birthday. Today."

Everything in her went still. "Grandmother, what are you talking about?"

"Your inheritance. It's all here in these files. Stocks, bonds. It's quite a bit of money. I just hope you're responsible enough to handle it."

Her body tense, Joy leaned forward in the chair. "Why didn't I know about this?"

The older woman straightened the already perfect pile of folders before her. "I was hoping you would be more settled by now, but there's nothing that can be done at this point. It was set up so you would have access to it when you turned thirty." She drew her lips into a frown. "Now you are."

Joy was speechless. "I can't believe this—that you never told me. Why not? Why didn't you trust me?"

"You don't have the best record when it comes to responsibility, Joy. Just look at tonight. Look who you brought to dinner with you."

"What's wrong with Ash?" she asked in a low voice, her blood pounding in her ears. Anger raged through her, and she fought for control before she lost it.

"Men like that—*that artist*—will prey on girls like you."

"Girls like me. What kind of girl is that, Grandmother?"

Grandmother met her gaze. "Girls who don't think. You're an easy target."

"You told my brothers on their thirtieth birthdays, too?" Joy asked.

Grandmother looked at her desk. "Not exactly."

"What do you mean, 'not exactly'?" Joy asked in a steely voice.

"They received their inheritances when they turned twenty-one."

Joy just sat there, frozen. Her parents' will had given her brothers their money nine years before her? "What? Why?"

"Because your parents were smart. I pointed out that if something ever happened to them, any scoundrel could swoop in and take full advantage of your spirited nature. I didn't want you to spend your inheritance on frivolous things. I wanted you to go to college and follow in your father's footsteps!" she said, her expression fierce. "I wanted you to be like your brothers and become a doctor or a lawyer, not some lazy heiress."

Joy's voice was stone-cold. "I love what I do. I'm sorry if I don't fit into your idea of success, Grandmother. But I would do what I do no matter what. It wouldn't have mattered if I had money or not. Don't you get that?"

"I just wanted you to be self-sufficient, Joy."

"I am."

She stared at her grandmother for a second before she said, "Why me? Why not my brothers?" She had to know.

"They're boys, dear. And they've always been serious about their studies and their careers."

"So was I," Joy said in a low voice. "I went to Stanford for fuck's sake! I got accepted into one of the most competitive art history programs in Paris!"

Grandmother gasped. "Joy! Watch your mouth."

"No. I curse like a sailor, Grandma. Better get used to

it." On shaking legs, she stood. "In fact, you better get used to a lot of things."

"Joy . . ."

"I'm not fat. I like Ash. I'm smart. And I'm sick of you manipulating me!"

"Everything I've done has been for your own good."

"Really? Or is it because my perfect brothers can't even be bothered to be a part of this family and I'm all you have? So you do whatever it takes to keep me under your thumb. Let me see the paperwork."

Grandmother handed over the files, and Joy flipped open a folder. When she saw the various balances, her stomach dropped in shock. "I can't believe you've been keeping this from me."

"It was for your own good," she repeated, and Joy heard desperation there. She ignored it.

"It was for my own good to treat me like some kind of birdbrain in this family just because I'm a girl?"

"Because I love you." Her grandmother's blue eyes turned watery—was she actually tearing up? "I've just done what I think is best for you."

"This—" Joy picked up the file and waved it at her grandmother. "Keeping this from me while my brothers were all privy to the information was *not* best for me."

Grandmother stood, her tears quickly drying. "You're a good girl, Joy. But you're flighty and you don't think. That"—she lowered her voice—"man out there is a perfect example."

"You don't even know him." Shaking in rage, Joy spun on her heel and yanked the door open. She marched down the hallway, not even pausing when she yelled, "Come on!" to Ash as she passed the sitting room.

"Joy, wait," she heard her grandmother calling after her. "What about dinner?"

Chin raised, Joy turned and faced her mother's mother. "Guess what?"

Her grandmother just stared at her.

"You've finally managed to kill my appetite. And you know what else?"

"What?" her grandmother said uneasily.

"I look fucking fantastic in these jeans!" What would have been a fabulous exit line was ruined by her frenzied digging through her purse, looking for the keys to her Mercedes. She began handing items to Ash: reading glasses, lotion, a bottle of perfume. She dug deeper, her mind so distracted by now she didn't even realize when she took out a small but heavy piece of marble. She was about to hand it to Ash when she realized what she'd done. He stared at it, his expression one of total confusion. And then disbelief. When he looked back at her, his eyes seemed ice-cold.

He reached out to take the sculpture, but her hands were shaking so badly she could barely hold it steady, and just before he reached for it, the beautiful sculpture dropped onto her grandmother's slate floor, shattering into an array of chunks and chards.

"What is this, Joy?"

"I can explain—"

"Where did you get this?" She'd never heard his voice sound so deadly.

"I took it, but I was going to give it back!"

"You took it?"

She nodded.

"You mean you stole it."

"Yes, but I had a good reason."

She saw him bite the inside of his cheek, fighting for control. "A good reason to steal. From me."

She went to touch his arm, but he jerked back. "Listen, Ash. Can I just explain?"

"What's there to explain? You took something that didn't belong to you. That makes you a thief."

"It was for your own good!" She cringed. Hadn't her grandmother just said those very words to her only moments ago?

His gaze sharpened, and she nearly recoiled. "I thought I could trust you," he said.

"You can."

Slowly, he shook his head. "No. I can't." All the items he'd been holding fell to the floor.

The hurt of betrayal burned in his eyes, and she felt her own eyes water. "Ash, please . . ."

But he ignored her. Instead he turned and walked out the door.

She looked up to see her grandmother, who'd silently witnessed the whole thing, shake her head and walk back to the study. Then Joy was alone, surrounded by random items from her purse and the ruins of Ash's sculpture. There was nothing left to do now but clean up the mess and go.

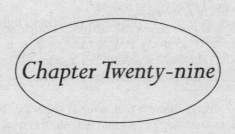

Chapter Twenty-nine

As she entered her apartment later that night, she was still reeling from the night's events. Ash, the money, the argument. It was all too much.

So much betrayal, so much hurt.

She dropped the pile of files onto the kitchen counter. She'd been lied to by her grandmother and her three brothers for nearly a decade.

A fucking decade!

As she jerked open the freezer door and pulled out a carton of rocky road, she laughed bitterly. Just days ago, her grandmother had made her feel horribly guilty when Joy had asked her for a loan. What a joke!

She began shoving bites of ice cream into her mouth. She could almost accept the fact that her grandmother had deceived her this way, but to know that her brothers were in on it, that they believed she was as irresponsible as her grandmother thought she was, hurt Joy to the bone.

Was this how everyone saw her?

But she already knew the answer; enough people had told her so. If so many people thought that, it must be true, and as she looked around her apartment, she saw in the chaos of her home what everyone else saw in her: a mess.

She'd always thought that, even if she was a bit disorganized, at least she was a good person. But now she was even beginning to doubt that.

Absently she began piling up papers on her kitchen table. Why *was* she so messy? She had a desk by the entryway; why didn't she ever think to use it? She glanced to the writing desk she'd bought from the import store. It was piled with miscellaneous items like photographs, a bottle of water, a windup toy, a bra. . . .

She went to the desk and cleared the surface, putting every item in its proper place. Then she gathered the piles of mail and bills scattered around the house (why had she put her checkbook in the bathroom?) and organized the desk appropriately. Standing back, she crossed her arms over her chest and was surprised at how satisfying it was to look at all the paperwork stored in its correct area.

The kitchen was next. She drank wine as she organized the cookbooks and cleaned the counters. There was her favorite fake-jeweled hair comb! Why was it behind the toaster? She found a basket in the fireplace and took it to the bathroom, and from then on, whenever she found a ponytail holder or other hair accoutrement, she placed it in the basket.

It was like she was possessed. When the kitchen looked like Martha Stewart's cleaning team had been through, Joy moved on to the living room. She gathered bag after bag of old magazines and newspapers, making about twenty trips to the apartment recycle bins. She gathered all her art history books and organized them in the bookshelf next to the fireplace. She arranged the colorful ethnic throw pillows on the sofa and draped the brightly woven blanket she'd picked up in India over the back of a chair. She stacked the current magazines she hadn't yet read on the rustic coffee table and then positioned all the candles she'd uncovered next to them.

Next she attacked her bedroom, sorting clothes and drawers and putting things away. She took everything out of her closet and replaced the items in a neat, ordered fashion. She even organized her blouses and skirts in sections by color, going from white to pink to red, all the way down to black.

By the time she had cleaned the entire apartment, it was close to dawn.

She was a sweaty mess, but she felt good. Cleansed. This was a good start; she was ready to make some changes in her life.

Erica was grinding spices for her own curry paste when she heard a soft knock on the door. Blaine. Instinctively, she knew it was him.

She peered through the eyehole. Her heart skipped before she could stop it. What was he doing here?

Unsure, Erica continued to stare through the small hole of glass. Why did the man have to be so damn gorgeous? He wore another of his tight, long-sleeved T-shirts and those damn khaki pants that seemed anything but preppy now that she knew exactly what was underneath them.

"Erica. I know you're in there; I can smell the curry. Now open the door."

She paused, her heart pounding. She wanted him to go away. And she wanted to pull him inside and wrap her arms around him.

But that would just make everything so much worse.

"Come on, Erica. You can't avoid me forever."

"Fine, but only for a second. I'm busy." She pulled open the door.

"Smells amazing," he said, entering her apartment.

She crossed her arms over her chest. "What do you want?"

"To find out why you've been avoiding me since that day in the restaurant."

"I haven't been avoiding you. I see you every day at school."

"Yeah, but each time I try to talk to you, you run away."

She moved past him, heading for the kitchen. "I do not run away. I'm just busy."

He grabbed her arm, stopping her. "Don't lie to me. What's going on?"

Raising her chin, she met his gaze. "Nothing. I just don't want to be your plaything anymore."

He blinked slowly. "My plaything? What are you talking about?"

She jerked out of his grasp. "Come on, Blaine. I saw you with your lawyer friends." *And that girl.* "Your friend even said it: You're going back to being a lawyer."

"No. What he said was that they want me to."

"And based on how you were dressed that day, I would assume you will."

"And you'd be wrong."

"Then what were you doing there?"

"They were celebrating the end of a three-year case, one I was involved in."

She scoffed. "A messy divorce? It took a team of lawyers to divide up the Jaguars and the houses?"

"No. It was a domestic violence case. A poor woman trying to leave her abusive asshole of a husband. A rich jerk who beat her up but didn't want to give her custody of her three children."

That stopped her cold. "A-a poor woman? But how can she afford you?"

"Pro bono. We're not all a bunch of selfish assholes, you know."

Her stomach churned, unsettled. "What about that blond woman? The one sitting next to you that day?"

"You mean Bitsy?"

"*Bitsy?*" Seriously?

"She was on the case, too."

"Is she your girlfriend?"

Now it was his turn to look uncomfortable. "Um, not anymore."

"But she was."

"Yes."

A bitter laugh escaped her throat. "Bitsy and Beaumont. How perfect."

"I'm not seeing her anymore."

"But she wants to."

"Maybe. I don't care about her, Erica."

"Okay, I need you to leave now."

He stared at her, and she could tell he was fighting back anger.

But she couldn't think, didn't know what to think.

Everything was so much easier when he fit into the box she'd created for him.

But now he'd blown that box into shreds, and she didn't know how to put it back together.

"Please, Blaine. Just go."

He continued to hold her gaze before finally stepping back. "Fine. But I mean what I said before."

"What?" she asked, her voice shaky. Her head was spinning; nothing made sense.

He went to the door and opened it. Then, with one last look, he said, "I won't wait forever." And then he shut the door quietly behind him.

She stared sightlessly, fighting the urge to run after him. Because she wanted to. She wanted to so badly it scared the daylights out of her. So instead, she went to the kitchen and pounded away at the spices. And as she worked, she couldn't help but feel like it was her own heart she was grinding into tiny specks of powder.

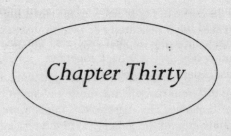

Chapter Thirty

One week later and Joy still hadn't heard from Ash. He'd delivered all the art on Sunday. He knew she didn't work Sundays, so he must have purposely come on that day so he wouldn't have to see her.

She got the hint.

Her heart had ached all week, and she felt as if her throat was constantly on the verge of closing up. But she'd done what she'd done, and now she had to live with the consequences. It was her recklessness that had gotten her into this mess, and she vowed to be more careful in the future. She was thirty now. No more bad choices, no more chaos. She'd learned her lesson: It was time to start thinking before she acted.

Andrew hung the last of Ash's photographs on the wall, and Joy stood back to admire the newly transformed space. If she looked at all the images objectively, she had to admit the images he'd taken of her were very nice. The way he used light and shadow to emphasize the dip of her waist or the curve of her breast was breathtaking. And the best part was, he'd obscured her face in just such a way that it was nearly impossible to identify Joy as the model the images featured.

There were others, too. She'd arranged a mix of pieces featuring different models, the uniting element being the theme of bondage. His marble sculptures were perched on pedestals around the gallery, with the one large piece taking center stage in the space. Despite her sadness over losing Ash, she had to give herself some credit. She'd curated a damn good show.

In the bathroom, she changed into the outfit she'd bought just for tonight. A simple black sheath dress with a high collar and a hem that fell just below the knee. She wore black mules with just the tiniest kitten heel, and she'd pulled her hair into what she hoped resembled a French twist. Now she applied the makeup she'd purchased just for tonight. On Wednesday, she'd hit the MAC counter and had a makeover. A professional look—that's what she'd asked the makeup artist to create for her, and he'd done a perfect job. Now she applied the bronze eye shadow, brown eyeliner, and peach blush just as he'd instructed her. Stepping back, she looked in the mirror, her reflection gazing back at her.

She looked good. Put together, sophisticated, professional. She looked ready to sell art. Ash's art.

Her heart cracked, but she ignored it. Deep breath. In, out. She was a proficient art dealer, and this was the most important event of her professional career so far. She hardly ever allowed herself to think of her parents, but she couldn't help but wish they were here tonight. After all, this was one of her greatest professional achievements, and it would be nice if they could have been here to share it with her. Would they be proud? She believed they would—she *had* to believe they would.

When she looked in the mirror, she saw her mother's hazel eyes. Joy's chest tightened. It was so hard. When she'd first heard about her parents, that they'd died in a plane crash in Spain, Joy had been devastated. She remembered dropping to her knees, because her legs couldn't hold her up any longer. She remembered lying in bed, curled up on her side, sobbing uncontrollably as her heart was ripped in two.

The worst thing a person could ever experience was losing a child. That's what her grandmother had told her. That's what, at sixteen years of age, Joy had believed. Guilt ate at her because she was so sad. She missed her parents, but didn't her grandmother have it so much worse? Her mother was Grandmother's only child. And then she was gone. At least Joy still had her brothers. Even if her brothers were too preoccupied in their own lives to pay Joy any attention, they were family, and Joy held family above all else.

With a sigh, she turned and picked up her brand-new Chanel purse. It was a quarter the size of her other purse, but it was Joy's birthday present to herself. It was time to give up her old oversized, overpacked, disorganized purse and move on. Women in their thirties, women who wanted to present themselves as polished, sophisticated organized adults, did not carry suitcases full of crap everywhere they went.

She glanced at her new Rolex: 5:45. She already knew Ruby was in the gallery overseeing the caterer, and Andrew was welcoming guests. Several of the pieces already had little red stickers on the frames, indicating that they'd been sold. The night was going to go fine. Smooth as silk.

If only her palms would dry up. If only her pulse would slow down.

Ash.

She was going to see him tonight. She was going to smile and act professionally and sell his work. She was going to do her job, because when it came down to it, this was what she loved. To be in the trenches. The art world was cutthroat, and even as her tummy fluttered with nerves, a buzz of excitement shot through her veins in a thrilling rush. She loved selling art. Real art. Original pieces of beauty. She loved knowing that, through her efforts, something new and amazing was going to hang on the wall of someone's house, and they were going to experience joy whenever they looked at it.

This was what she lived for.

And even if Ash hated her, she was still going to do her job and do it the best she could. With one last glance in the mirror, she took a deep breath and emerged into the main gallery, ready to do her job.

"Montgomery, you've actually pulled this off."

Joy glanced over at her boss and pretended to sip her champagne. "Thank you, Mr. Panos."

All night she'd been flitting through the crowded gallery, talking to clients and placing red stickers on Ash's pieces every time she sold one. By any standards, the show would be considered a success. Nearly every one of his works had been purchased, and several people had already approached her to request information on commissioning their own masterpieces.

Even Prickhead Panos seemed to be happy with her. Everything she'd wanted out of her career was coming to fruition, and yet she couldn't get rid of the swelling feeling of sadness that floated in her heart like a balloon ready to pop.

Ash hadn't even looked at her all night.

He'd arrived, and then he'd parked his long, lean form in a corner and waited for guests to approach him. He looked phenomenal, of course. He'd actually shaved tonight, and her heart simply melted at the sight of the sharp lines of his newly exposed clean-shaven jaw. He seemed to have put some sort of product in his hair that made it glisten under the lights, giving him an unkempt, bad-boy look that had nearly every female in the room swooning.

Mine, Joy wanted to yell. *He's all mine!*

But, of course, she bit her lip and kept her mouth shut. Because Ash wasn't hers; she'd made damn sure of that.

Despite his more than usual grooming, he still wore jeans, a T-shirt, and his steel-toed boots. But tonight, he'd donned a black blazer that emphasized his broad shoulders, and Joy couldn't help but feel a shot of desire as she remembered exactly what his strong body had felt like under her hands. Over her body. Between her legs.

Goddamn, she'd fucked up.

Just then he looked up and caught her eye. Her heart stopped. His gaze flickered to the marble sparrow she wore at her neck, and for just one second, she thought she saw his expression soften, but then, in a flash, he shut her out; those green eyes went cold as a glacier. She had to look away.

"Joy, you little minx. I never would have thought you had it in you."

Her skin prickled. She knew that voice, knew that accent. Slowly she turned around.

"William?" she said with shock. "What are you doing here?"

He grinned the grin that had once had her on her back in ten seconds flat. "It's my gallery, isn't it?"

"Yes, of course. But I didn't know you were coming." She felt her skin go hot and her stomach turn. The last time she'd seen William Cartwright she'd been about to fall asleep next to him in a hotel bed.

"I've been e-mailing you."

"I've responded," she said, sipping her champagne.

"Not to the good parts."

"Poor you."

Her sassiness brought out one of those charming smiles of his. Even though she despised him, she had to admit he was handsome. His thick brown hair fell in a wide, charming lock over one of those mesmerizing blue eyes. He had a way of focusing on her as if she were the only person in the room, which was deadly, of course.

Fortunately she was totally immune to that phony charm now. It seemed so fake, so contrived. She couldn't believe she'd once fallen for it, but that Joy seemed like a whole other person now.

He wore a perfectly fitted suit that reminded her of the Beatles, and his loafers were shiny but not too fancy. He had style.

Her stomach turned just being next to him. Compared to Ash he seemed so sleazy, so untrustworthy. . . .

Kind of how Ash currently thought of her.

"Listen, darling. I need to discuss something with you.

Strictly business, of course." He gave her one of those smiles, and she barely refrained from rolling her eyes.

Joy held her elbow in her hand as she sipped champagne. "Talk."

"Don't be too snooty, love. I am your boss, after all."

Not for long. "William, what can I do for you?"

He plucked her champagne flute out of her hand, drained it, and placed the empty glass on her desk. Then he took her hand and led her into the back storage room.

Once inside, he turned to her. "Looking at all those erotic photographs of you has me positively dying to get in your knickers."

She took a step back. "William. There is no way that's going to happen."

"Are you sure?" He moved forward, and she backed away, until she was pressed against the wall. Then he came close, too close, and put a finger to her lips. "Stop being coy, love. We can play all those games later."

"I'm not playing any game, William."

He leaned in until his lips were at her ear. "You know you want it. Remember how I used to make you scream for me?"

Unfortunately she did. And it made her feel sick.

"William. I'm not kidding. Leave me alone."

He paused, and she felt something in him shift. In an instant, he went from charming Englishman to a man who looked scarily intent on having his way with her. Suddenly the hairs on the back of her neck stood on end, the way they'd done that day in the alley when she'd been robbed.

He put a hand on her shoulder and gripped her tight. Too tight.

"William, that hurts."

"I mean it, Joy. I'm going to have you. Right now. Willingly or not." He whispered the words coldly into her ear, and a chill went through her.

She reached between his legs and cupped his balls. "Is that so?" she whispered back.

"That's more like it, love. I knew you were playing games. I knew you couldn't say no to me."

"Yes. I can." She tightened her grip and twisted his testicles until he gasped in pain. He slumped forward.

"Don't you fucking come near me again," she whispered back into his ear in her sweetest voice. Then she squeezed his testicles even harder and twisted some more, until he cried out. Funny, the sound was similar to the one he made when he came.

She continued to whisper into his ear, her words like sugar. "Don't e-mail me. Don't call me. Don't touch me."

"Joy, please . . ." He groaned.

And that's when she looked over her shoulder and saw Ash standing there.

Her voice froze in her throat. She watched his gaze assessing the situation, and her blood went cold. Visualizing the scene through his eyes, she knew exactly what it must look like.

She was backed against the wall with a man leaning into her body. She was whispering into his ear, and his balls were in her hand.

But she was immobile. She couldn't speak or think or breathe. She was helpless as Ash gave her one unreadable look, turned on his heel, and walked away.

"Fuck!" she exclaimed, finally finding her voice as she pushed William off her.

He keeled over, clutching his crotch. "You bloody bitch," he bit out.

"Fuck you, William. I quit." And then she walked out the door, leaving him clutching his balls.

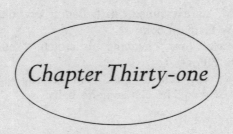

Chapter Thirty-one

By the time Joy returned to the reception, Ash had disappeared. She scanned the crowd, but she knew it was useless. Her mind somehow sensed the lack of his presence.

Erica came to her side. "Joy, what's wrong?"

She quickly told the story to her friend. "And now I don't know what to do. He already thinks I'm a thief. Now he thinks I was getting it on with my boss."

She noticed the corners of Erica's lips were twitching, like she was trying to hold back a laugh.

"What's so funny?" Joy demanded.

"You fucking crushed Cartwright's balls. Literally." She jerked Joy into a tight hug. "I love you so much right now."

"Yeah, well, he's going to come out here any minute, and he's going to be pissed."

Erica released her. "Yeah, maybe it's best if you get out of here."

"Let's go." Joy snatched her bag and coat, and, like schoolgirls ditching class, they dashed out the door.

"Wait!" Joy said, halting Erica on the sidewalk. "I can't just leave Andrew in there to deal with everything."

"Screw it. Let Cartwright run his own gallery for once. You don't work there anymore."

Joy let that sink in. Then, "Yeah. Fuck it. There's nothing as freeing as walking out on the most important day of your career." She had to laugh, and heard the hysterical edge to the sound.

Erica grabbed her shoulder and tugged. "Let's go."

They scurried to the nearest pub, where they settled into a booth in the back. They ordered, and the waitress brought a beer for Erica and a vodka tonic for Joy.

After they'd had a few sips, Joy looked at her friend. "I don't know what to do about Ash."

"Have you tried talking since the sculpture incident?"

"Only about gallery stuff, and even that was a challenge. He obviously doesn't want anything to do with me." Joy absently stirred her cocktail with the mini red straw. "And I didn't even tell you the best part." She went on to explain about her inheritance and how she'd specifically been made to wait because she was the only girl in the family.

Erica sat back, her eyes wide. "Wow. That's fucked up."

"Pretty much." Joy poured some of her drink down her throat.

"Still," Erica said. "Ash went looking for you for a reason."

"Yeah, and look what he saw me doing."

"So are you just going to let him go?"

"What else can I do?"

"Fight for him."

Joy glanced up. "Like you're fighting for Blaine?"

Erica shifted. "That's different."

"How?"

"It just is," Erica said.

"You pushed him away. Why don't you pull him back?"

"It's not that easy. I just can't wrap my head around the fact that I could fall for . . ."

"A preppy?"

"That's the thing. I'm not sure he is. And if it even matters."

Joy reached across the table and took her friend's hand. "Sometimes we just have to admit we're wrong and go for what we want, right?"

Erica nodded absently, staring into her drink.

"Fuck this," Joy said, suddenly leaning forward and downing the rest of her drink. She slammed the empty glass onto the table, where it landed with a satisfying thunk, like a judge's gavel.

"I'll make you a deal," Joy said.

"What?" Erica asked, obviously wary.

"I'll go after Ash if you'll go after Blaine."

Erica jerked back. "What?"

"I'm serious. We're both sitting here, drowning our sorrows in alcohol. I don't know about you, but I'm ready to be done with this whole sad business. So let's make a deal. I'll go to Ash and you'll go to Blaine."

Erica just stared at her, and in her eyes, Joy could see the debate going on in her head. Finally Erica leaned forward so she was resting her elbows on the table, mirroring Joy's position. "What am I supposed to say to him?"

"That you're sorry for being an idiot, and you want to try to make things work. Just like I'm going to say to Ash."

"Lordy," Erica said, shaking her head.

"I know."

"Am I really considering this?"

"What do you have to lose?" Joy asked.

"I can't believe I'm considering this."

"Trust me. What I'm planning has the potential to be much more humiliating than anything you'll experience with Blaine."

"The only reason I'm willing to try is because I want to see you make things work with Ash. And I happen to know Blaine's at a workshop tonight, so I know where to find him."

"There you go!" Joy exclaimed. "It's fate."

She just hoped fate was on her side, too.

An hour later, Erica was loitering outside the culinary school entrance. Blaine was one of the last people to leave the building, and the minute Erica spotted him, her pulse started racing. He looked like such a conservative boy, but she knew that underneath his appearance there was a bad boy waiting to get out.

She wanted to open that door.

Still, what if he rejected her? *I won't wait forever*. Had her chance come and gone?

For a second she considered turning around before Blaine saw her, but she'd made a deal with Joy, so she stayed where she was. She would do this. For better or for worse, Erica was going to talk to Blaine.

God, the man was gorgeous. How could she have ever

found him boring? His brown hair was just a bit too long; his jaw was sharp. And those eyes, so big and brown and luscious.

Erica wanted him with a fierceness that brought every nerve in her body alive.

"Hi," she said, stepping in front of Blaine.

Shock registered across his face before he masked his expression.

"Hi, Erica."

"Um." Erica adjusted her dress. "I wanted to talk with you."

"About?"

God, was he going to make her do this here? Now?

He was. Crossing his arms over his chest, he waited for her to speak.

"I wanted to apologize." Jeez, this was even harder than Erica had thought it would be. She felt sweat pricking at her brow as her stomach did a flip. Maybe this wasn't such a good idea. . . .

Blaine looked expectant, and was that a gleam of humor in his eyes? "What did you want to apologize for, Erica?"

Screw it. She stepped closer to Blaine and met his gaze. "For being a stupid, scared, prejudiced bitch."

Something fluttered across Blaine's face, and after a minute, his mouth twitched into the tiniest of smiles. "Well, admitting you have a problem is the first step toward recovery."

"What's the second step?" Erica asked, her heart going crazy in her chest.

"I'd say the second step is kissing me."

Erica didn't need any more of an invitation. She

yanked Blaine against her body and kissed him. He tasted like cinnamon, and it was sweet, so sweet, to feel his body pressing against hers, to feel his solid chest rubbing against her sensitive nipples.

Smiling, she pulled back. "So. Are we good?"

He kissed her again, until her body swirled with desire. Then he looked down at her, his eyes glimmering in the soft light. "Sweetheart, let's go back to my place and I'll show you how good we can be."

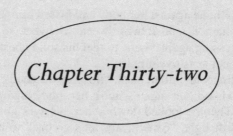

Chapter Thirty-two

Please answer, please answer . . .

Standing on his doorstep shivering, not from the cold but from nerves, Joy prayed Ash would answer the door. She just needed to see him, to try to convince him to forgive her, to show him she would do anything to make up to him what she'd done.

Please answer, please—

The door opened and he was there, staring at her. His face was totally blank; she had no idea what he was thinking.

She pushed inside.

Turning, she said, "Ash. Please sit on the sofa and let me show you something."

He didn't say anything, but at least he didn't tell her to get the hell out of his house. But her hands were shaking as she carried her bag—she'd switched back to the big old one—and went into the kitchen. The first thing she did was take a big shot of his whiskey. Then she removed her coat and began pulling the things she needed out of her purse.

Oh my God, I can't believe I'm doing this.

She kicked off her shoes. She was already wearing the silk skirt low on her waist, and she tied a scarf edged with coins around her hips. Then she took out the gold arm ornaments and slid them on so gold thread covered her skin from elbow to wrist in a gold web.

Then she bent over and gave her hair a good upside-down toss, trying to get it nice and wild-looking. Before she picked up the small boom box, she downed one more shot of whiskey, just for luck, and then she was ready.

When she saw Ash, a shiver raced down her spine. She experienced a moment of discomfort when his gaze fell on her skin, exposed from just under her jingly bra to where her scarf and skirt rested low on her hips, several inches below her belly button. She never even wore a two-piece bathing suit at the beach, and now she was about to perform for Ash at her most vulnerable?

But that's exactly why she was doing it. She wanted Ash to know how much she trusted him, and she needed him to know she'd do anything to prove her love for him, even if it meant she did the one thing she swore she'd never do.

But she loved him. That was the only reason she was here, the only reason she was taking this chance of possible humiliation and rejection. If that happened, it would be devastating, but at least she had to try.

She wanted him so badly—she wanted to own him as much as she wanted to be owned *by* him. And that want fueled her. She turned on the music and positioned herself directly in front of his gaze.

Hell, if she was going to do this, she was going to do it right. She met Ash's gaze and smiled. She placed her arms out elegantly, one raised above her head with her fingers pointed toward the ceiling, the other arm at her side, her fingers positioned gracefully.

Slowly, the exotic beat of Middle Eastern music drifted into the room. The slow, sensual sound of a flute signaled her, and she began to move her hips.

She danced. With her attention focused solely on Ash, she moved her hips and arms along with the music. The steady beat of a drum joined the flute, and it seemed to pull her hips from side to side. The music entered her body, and it was impossible not to feel sexy as she spun in a circle, letting her hair arc behind her. She paused a few feet from Ash to undulate her stomach to the beat.

She put everything she had into her dance. Her heart seemed to be in her throat as she used every muscle, every curve of her body, to dance. Her skirt spun around her ankles; her hair fell in front of her face. She continued to focus on him, but he faded as she moved toward the crescendo. The drum beat faster, stronger, and she jerked her hips up and down and side to side. She felt the strength in her core moving seductively, and she used that part of herself to entrance her audience even more.

And then she realized she liked this, liked performing for him. A quick glance at his crotch, and she saw he seemed to be enjoying it, too.

The fact that he was becoming aroused made her own sex dampen. As she shimmied her arms, she lowered her chest, allowing him to see right down her bra top to her breasts.

She stepped back and raised her arms above her head.

As if her wrists were bound, she pressed the heels of her palms together, and then as slowly, as delicately as she could, she lowered herself until she was kneeling on the ground.

She stayed in that pose as the flute piped its last few notes. And then it was silent, but she remained in the position, eyes downcast. The dance had left her breathless, and her chest rose and fell as she panted before him.

And yet . . .

Nothing. He neither spoke nor moved. What seemed like an eternity went by, and her heart began to crack.

It hadn't worked.

Her eyes stung as she began to lower her arms from the pose. He didn't want her. Mortified, she just wanted to get out.

"Don't you dare move."

She glanced up at him. "W-what?"

"Stay there." He pushed himself off the sofa and disappeared for a few moments. Joy's heart rate skyrocketed as she waited for him. What was he going to do? What did he want? The uncertainty was killing her as she remained in the position he'd ordered her to stay in.

Her arms started to shake from the effort of holding them over her head, and just when she thought they would collapse, he was there before her.

And he had a length of red rope in his hand.

Her skin pebbled as an erotic awareness went over her. Was he . . . ?

"You've been a bad girl, haven't you, Joy?"

She nodded.

"Stealing is wrong, isn't it?"

"Yes."

"You know what happens to thieves, woman?"

"They get punished?" She couldn't help the little hopeful note in her voice.

"That's right." He started wrapping the rope around her wrists. She felt the soft nylon binding, and, just like that, she began to lose herself. To him.

But so many things were unresolved. "Ash, we need to talk."

"We will. After I punish you."

His words sent a jolt of lust shooting through her, and she nearly let it drop.

But she shook her head. "No. That's partly why we got into this mess in the first place. I let myself be persuaded too easily."

When he looked down at her, she saw his eyes weren't shuttered any longer. He looked . . .

Happy.

He sank to his knees so they were face-to-face. Like she was some kind of prisoner, he lowered her hands so her bound wrists were in front of her.

She took a deep breath. "Ash. I know you think I was getting it on with Cartwright, but I promise it wasn't how it looked."

"I know."

"I mean, I'm sure you think you can't trust me but . . . Wait. What do you mean, you know?"

"I saw everything. I heard everything. And it was obvious you could take care of yourself." He placed a soft kiss on her nose. "I was so proud of you."

She searched his eyes. He was dead serious. "But what about the sculpture? Aren't you mad about that?"

"Oh, yes." But he was grinning. "And I'm looking forward to making you pay for that."

Leaning down, he lifted her skirt. "Good girl, you're not wearing panties." He kissed her clit, then started to flick at her in that way that could shoot her to climax in exactly one minute.

He pulled back. "You have the most beautiful pussy," he murmured. "I bought you something on my way home."

He stood, and she saw him pull something out of his back pocket. It looked like a plastic butterfly. Awareness dawned on her as he untangled the straps around the purple butterfly and smiled.

"This is a remote-control vibrator."

She felt the muscles of her belly quiver as he strapped it around her thighs. The butterfly hugged her pussy, with a pointed tip pressing right against her clit, already swollen and sensitive from Ash's mouth.

"After seeing you tonight, all I wanted was to punish you." He tightened the straps around her ass and gave it a buzz from the wireless remote in his hand. "Hear you scream for me."

She jerked as a shock went through her belly with the sudden pulsing at her pussy.

"You like that, sweetheart?"

"Yes," she said above her beating heart.

He turned it off, and she gasped. Even though the butterfly had stopped buzzing, her clit still pulsed. "Ash . . ."

"I'm punishing you, remember?" he said with a deliciously wicked grin.

"Asshole."

"So I've been told. Be right back."

He left her there, helpless with her arms tied. Her

arousal should have abated, but with each passing second, her body became more alive with anticipation. Her breasts were hard points under her bra, heavy from the coins and decoration, and her sex was throbbing with want.

Then he was back, and she felt him cutting her bra off her shoulders.

"Hey!" she said. "That was expensive."

"I'll buy you an entire closetful of them. I plan on having you dance for me on a regular basis."

Her heart swelled. "You mean you liked it? You really liked watching me?"

"Oh, hell yeah. I think it was the fucking sexiest thing I've ever seen."

Joy didn't believe him; he'd taken some of the most erotic images she'd ever seen. Still, it was a nice compliment.

"Just don't think you're going to go out dancing for anyone else. That's for my eyes only."

His possessive words made her smile.

He kissed her again, and just when his tongue entered her mouth, he turned on the butterfly, and she cried out. Bucking her hips against the humming vibrator, she kissed him hungrily, her wrists straining as she leaned forward, pulling the rope taut.

Just when her entire body was shaking with need, he left her, circling her like an animal circles fallen prey.

She'd noticed what looked like a bamboo stick in the corner, and now he went and picked it up. He tapped it lightly on his palm.

"Ash?" she said, suddenly a bit scared. Yeah, she liked a bit of pain, but did she really want to be caned?

"I told you," he said. "You need to be punished for

your misdeed." And then he gave the butterfly a pulse, and she gasped as pleasure shocked her to the core.

He circled her again, changing the vibrator's speed from low to high, until she went from low moans of pleasure to loud cries like she'd heard only out of porn stars.

What had he done to her? She had absolutely no inhibitions any longer.

And it felt amazing.

When he flicked the cane in the air, only about a foot away from her body, she gasped as the sound whipped through her ears. It was going to hurt.

And she wanted to feel it.

"Do it," she said, her voice gravelly.

He kept the vibrator going, and just when she thought she would climax, the buzzing ceased. The first sting of the cane made her scream. From pain or pleasure she wasn't sure, but then the vibrator started again, and it was only pleasure.

He continued the sweet torture. Whipping the fleshy part of her ass and then pausing to buzz her clit with the vibrator only he controlled.

In between, he'd place soft kisses on her neck, her shoulders. The combination of sensation overwhelmed her, and she felt as if everything in her body had evaporated, leaving only a euphoric numbness that blanketed her. She felt the vacant smile on her face.

He caned her ass again, this time not stopping in between strikes. He was literally whipping her into a frenzy; each time he hit her flesh, she screamed, and she heard herself asking for it harder and harder. . . .

But then he stopped. When he released her, she was in a fog, endorphins rushing through her body in a wonderful charge. When he picked her up, she smiled at him. "I love you so much."

Kissing her forehead, he said, "I love you, too, baby. You're mine now. You know that, right?"

"Yes, Ash. And you're mine, too."

"Yeah, that's the fucking truth."

He carried her upstairs and placed her gently on the bed. Then he removed the vibrator and stripped down in front of her.

She watched his beautiful body as he moved, loving the way she could see his toned muscles under his skin. Loving the way his jaw-length hair fell in front of his eye. Loving the fact that it all belonged to her.

He'd said so.

"Come here," she said, spreading her legs wide.

He rolled on a condom and then climbed on top of her, settling right between her thighs.

"Make love to me, Ash."

He held his head a few inches above hers and locked his gaze onto hers.

"Yes, baby. Anything you want."

Cupping her breast in the palm of his hand, he kissed her so gently it was like a whisper on her skin. It was nearly unbelievable that this sensitive lover was the same dominant man who'd held a cane in his hand moments ago.

He continued to kiss her breasts, her ribs. She trembled beneath his touch, and when he again pressed his lips to hers, she welcomed him.

She explored his mouth with her tongue, thinking she could kiss him forever.

But there was a pulsing need between her legs, and she needed to feel him in her, needed to be one with him.

"Ash," she whispered. "Please."

"Oh, Joy." She felt him tilt his hips back, and in one solid move, he entered her. Hard and deep and solid. She arched her neck as her body welcomed him. She couldn't remember ever feeling quite so complete. He leaned down to kiss that place below her ear, so softly and tenderly she gasped.

She spread her legs wider and bent her knees, tilting her pelvis so she could feel him as much as possible. He lifted his head to look at her, and their gazes were still fixed on each other as he pulled out and drove into her again.

"Ash, oh . . ."

He pulled out, slowly, and entered her once again.

"Joy, my Joy."

"Yes, yours," she breathed as he continued the lovely, slow rhythm of making love to her.

"Come for me, sweetheart. I want to watch your face as you come."

"Yes." Staring sightlessly, she clung to him as wave after wave of tremors rocked through her.

He kissed her back to earth and then drove into her three more times. She traced her fingers down his back, and then she felt his own orgasm pulsing inside her.

"That's it, honey," she whispered, holding him close. She could feel his heart pounding hard against her own.

When they came back down, he rolled off her and lay on his back, pulling her against him. She could hear his heart still hammering in his chest. Idly, she drew circles around his nipple with her fingertip.

She bit her lip. Yeah, the evening had been amazing, but what did it mean?

"What are you thinking, sweetheart?"

She continued to draw on his chest and tried to sound casual. "So . . . does this mean we're, um . . ." She swallowed. "Boyfriend and girlfriend?"

"Is that what you want it to mean?" She wasn't sure, but she swore he held his breath.

"Yes," she said in a tiny, insecure voice.

He exhaled. "Good. Because so do I. But, Joy?"

"Yeah?"

"There's one thing I'm going to demand if we're going to be together."

Her heart stopped. "What?" She didn't want to give up her career or her friends or her freedom. Is that what Ash would want?

"I'm not sure you're going to like it. . . ."

"What is it?" she demanded, resting on one elbow and staring down at him.

"Well . . ."

"Ash, what is it?"

"You're going to learn how to change a tire," he said with a grin.

She punched his shoulder—his good shoulder. "You asshole."

"I love it when you call me names."

"Good. Because I have a lifetime's worth to use up."

He brought her down for a kiss. "That's what I was hoping, baby. That's exactly what I was hoping."

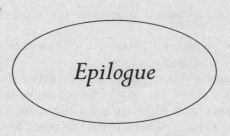

Epilogue

One year later.

Joy gazed around the crowded space with a sense of pride she'd never experienced. Tonight was the grand opening of the Montgomery-Hunter Gallery, and she couldn't believe the amazing response they'd had so far. She could hardly believe the massive turnout that had shown up for tonight's reception.

Ben, the graffiti artist who was actually named Ben, came up to her, his eyes sparkling with excitement. She knew he could hardly believe it, either. She'd already sold five of his canvases, and the city wanted to commission him to do a mural near the Embarcadero. He looked like he was over the moon.

"Joy," he said. "See that dude over there?"

She glanced at a tall man in a suit who happened to own the biggest winery in Napa. "Yes."

"He said he wanted to buy three pieces for his tasting room!"

"That's wonderful. I'll be sure to speak with him later. Can't be too eager, you know."

"Whatever you say, boss," he said with a smile. He'd been wary at first, but now he treated Joy as if she were some kind of god. She wasn't; she just believed in him as an artist, and everything else fell into place. Smiling, she watched Ben turn to speak with yet another admirer.

"You look stunning tonight," a voice whispered in her ear.

A shiver went through her as she felt Ash press up against her back. Over the past year, she'd only grown to love him more each day, and she had also discovered she loved working with him.

After she'd quit her job, they'd decided to open this gallery. Refusing to let her pay for everything, Ash had even dipped into his sacred savings account, a huge feat for him. He'd turned down any more security jobs in Iraq—thank God—to continue his art. After the übersuccessful show at the Cartwright Gallery, Joy had finally persuaded him to keep taking photographs and creating sculpture, and then, when she'd decided to open her own gallery, she asked him to be her partner. It had worked out perfectly. Ash was incredibly organized and took care of all the paperwork. Joy concentrated on finding new artists and selling their work. Their East Side gallery was doing phenomenally well.

Even her grandmother had to admit Joy had done something right. Eventually Ash had won the old lady over, and she'd even helped out by giving a large donation to the gallery. Now, Joy had to smile as she watched the older woman sitting in a chair on the other side of the room, chatting with a gentleman Joy knew to be one of the wealthier landowners in the Bay Area. Of course, Grandmother would know this, and the fact that Joy had such important clientele at her opening would be impressive even to Miriam.

In fact, there were a few eligible men in the room. Ash's mother smiled up at one of San Francisco's premier restaurant entrepreneurs, and Joy had to smile herself. The woman seemed ten years younger than when she'd first met her, and Joy knew Ash was finally realizing his family didn't need one hundred percent of his support.

His sister had proven more than capable of supporting herself. She'd come with her mother and was positively beaming as she gazed around a room filled with her brother's artwork.

Next her gaze fell on Erica and Blaine, huddled together in a corner. They could barely keep their hands off each other. Joy couldn't help but feel a bit smug as she watched them. Challenging her that night in the bar had been the best thing Joy had ever done. For both of them.

Erica had even come to like some of Blaine's friends, and a few of them mingled in the crowd. Joy noticed they were actually the rowdier of the bunch and could really suck back the champagne. Good. She wanted tonight to be fun as well as successful.

She leaned back against Ash. "I'm glad you like my outfit." She'd gone for elegant chic tonight and wore a pair of black slacks and a black-and-white silk blouse that tied at her neck. She still wore flats, but thanks to Ruby, they were *designer* flats, so it was, apparently, okay. Of course, at her throat hung the marble sparrow that Ash had given her on her thirtieth birthday. She rarely took it off.

"Well," Ash said. "I guess I better make a toast and thank everyone for coming."

"Good idea." She took two glasses of champagne from a waiter's tray and handed one to Ash. "Go get 'em, tiger."

He gave her one last kiss and then went to the front of the gallery and climbed onto a chair.

"Can I have your attention, please," he said, and slowly the conversation echoing throughout the room faded as all eyes turned to Ash.

"Joy and I want to thank you all for coming tonight. We truly appreciate the response we've had from you, and I know it fills Joy's heart with, well, joy," he said, and smiled as a soft chuckle came from the crowd. His gaze was on hers as he continued. "I know it fills her heart to see such a positive response to art. Promoting art is one of her passions, and we thank you for your support." He lifted his glass. "To art."

After everyone in the room tilted their glasses of champagne to their lips, Ash sharpened his gaze on hers. "I would also like to say something special to my partner in more than one way, my girlfriend, Joy. Or, if she answers the next question positively, my fiancée."

Joy spit out the champagne she'd just sipped, barely missing the bald head of one of Blaine's lawyer friends. Her heart started to race; had she heard Ash right?

He jumped off the chair and made his way toward her. She watched him, totally frozen to her spot, as he closed in on her. Then, when he was just a couple of feet in front of her, he bent down on one knee. He pulled something out of his pocket, and she put a hand to her mouth. "Oh my God," she whispered.

He held up a piece of marble, sculpted into the shape of a ring. "Joy Montgomery. Will you marry me?"

She felt tears pricking at her eyes, and though her throat was achingly tight, she managed to say, "With one condition."

"What?" he said, his eyes sparkling. He knew her too well, knew she couldn't say no to him.

"You'll never make me change my own tire."

His mouth broke into a grin. "Fine. You have a deal."

"Then give me that ring."

He took her hand and slid the delicate marble band onto her ring finger. She held up her hand and saw that, instead of a diamond, he'd carved a rose into the top of the ring. Surrounding the delicate flower were both their names.

"I love it," she said, her throat tight.

"I love you, Joy."

"Then kiss me."

He got to his feet and he did. Every day for the rest of their lives.

THE DISH

Where authors give you the inside scoop!

From the desk of Larissa Ione

Dear Reader,

"Family" is a word that means something different to everyone. Your family might consist of those who were born into it, or it might be made up of the people (or pets) you choose to bring into the fold. Your family members might be tight, or they might be estranged. Maybe they fight a lot, or maybe they get along beautifully. Often, family dynamics exist in a delicate balance.

So what happens when something happens to throw off that balance?

In ECSTASY UNVEILED, the fourth book in the Demonica series, I explore that question when the assassin hero, Lore, is forced to go up against his new-found brothers in a dangerous game of life or death.

In previous books, the conflicts each hero faced brought the demon brothers together to battle an enemy. In ECSTASY UNVEILED, the conflict is more internal, their bond is put to the test, and they become their own worst enemies.

Can love and trust overcome suspicion, tragedy, and an old enemy bent on tearing them apart?

When Idess, an angel bent on thwarting Lore's mission to kill someone close to his brothers, begins to fall for the coldhearted assassin, family ties are tested, betrayals are revealed, and a dark shadow falls over Underworld General Hospital.

Fortunately, "family" can also be a source of hope, and with Idess's help, Lore may yet find the family he gave up hoping for so long ago.

For more about the Demonica world and the families that make it come alive, please visit my Web site at www.LarissaIone.com to check out deleted book scenes, sign up for the newsletter, and enjoy free reads.

Happy Reading!

Larissa Ione

♥ ♥ ♥ ♥ ♥ ♥ ♥ ♥ ♥ ♥ ♥ ♥ ♥ ♥

From the desk of Laurel McKee

Dear Reader,

When I found out I had just a few days to come up with something for The Dish, I froze! There were just so many things I *could* write about that I couldn't decide. Should I talk about the rich history of late eighteenth-century Ireland? The beautiful Georgian architecture of Dublin? The gorgeous fashions? Irish music? The inspirations behind the characters? Or maybe a cautionary tale of my one attempt at Irish step dancing (there were head injuries—that's all I will say about that!).

I confessed my dilemma to my mom, who suggested we throw an Irish party with lots of Irish food and some Chieftains CDs, and then I could write about it (though there would be no dancing).

"Great!" I said. A party is always good. "But what are some Irish recipes?"

"Er—there's your grandmother's soda bread recipe," she said after some thought. "And, um, I don't know. Something with potatoes? Fish and chips? Blood pudding?"

"And Guinness," my brother added. "Every Irish party needs Guinness. And maybe Jameson."

I happily agreed. Fish and chips, soda bread, Guinness, Irish music, and you have a party! Blood pudding, though, can stay off the menu.

It was lots of fun to have what we called a "halfway to St. Patrick's Day" party. I just wish my characters, the Blacknall sisters and their handsome heroes, could have joined us. And if you'd like to try the soda bread recipe (which is supereasy—even I, officially the "Worst Cook in the World," can make it), here it is:

4 cups flour
1½ tsp. salt
1 tsp. soda
2 cups buttermilk

Preheat oven to 375 degrees.
Grease a round pan. Mix the ingredients
    thoroughly before kneading into a ball.

Cut a cross in the top, and bake for 50–60
minutes.
Serve with fresh butter and a Guinness!

And for some background on the history and
characters of COUNTESS OF SCANDAL and the
Daughters of Erin series, be sure to visit my Web site
at http://laurelmckee.net.

Enjoy!

Laurel McKee

♥ ♥ ♥ ♥ ♥ ♥ ♥ ♥ ♥ ♥ ♥ ♥ ♥ ♥ ♥

From the desk of Lilli Feisty

Dear Reader,

For those of you who have read my previous book,
Bound to Please, you may have noticed I have a bit of
a thing for music and musicians. My latest novel,
DARE TO SURRENDER, is not about a musician,
but it's still related to music. It's about a woman whose
emotional release is to dance. She won't dance in
public; she's much too shy for that. But she dances by
herself. A lot.

And it's not just any sort of dancing; she prefers to
belly dance. She's quite good at it, better than she

thinks. In fact, Joy is better at a lot of things than she gives herself credit for, and it was great fun helping her realize that. Because don't we all have our hang-ups? And working our way through them can be quite an exhilarating release.

If you read DARE TO SURRENDER, I'll tell you right now that there are a lot of similarities between the heroine, Joy Montgomery, and myself. She's a redhead. She's not necessarily comfortable with her curvy figure. She's totally disorganized. Her handbag is the size of a small suitcase.

There's more. She works in an art gallery—I owned one. She's very spontaneous, to the point of getting herself in crazy binds because of it. I do that. A lot. She drives an old Mercedes. So do I.

So you can see we have a lot it common. Except the dancing in public thing. To put it simply, I love to dance. Am I any good at it? Probably not. But I simply can't help myself. If I'm out, and I hear a good beat, I'm lured to the dance floor. In fact, I tend to dance at any opportunity, however inappropriate. It was quite pathetic, but just the other day, I was reprimanded at the grocery store for doing the Wang Chung in the frozen food aisle.

However, let me tell you, belly dancing is not as easy as it looks. To be good, you have to be able to move separate parts of your body at varying speeds and rhythms. For some people (me), it's not easy. But that's irrelevant—it's fun, and once you let yourself go, it really doesn't matter how good you are. You feel the music take over your body and you want to shimmy.

To undulate. To dance! I think belly dance is one of the sexiest, most feminine, mesmerizing forms of dance there is.

Some people assume belly dance was created for the sole purpose of entertaining men. In fact, this is not true. It was invented by women, for women. I think that's why it's such a sexy form of dance. When you belly dance, you're celebrating being a female. You use your hips, your arms, your waist. And, of course, your belly. And you don't need to worry if your belly is a bit round because it's about having fun and using your body to express yourself. And let's not forget the costumes. Belly dancing costumes are pretty darn gorgeous.

So this is Joy's hobby. And it's mine too. The only difference is that Joy is too shy to do so in public so she only practices in her own bedroom. (Also Joy is way better at it.) Of course, when she meets Ash Hunter, he slowly begins to chip away at Joy's inhibitions. But does he get her to dance in public?

Well, I won't give away the ending. But I will say, by the end of their story, Joy is ready to take the dare to surrender everything, even if it means embracing every facet of her femininity.

I hope you enjoy their story.

XXOO,

Lilli Feisty